GEORGIY SERGEYEVICH GARBUZ

Published 2024

Printed in the United States of America

First Edition
ISBN (softcover): 978-1-963380-59-0
ISBN (e-book): 978-1-963380-58-3

For information, address:
Holzer Books LLC
8 The Green, Ste. A
Dover, Delaware 19901 USA

For information about special discounts available for bulk purchases, sales promotions, and educational needs, contact:
info@holzerbooksllc.com
+1 (888) 901-7776

holzerbooksLLC®

Contents

Chapter 1

A Fractured World

The dull hum of the television cast a faint glow across the dimly lit bar. Headlines scrolled across the bottom of the screen in stark, bold letters: *Russia escalates conflict in Ukraine – NATO prepares response.* The news anchor's voice, tense but controlled, narrated scenes of devastation—buildings reduced to rubble, civilians huddled in underground shelters, smoke billowing from war-torn streets. It was the same story playing out across the world, an endless cycle of destruction.

Georgiy Sergeyevich Garbuz sat at the bar, his sharp eyes focused on the broadcast. He'd seen it all before. Not just the war itself, but the larger story behind it—a world teetering on the edge, held hostage by shifting alliances and economic power plays. Garbuz was no ordinary observer. He had been warning people for years about where this was all heading, but few had listened.

The bartender glanced at Garbuz as he wiped down the counter. "Another day, another disaster, huh?" he muttered, more to himself than anyone else.

Garbuz didn't respond immediately. His mind was elsewhere, processing the deeper implications of the conflict playing out on-screen. He was thinking not just about Russia and Ukraine, but about the bigger picture—the real battle that was being fought in the shadows. It wasn't just about territory or politics anymore. It was about control of the global economy. And at the center of that struggle was BRICS.

BRICS—the acronym for Brazil, Russia, India, China, and South Africa—had once been a loose coalition of emerging economies, created to challenge the dominance of the West in international finance. What started as an economic alliance had grown into something far more powerful over the past decade. Now, BRICS was not only pushing for greater influence in global markets but also for a complete restructuring of the world order.

As the Western world imposed sanctions on Russia for its actions in Ukraine, BRICS countries, led by China and Russia, saw an opportunity to strike back. They began a global push to de-dollarize—to reduce the world's reliance on the U.S. dollar as the reserve currency. This shift would upend the financial systems that had kept America and its allies at the top of the economic food chain for decades.

The economic might of BRICS was undeniable. With China's rapid industrial expansion, Russia's control of vast natural resources, India's burgeoning tech and service sectors, and Brazil and South Africa's strategic importance in Latin America and Africa, the alliance was becoming a force to be reckoned with. And the world was watching.

In Washington D.C., the halls of power buzzed with tension. Senator Elizabeth Warner sat in her office, flipping through a classified intelligence briefing. The latest reports from Europe were grim. Russian aggression was escalating, and NATO was preparing for what looked more and more like a military confrontation. But what really troubled Warner wasn't the war itself—it was what was happening behind the scenes. The U.S. dollar was under attack. If BRICS succeeded in creating an alternative global currency, America's economic dominance would crumble.

Her aide knocked lightly on the door before entering, a worried expression on his face. "Ma'am, another update just came in. BRICS is pushing hard for de-dollarization. They're making deals with African and South American nations, offering them better terms than we can."

Warner frowned. "How close are they to succeeding?"

"Closer than we'd like. If they pull this off, we're looking at a full-blown global recession."

Warner leaned back in her chair, her mind racing. The U.S. had relied on the strength of the dollar to maintain its position as the world's economic leader. But BRICS wasn't playing by the old rules anymore. They were building new alliances, carving out their own spheres of influence, and now, with Russia leading the charge, they had a real chance of shifting the balance of power.

"We need to get ahead of this," she said, her voice firm. "We can't let them take control."

Her aide hesitated before speaking again. "There's someone who's been trying to reach you. A man named Georgiy Garbuz. He claims to have a plan that could stabilize the global economy—but it involves space exploration. Something called the *International Intergalactic Space Federation*."

Warner raised an eyebrow. "Space exploration? In the middle of an economic war?"

"Yes, ma'am. He's been persistent. He says it's the only way forward. Something about creating a unified space alliance to shift the focus from Earth's dwindling resources to the vast potential in space. He's written to the President, the State Department, even the UN."

Warner stared out the window, considering the idea. She had heard of Garbuz before, though she didn't know the details. A visionary, some called him. Others labeled him a dreamer. But right now, the world was short on visionaries, and a dreamer might be exactly what they needed.

Across the Atlantic, in Moscow, Russian President Vasily Orlov paced in his private study. The BRICS alliance was his crowning achievement. For years, Russia had been sanctioned, isolated, and squeezed by the West. But now, with BRICS gaining momentum, the tables were turning. Orlov had a vision—one in which Russia, not America, would lead the world into the future. And he was willing to do whatever it took to make that vision a reality.

Still, Orlov couldn't shake the memory of a proposal he had once dismissed. Years ago, Georgiy Garbuz had come to him with an idea for an international space federation—a project that would unite the world's powers in a mission to explore and colonize space.

Back then, Orlov had been more focused on earthly concerns. Space was a luxury Russia couldn't afford. But now, with the global economy on the verge of collapse, Garbuz's idea didn't seem so far-fetched. Whoever controlled space would control the future. And Orlov wasn't about to let that future slip away.

Back in the quiet Chicago bar, Garbuz finished the last of his water and stood up, pulling a neatly folded envelope from his pocket. Inside was a proposal—a plan he had spent years perfecting, a plan that could change the course of history. He left the envelope on the bar, a small token of his presence, and nodded to the bartender.

"Take care," he said quietly before stepping into the cold night air.

Outside, the wind bit at his skin, but Garbuz barely noticed. His mind was already racing ahead, calculating his next move. He had spent decades watching the world stumble from one crisis to the next, but he had never lost faith in his vision. The world was breaking apart at the seams, and no one was looking to the stars for answers. But Garbuz was.

He pulled out his phone, a message lighting up the screen.

Senator Warner is ready to meet.

A faint smile tugged at the corner of his lips. The pieces were finally falling into place. It was time to take the world beyond its borders—beyond its limits. The stars were waiting, and with them, the future of humanity.

Chapter 2

The Economic Collapse

The once-bustling heart of downtown Chicago now felt hollow. The empty shelves in grocery stores, the boarded-up windows of once-thriving small businesses, and the endless line outside the unemployment office told a story that words couldn't capture. Across the world, economies were collapsing under the weight of sanctions, inflation, and political instability, but the real devastation was happening on the ground—in people's lives.

In a small, family-owned grocery store, Maria Vega stood in the frozen foods aisle, staring at the price tags. Everything seemed out of reach. The bread she used to buy for $3 now cost $9. The milk, a staple for her two kids, was priced like it was liquid gold. She held a jar of peanut butter, weighing it in her hands, before reluctantly placing it back on the shelf.

She pulled her cart into the next aisle, where her husband, Carlos, was staring at his phone, his expression growing more frustrated with each passing second.

"They raised the price of gas again," he muttered, his voice low and full of defeat. "It's at five dollars a gallon now. We barely have enough to fill the tank for the week."

Maria clenched her fists around the handle of the cart, feeling the weight of every dollar, every choice they had to make. Their family was being squeezed from every angle. The rising cost of living, the stagnant wages, the relentless pressure of an economy spiraling out of control—it was all becoming too much.

"It's getting worse, isn't it?" Maria asked quietly, though she already knew the answer.

Carlos nodded, his jaw tight. "Yeah. It's worse."

The Vega family was not alone. The scene in Chicago was mirrored across the country and around the world. Inflation was at a historic high, and wages hadn't kept up. People's savings were vanishing, businesses were closing, and entire industries were on the verge of collapse. It wasn't just an economic downturn—it was the beginning of a full-blown collapse.

On the other side of the world, in London, similar scenes were unfolding. Crowds gathered outside Parliament, their chants echoing off the stone walls. "End the austerity! Save our jobs!" The protests had started out small, a response to the government's economic policies, but as the cost of living crisis deepened, the demonstrations swelled.

Inside Parliament, Prime Minister Harold Conway faced a growing storm. His cabinet room was tense, filled with economic advisors, political strategists, and security officials. Conway himself was pale, the weight of the nation on his shoulders.

"We're running out of options," said one of his senior economic advisors. "The sanctions on Russia have triggered an energy crisis that's hitting us harder than we anticipated. Our gas reserves are drying up, and the rising costs of food imports are crippling households."

Conway leaned forward, his fingers steepled as he absorbed the grim news. "And what's the latest from BRICS? Have they made any further moves on de-dollarization?"

A foreign policy advisor cleared his throat nervously. "China and Russia are ramping up negotiations with African and South American countries. If they succeed in de-dollarizing those regions, we could see a significant drop in the value of the pound."

Conway closed his eyes for a brief moment, trying to block out the weight of the room. "So we're looking at potential energy shortages, mass unemployment, and a devalued currency all within the next few months?"

The advisor nodded.

Conway opened his eyes, letting out a slow breath. "Then it's no longer potential. It's inevitable."

In India, the markets were far less stable than in London. In the crowded streets of Mumbai, the bustling energy of trade was being replaced by desperation. Once, the city had been the beating heart of India's economy, but now it felt as though it was running on borrowed time. Ramesh Patel, a vendor in the infamous Crawford Market, watched his stall of fresh produce with growing anxiety. His fruits—once a luxury for some and a staple for others—were starting to rot in the heat.

"Ramesh!" his neighbor, Sunil, called from his nearby stall, wiping sweat from his forehead. "Did you hear? The transport workers are going on strike. They're saying the fuel prices are too high for them to keep operating."

Ramesh swore under his breath. "How am I supposed to get more goods if they stop delivering? It's already impossible to pay for transport!"

Sunil shook his head, equally frustrated. "I don't know, brother. I'm barely selling anything as it is. No one has money."

Ramesh looked around the market, seeing the same reality reflected on every face. India, like the rest of the world, was choking under inflation and the rising cost of essentials. Fuel prices were skyrocketing, making it impossible for suppliers to transport goods. Food prices were tripling, and soon, Ramesh feared, even basic necessities would be out of reach for most families.

He knew people weren't buying because they couldn't afford to. But what did that mean for his future? What did it mean for his children?

While ordinary citizens were feeling the full force of the economic collapse, the elite gathered in Davos for the annual World Economic Forum. There, in the snowy luxury of the Swiss Alps, the world's most powerful business leaders, politicians, and economists met behind closed doors to discuss the crisis.

Georgiy Garbuz stood at the window of a private conference room, looking out at the pristine landscape. From here, the world's problems felt distant—abstract. But he knew better than anyone how close to the edge humanity was teetering. He'd seen the signs long before others had noticed, but they had dismissed him. Space exploration? A united global initiative to expand beyond Earth? They had laughed at the idea. But now, with the global economy collapsing, the future was clear to Garbuz.

There was no future on Earth. At least, not one where humanity could thrive. The resources were finite, and the politics were too fragmented. The only way forward was up—into space.

As he turned back to the room, Garbuz straightened his suit. Today, he wasn't here to convince them to save the planet. He was here to convince them to look beyond it.

He strode toward the large oak table, where several powerful figures were seated—global CEOs, heads of state, and thought leaders. All eyes turned to him as he approached. They knew him, of course. He wasn't just another entrepreneur with a wild dream. Garbuz had built his reputation on practical vision—one that didn't just look toward the stars, but understood how to get there.

"It's no longer a question of if we need to change," Garbuz began, his voice calm and commanding. "It's a question of when. And that when is now."

The room was silent, waiting for him to continue.

"Our current economic systems are collapsing. We've seen the reports, we've seen the unrest. What we haven't seen is a solution that works. Until now. Space isn't just the final frontier—it's our only frontier. The *International Intergalactic Space Federation* is no longer a distant dream. It's a necessary reality."

He placed his proposal on the table, a small, leather-bound book. On the cover, the title gleamed: *Follow in the Future with the Shadow*.

The world's most powerful eyes were now on him, and Garbuz knew this was his moment. He had one shot to make them see what he saw—that survival wasn't on this planet. It was beyond it.

Chapter 3
Rising Tensions

The lavish halls of the Kremlin glowed in the fading evening light. Inside, President Vasily Orlov sat at the head of a long mahogany table, flanked by his top military advisors. Maps of Eastern Europe were spread across the table, crisscrossed with red markings indicating troop movements, military installations, and potential strike zones. Orlov's steely eyes scanned the room, taking in the grim faces of his generals and ministers.

"The time has come," Orlov said, his voice low but firm. "We must make our next move. The West is weak, divided by their own internal chaos. The longer we wait, the more ground we lose."

One of his top generals, a man with silver hair and a hardened face, leaned forward, his finger tracing a path along the Ukrainian border. "NATO forces are increasing their presence in Poland and Romania. If we push further, they'll respond with more sanctions, perhaps military force."

Orlov gave a slow, deliberate nod. "Let them. We have allies—strong ones."

Russia's participation in the BRICS alliance had transformed its standing on the global stage. The BRICS nations—Brazil, Russia, India, China, and South Africa—had grown from an economic coalition into a political powerhouse, directly challenging Western dominance. What had begun as a shared interest in economic growth had turned into a full-scale geopolitical movement, aimed at de-dollarizing the global economy and weakening the influence of the U.S. and Europe.

The BRICS nations had weathered the storm of sanctions, using their combined resources to create alternative trade routes, new financial systems, and a growing sphere of influence that stretched from Asia to Africa and beyond. But even within BRICS, cracks were beginning to show.

Thousands of miles away, in the heart of Beijing, Chinese President Zhang Wei was facing a dilemma of his own. While China and Russia were united in their opposition to Western dominance, tensions between BRICS members were simmering beneath the surface. India and China, the two largest powers in the group, had long-standing border disputes and competing economic interests that threatened to fracture their alliance.

Zhang stood in his office, staring at a wall of screens that displayed live feeds from across the world—stock markets, military positions, satellite images. The Chinese economy, though still a global powerhouse, had been hit hard by the recent disruptions in international trade. Inflation was rising, and internal dissent was becoming more pronounced. The government had managed to keep protests at bay, but only just. If the de-dollarization effort didn't succeed soon, China's own stability could be at risk.

Zhang's advisor entered the room quietly, bowing slightly before speaking. "President Zhang, the Indian delegation has requested another meeting to discuss the border issue."

Zhang's expression darkened. "And what of their support for BRICS? Are they still committed to the de-dollarization plan?"

"They've expressed support publicly, but privately...they are wavering. India is positioning itself to maintain strong ties with the West, particularly the United States. They are reluctant to go all-in on our strategy."

Zhang turned away from the screens, his gaze sharp. "The Indians think they can play both sides. They are mistaken."

The room fell silent. Zhang knew the stakes. China had invested too much into BRICS to allow internal dissent to derail their mission. Yet, even with their shared goal of countering Western influence, the friction between China and India was growing by the day. The

BRICS alliance was strong, but fragile. Any significant disruption could send the entire effort crashing down.

In New Delhi, Prime Minister Ravi Sharma sat in a high-level meeting with his national security advisors, all of them wary of the growing tensions with China. The border disputes between India and China had escalated over the past few months, with military skirmishes taking place along the Line of Actual Control in the Himalayas. Though both nations were part of BRICS, their rivalry was deep-seated, and the mounting pressure on India to choose between its alliances was becoming impossible to ignore.

"We cannot afford to antagonize China right now," one of Sharma's senior advisors warned. "Their support is crucial if we want to avoid being caught between the U.S. and BRICS. But we also can't let them dictate our actions."

Sharma, his face lined with exhaustion, leaned back in his chair. "And what of Russia? Where do they stand in all this?"

"Russia is firmly aligned with China, but they're preoccupied with the situation in Europe. They've been pushing us to fully support the de-dollarization plan, but we have too much at stake with our Western partners. We can't afford to alienate the U.S. or the European Union."

Sharma sighed heavily. The balancing act was becoming more dangerous by the day. India needed the economic strength of BRICS to continue its growth, but at the same time, the country couldn't sever ties with the West. The U.S. was still a key trading partner, and the technological cooperation between Silicon Valley and India's tech sector was essential for maintaining the country's competitive edge.

Back in Moscow, Orlov continued to lay out his plans. Despite the growing tensions within BRICS, Russia was moving forward with its agenda. Orlov knew that as long as China stood by them, the alliance could withstand the pressure from both within and outside. His real concern was the future—not just of Russia, but of the world.

Orlov paused, leaning back in his chair. "We've been too focused on Earth. Our future doesn't lie in fighting over borders or currencies. The real game, the game that will define the next century, is in space."

The room fell silent. The generals exchanged glances, unsure of where Orlov was going with this.

"Georgiy Garbuz," Orlov continued, his voice low, "came to us years ago with an idea. An idea we dismissed as too ambitious at the time. The *International Intergalactic Space Federation*. He wanted to unite the world's powers in space exploration, to shift our focus away from Earth's dwindling resources and into the vast potential of the stars."

One of the generals raised an eyebrow. "Space exploration? In the middle of a global economic collapse?"

Orlov gave a small, calculated smile. "It's not as absurd as it sounds. BRICS has proven that when we unite, we can challenge the West. But if we want to truly reshape the world order, we need to think bigger. Garbuz's vision was about more than exploration. It was about survival. Control of space will mean control of the future. Whoever leads the charge into space will set the rules for the next century."

The general nodded slowly, beginning to understand. "You believe we should revisit Garbuz's proposal?"

"I believe," Orlov said, his eyes gleaming, "that we should lead it."

As the BRICS alliance wrestled with its internal tensions and ambitions, Garbuz's name once again began to surface in high-level discussions. What had once been seen as a distant dream was now becoming a strategic necessity. For Garbuz, it was just a matter of time before the world realized that space was not just the final frontier—it was the only frontier worth fighting for.

And he would be the one to lead them there.

Chapter 4

A World on the Brink

The glass doors of the World Economic Forum slid open with a quiet whoosh, allowing Georgiy Sergeyevich Garbuz to step into the grand atrium of the conference center. It was an imposing space, filled with towering columns of glass and steel, designed to symbolize the transparency and strength of the global economy. But Garbuz, with his sharp instincts honed over decades of navigating political and economic storms, knew better. Transparency was an illusion. Strength was fleeting. The real game was being played in the shadows, where power was consolidated and empires built—often on the edge of collapse.

As he moved through the halls, surrounded by the world's elite—CEOs, heads of state, economists, and diplomats—Garbuz could feel the weight of their anxiety. He had been invited to speak, not because they believed in his vision, but because they were desperate. The collapse of the global economy had left them scrambling for solutions, and his proposal—once dismissed as a dreamer's folly—now seemed like a potential lifeline.

But even in desperation, they would resist him. Garbuz knew that. Visionaries were always met with skepticism until they were proven right.

Years before, when he first conceived the *International Intergalactic Space Federation* (IISF), Garbuz had seen the writing on the wall. The global economy, tied to finite resources and short-term thinking, was destined to break down. The constant cycle of war, trade disputes, and political instability was unsustainable. Humanity's only hope for long-term survival was to look beyond Earth, to the limitless possibilities of space.

He had written his first proposal in 2007 and presented it to the Russian government, believing that space exploration would offer a way to unify warring nations under a single, global mission. But the politicians and military brass had been too focused on territorial disputes, too concerned with the geopolitics of the moment, to see the bigger picture. They had dismissed him as naive, a dreamer with too much ambition.

Yet Garbuz hadn't given up. He had refined his vision, built alliances, and quietly laid the groundwork for what would become the IISF—a space-faring organization that would not only explore but also colonize other planets, ensuring humanity's survival beyond Earth's limited resources. He envisioned a future where space academies trained the next generation of astronauts and scientists, and where multi-trillion-dollar industries based on space technology and interplanetary commerce would fuel the global economy.

His book, *Follow in the Future with the Shadow*, had been a blueprint for this vision, but it had only reached a small audience. Now, with the world on the brink, people were starting to listen.

Inside a private conference room at the forum, Garbuz sat down with the key decision-makers who had agreed to hear him out. Around the table sat powerful figures: the U.S. Secretary of Commerce, the German Chancellor, a high-ranking official from the Chinese government, and representatives from several of the largest corporations in the world. They were here not because they believed in space exploration, but because they were running out of options.

"Mr. Garbuz," began the U.S. Secretary, a stern woman in her fifties with sharp features, "you've made some bold claims in your proposal. But we need more than vision. We need practical solutions to the immediate crisis. Space exploration may have long-term potential, but right now, the world needs answers that will stabilize our economies."

Garbuz leaned forward, his calm demeanor never wavering. "What you need," he replied, "is a new frontier. The solutions you're looking for—temporary bailouts, shifting trade alliances, currency manipulations—won't save you. They'll only delay the inevitable collapse. The real answer lies in expanding our horizons. Space isn't just the future. It's the only path forward."

The German Chancellor, a pragmatic man with a reputation for cautious decision-making, spoke next. "But space exploration requires vast resources, time, and cooperation between nations that can barely agree on trade policies. What makes you believe the IISF can succeed where other international efforts have failed?"

"Because the alternative is extinction," Garbuz said bluntly. He paused for a moment, letting the gravity of his words sink in. "The resources on Earth are finite. Energy, minerals, food—it's all running out. And the wars you're fighting, the economic collapses you're facing, they're all symptoms of that scarcity. Space is the only place where we can find the resources we need to sustain civilization for the next millennium."

There was a murmur of unease around the table. They all knew the truth of what Garbuz was saying, even if they weren't ready to admit it. The global crises they were facing weren't temporary. They were the beginning of the end, unless something changed.

Garbuz continued, his voice calm but insistent. "The IISF is more than just an exploration initiative. It's a way to restructure the global economy. Imagine this: instead of competing over dwindling resources, the major world powers join forces to harness the untapped wealth of the cosmos. We build space stations, mine asteroids, colonize planets. The scientific breakthroughs alone—new energy sources, medical advancements, technological innovations—will create industries worth trillions. And all of it will be shared among the nations who participate in the IISF."

The Chinese official, who had remained silent until now, finally spoke up. "And what role do you see for China in this federation?"

Garbuz didn't hesitate. "A leading one, of course. China has the industrial capacity and technological expertise to be a major player in space. The IISF will need every nation's strengths—America's innovation, Russia's aerospace capabilities, China's manufacturing power. Together, we can build something that benefits everyone. But it has to be a true partnership. No one nation can dominate."

The official nodded, considering his words carefully.

As the meeting went on, Garbuz laid out the specifics of his plan. The IISF would be founded by six major powers—America, Russia, China, Germany, India, and England—each bringing their own resources and expertise to the table. In exchange for their participation, these nations would receive exclusive rights to the technological advancements and economic benefits that would arise from space colonization. Additionally, the IISF would establish Space School Academies in each founding country, providing free education to children and training them for the new frontier.

It was an ambitious plan, but Garbuz knew that ambition was exactly what the world needed. The old ways weren't working anymore. The political squabbles, the wars over land and resources, the endless cycles of boom and bust—they were all leading to the same outcome: collapse.

As the meeting came to a close, the U.S. Secretary of Commerce stood, her expression thoughtful. "You've given us a lot to think about, Mr. Garbuz. But I'm still not sure we can afford to focus on space when there are so many urgent issues here on Earth."

Garbuz smiled slightly. "That's exactly why you can't afford not to."

Outside the conference room, as the attendees filed out, Garbuz lingered for a moment by the window, looking out at the snowy peaks of the Swiss Alps. The world was on the edge of a precipice, but he could see a future where humanity thrived—if they were brave enough to take the leap. His phone buzzed with a message:

Senator Warner has confirmed. She's ready to meet.

It was time to make his next move. Garbuz knew that the road ahead would be difficult, filled with resistance and doubt. But he had spent years preparing for this moment. The rise of the IISF was inevitable. The question now was how many would join him before it was too late.

Chapter 5

Allies and Enemies

The sound of camera shutters clicking filled the press room of the White House, where Senator Elizabeth Warner stood at a podium, speaking with characteristic precision. Her dark hair was tied back, and her tone was measured, but the intensity in her eyes spoke volumes.

"The global economy is in crisis," Warner began, addressing the reporters assembled before her. "But this crisis also presents us with an opportunity. Georgiy Garbuz's proposal for the IISF offers us a chance to take control of our future—both here on Earth and beyond. This is not just about space exploration. It's about jobs, innovation, and securing America's leadership in a new global economy."

As she spoke, Warner's mind was racing. She had spent years working within the political system, navigating the ever-changing landscape of power and influence. Now, she saw Garbuz's vision as a lifeline—a way to restore American dominance while simultaneously addressing the economic collapse. But she also knew that not everyone in Washington shared her enthusiasm.

Behind her, the cameras zoomed in on the figures seated at the back of the room—her political opponents, watching silently as she made her case. Senator Michael Trent, a fierce critic of Garbuz's plan, sat with his arms crossed, his expression dark. Warner knew that the battle ahead wouldn't just be fought in boardrooms or the halls of the UN—it would be fought here, in the heart of Washington.

Thousands of miles away, in Moscow, President Vasily Orlov stared out the window of his office, deep in thought. Snow drifted lightly outside, coating the Kremlin's grand spires in white. Orlov's mind, however, was on something far beyond Russia's borders.

The IISF proposal had stirred something in him—a mixture of curiosity and ambition. Russia had always prided itself on its space legacy. It had been the first to send a human into space, after all. Garbuz's vision of a unified space-faring federation was both appealing and dangerous. If Russia joined, it could regain its former glory. But if it didn't, it risked being left behind in the race for control of space.

Orlov's advisor, Viktor Karpov, entered the room, carrying a folder thick with intelligence reports. "The West is pushing hard on the IISF," Karpov said without preamble. "Warner is rallying support in Congress. The Germans are on board. And Garbuz has started reaching out to private companies to secure funding. He's moving fast."

Orlov nodded, his gaze still fixed on the falling snow. "And BRICS?"

Karpov hesitated before answering. "China is wary. They have their own space program, and they're concerned that the IISF will dilute their control over space development. India is sitting on the fence, as always, trying to maintain good relations with both sides. South Africa and Brazil are too busy with their internal problems to make any firm commitments."

Orlov turned to face Karpov. "And what of Garbuz himself? Have we received any overtures?"

"Not directly," Karpov said, "but the channels are open. If we want to talk, he'll listen."

Orlov nodded thoughtfully. "Keep the lines open. For now, we maintain our position within BRICS. But we cannot let the West control space. If Garbuz succeeds without us, we will be at their mercy for generations."

Meanwhile, in Beijing, President Zhang Wei sat at the head of a long conference table, reviewing reports with his advisors. The Chinese government had invested billions into its own space program, and Garbuz's IISF plan was seen as both a threat and an opportunity.

Zhang's chief advisor, Lin Cheng, presented the latest intelligence. "Garbuz's IISF will require international cooperation on a scale we've never seen before. But if China joins, we will have influence over the direction of the project. However, there are risks—chiefly, that it will dilute our control over space technology and allow the West to dominate."

Zhang nodded slowly, his fingers tapping lightly on the table. "We must be cautious," he said. "The West would like nothing more than to use the IISF as a way to regain their economic advantage. But if we refuse to participate, we risk being excluded from the future. Prepare a proposal. We'll open negotiations with Garbuz, but on our terms."

Lin nodded and left the room, leaving Zhang to ponder the next move. The Chinese president knew that the IISF represented more than just a scientific endeavor—it was a battleground for global supremacy. If China wanted to maintain its position as a rising superpower, it would need to play both sides carefully.

As the days passed, Garbuz's proposal sent ripples through every corner of the globe. In Europe, the German Chancellor publicly voiced support for the IISF, calling it "the most visionary project of our time." France and the UK, though wary, began exploratory talks with Garbuz's team. In India, Prime Minister Ravi Sharma struggled to navigate the geopolitical minefield, balancing India's relationship with both BRICS and the West.

The reactions varied, but one thing was certain—no one could ignore the IISF. Whether they supported or opposed it, world leaders knew that the future of their nations hung in the balance.

Back in Washington, Senator Warner's office was a hive of activity. Staffers rushed in and out, briefing her on the latest developments. Warner herself sat at her desk, reviewing a list of potential allies in Congress. She knew the fight was only just beginning. There would be powerful opposition from both sides of the aisle—some would see the IISF as too risky, too ambitious. Others would resist any form of international cooperation, viewing it as a threat to American sovereignty.

But Warner was determined. She believed in Garbuz's vision, and she knew that if the U.S. didn't lead the charge into space, someone else would.

She looked up as her chief of staff entered the room. "Senator," he said, "we've got a problem. Senator Trent is mobilizing a coalition to block funding for the IISF. He's calling it a waste of taxpayer money."

Warner nodded. "I expected that. Set up a meeting with Garbuz. We need to counter this before it gains too much traction."

The chief of staff hesitated for a moment. "Senator, are you sure this is the right move? If this fails..."

"It won't," Warner interrupted, her voice firm. "We can't afford to fail. The world is watching. And if we don't act, we'll lose everything.

Chapter 6

Building a Coalition

The weight of global expectation pressed on Georgiy Garbuz as he sat in a sleek black SUV driving through the heart of Washington D.C. Outside the tinted windows, the city buzzed with its usual hum of activity—congressional staffers rushing between buildings, lobbyists making deals on the sidewalk, protesters waving signs about the crumbling economy. But inside the vehicle, Garbuz's mind was elsewhere. He was preparing for the most important meeting of his career: rallying the support of the world's most powerful players to bring the IISF to life.

He knew that the future of the IISF—and humanity's future beyond Earth—rested on the decisions made in the coming weeks. He had won a few early supporters, but now he needed to build a coalition strong enough to resist the inevitable political, corporate, and international backlash that was coming.

At the same time, in New Delhi, India's Prime Minister Ravi Sharma sat across from Garbuz in a private meeting room within the grand Rashtrapati Bhavan. The air was thick with the scent of sandalwood, and outside, the manicured gardens basked in the afternoon sun. Sharma's brow furrowed as he studied the detailed proposal Garbuz had laid out.

"The IISF could redefine the global balance of power," Sharma said slowly, his eyes not leaving the document. "But for India to join, we need assurances. The BRICS alliance will see this as a Western project, even if it claims to be international. They won't look kindly on our participation."

Garbuz nodded. "I understand your concerns, Prime Minister. But this isn't just a Western initiative. India is poised to play a critical role in the IISF. Your technological advancements in space science, as well as your growing economy, make you a necessary partner. This is about creating a new frontier—one that belongs to all of us."

Sharma leaned back in his chair, his face thoughtful. "What you're proposing could elevate India's status on the global stage. But the BRICS nations, particularly China, will see this as a threat. How do you propose we balance that?"

Garbuz met Sharma's gaze, unwavering. "China may not like it, but the IISF is about survival. The economic and political crises on Earth will only intensify. Space offers the resources we need to stabilize our world economies, to create jobs, and to maintain peace. India can choose to stand on the sidelines and risk being left behind, or you can lead."

There was a long pause before Sharma spoke again. "I will consider your proposal. But this decision will require careful diplomacy on our part. We cannot afford to alienate China."

Garbuz smiled, sensing the door was open. "I understand. Take your time, but know that the IISF is the future. And that future is happening now."

Back in Europe, Garbuz made his next move. In Berlin, the mood was cautiously optimistic. The German Chancellor, a pragmatic and respected leader, had expressed interest in the IISF from the beginning, seeing it as a way to revive Europe's shattered economy and restore its place as a technological powerhouse.

The meeting was held in a grand conference room within the Reichstag. The Chancellor, a tall man with salt-and-pepper hair and a reputation for meticulous planning, sat at the head of the table. Around him were advisors, economists, and representatives from Europe's largest corporations.

"As you know," Garbuz began, standing at a podium, "the world economy is collapsing under the strain of inflation, resource shortages, and political instability. The IISF represents a new beginning—not just for space exploration, but for global economic recovery."

The Chancellor raised an eyebrow. "We're listening, Mr. Garbuz, but Europe has its own space agency. What can the IISF offer that we cannot achieve ourselves?"

Garbuz didn't hesitate. "Scale, Chancellor. The IISF will bring together the world's greatest minds and the most powerful economies to achieve something that no single nation can accomplish. We're talking about mining asteroids for resources, building space colonies, and creating a multi-trillion-dollar economy based on interplanetary commerce. And Europe's participation will ensure that you remain at the forefront of this revolution."

The Chancellor exchanged glances with his advisors. "And what about the risks? The political fallout? The world is not in a cooperative mood these days."

Garbuz nodded. "That's exactly why the IISF is so important. The more fractured the world becomes, the more we need something to unite us. Space exploration is that unifying goal. It offers something no war, no trade agreement, no temporary economic measure can—a vision for the future."

There was a silence in the room as the weight of Garbuz's words sank in. Finally, the Chancellor spoke. "You make a compelling case, Mr. Garbuz. Germany will support the IISF, under the condition that Europe is given a leading role in the scientific and technological development. We want to be at the heart of this new economy."

Garbuz smiled. "You have my word. Europe will be a leader in the IISF."

While Garbuz secured critical allies in Europe and India, opposition was gathering strength elsewhere. In Beijing, President Zhang Wei was deep in discussions with his top advisors about the risks the IISF posed to China's ambitions.

In a sleek, minimalist office inside the Zhongnanhai complex, Zhang studied a series of reports detailing Garbuz's growing support among the world's leading nations. His chief advisor, Lin Cheng, stood by his side, outlining the possible scenarios.

"Germany is on board," Lin said. "India is wavering, but they could go either way. If they join the IISF, China's influence in BRICS will be weakened."

Zhang's eyes narrowed. "We cannot allow Garbuz to monopolize space. If the West controls space, they control the future."

Lin nodded. "We could push harder on our own space initiatives, accelerate our program, and make sure China's interests are protected. Or…"

Zhang turned to face him. "Or what?"

Lin hesitated. "Or we make a play to control the IISF from within. If China joins the IISF, we will have a say in its direction. We can shape it to suit our interests."

Zhang considered this carefully. "And if we don't join?"

"Then the West will dominate the next century, and China will be relegated to the sidelines."

Zhang's expression hardened. "Prepare a proposal. We will open talks with Garbuz—but we will do so from a position of strength. The IISF may be his vision, but if China joins, we will control the outcome."

As Garbuz traveled the world, building his coalition, it became clear that the IISF was becoming more than just a proposal—it was a battleground for global supremacy. Every nation that joined would bring its strengths, its ambitions, and its hidden agendas. And every nation that resisted would see the IISF as a threat to their future.

Back in the U.S., Senator Elizabeth Warner was doing her part to rally domestic support. At a private dinner in New York, she sat across from the CEOs of the nation's largest tech companies—giants like SpaceX, Google, and Amazon. The stakes were high, and she knew she needed to secure their financial backing.

"Garbuz's vision will require funding on a scale we've never seen before," Warner said, her voice steady. "But the payoff will be extraordinary. The IISF will create a new industry, one that will drive technological advancement for generations. We're talking about everything from space travel to asteroid mining to new energy sources. This is the future of American innovation."

The CEOs exchanged intrigued glances. One of them, a man with salt-and-pepper hair and the sharp gaze of a tech titan, leaned forward. "We're interested, Senator, but space is a risky investment. What guarantees do we have that the IISF won't collapse under the weight of global politics?"

Warner smiled. "No guarantees, except this: those who invest in the IISF will shape the next century. And those who don't will be left behind."

The room fell into silence, the enormity of the decision hanging in the air.

Chapter 7

Sabotage and Subterfuge

On a chilly evening in Moscow, President Vasily Orlov met with a select group of advisors deep within the Kremlin. The usual grand halls and opulent decor were absent in this clandestine meeting. The room was small, the lights dimmed, the air thick with tension. Orlov sat at the head of a round table, his face illuminated by the glow of a laptop in front of him. On the screen was a detailed report of Garbuz's progress—one that was deeply concerning to Russia's inner circle.

"This Garbuz… he's more of a threat than we anticipated," said Viktor Karpov, his most trusted advisor. His voice was calm, but the concern in his eyes was unmistakable. "His proposal is gaining momentum faster than we thought. Germany is on board. India is leaning toward joining. Even China is considering negotiating."

Orlov's fingers drummed against the table, his eyes narrowed. "And yet, his plan is still vulnerable. It's not fully realized yet."

Karpov nodded. "True. But the longer we wait, the more dangerous it becomes. Once the IISF is established, our influence in space will be overshadowed. Russia cannot afford to be sidelined."

Orlov's gaze darkened. "Then we strike now, before his coalition solidifies. We need to disrupt his progress, weaken his alliances."

Karpov leaned in slightly, lowering his voice. "We have already begun preparing. Our agents have infiltrated several key sectors of his operation—primarily in the U.S. and Europe. The first step will be a cyber-attack. We've identified vulnerabilities in his university collaborations, particularly the research labs at the University of Minnesota."

Orlov's lips curled into a slight smile. "Good. Make it happen. And ensure it cannot be traced back to us."

Halfway across the world, in Minnesota, the lights inside the University of Minnesota's Space Research Center flickered ominously. Dr. Alison Park, the lead scientist on a critical research project tied to the IISF, glanced up from her desk, her fingers frozen over her keyboard. She furrowed her brow and turned to her colleague, Dr. Ethan Martinez, who was engrossed in reviewing data across the room.

"Did you see that?" Alison asked.

Ethan shrugged, not looking up from his monitor. "Power surge, maybe? Weather's been weird lately."

Alison frowned, her instincts telling her something was off. She was about to return to her work when the lights flickered again—this time longer. The hum of the computers slowed, and the screens around the room suddenly went black.

"What the—?" Ethan began, but his sentence was cut off as a red flashing light appeared on the central server screen. A siren began to blare through the building. The sound was cold, mechanical, and unmistakable.

"Cyber-attack," Alison whispered, her eyes wide. "We're being hacked."

In the following hours, chaos erupted at the Space Research Center. Critical data, research results, and years of work related to space propulsion technology and asteroid mining—all tied to the IISF—were wiped from the university's servers. Security protocols had been bypassed with shocking precision, and it quickly became clear that the attack was far more sophisticated than anything they'd anticipated.

Garbuz was alerted almost immediately. From his office in Washington, he stared at the report in disbelief. Years of research—gone in minutes. The ramifications were immense. Without that data, a significant portion of the IISF's technological foundation was crippled.

"Who did this?" Garbuz demanded, his voice low but laced with fury.

His chief security officer, Elena Markov, shook her head, her expression grim. "We don't have conclusive proof yet, but the attack has all the hallmarks of a state-sponsored cyber-strike. My guess is Russia."

Garbuz clenched his fists. He had expected resistance, even sabotage, but not this soon and not at this scale. He knew Orlov and the Russian elite were wary of the IISF, but he had hoped they would stay on the sidelines for longer, weighing their options before making a move.

"Can we recover the data?" Garbuz asked, though he already knew the answer.

"We're working on it," Elena replied. "But it'll take time. And even if we do, the damage to our credibility—especially with the universities and private sector partners—is done. They'll see this as a vulnerability."

Garbuz stood silent for a long moment, his mind racing. The attack was a direct threat, not just to the IISF, but to the fragile coalition he was trying to build. If word spread that their research was vulnerable, other nations and corporate partners would think twice before committing. He needed to act fast to reassure his allies and stop the momentum of opposition.

As the digital sabotage unfolded, the media began to play its part in undermining Garbuz's efforts. In New York, an influential cable news network, long known for its conservative stance, aired a special report titled: *The IISF: A Billionaire's Fantasy or a Globalist Plot?*

The host, a middle-aged man with a sharp, accusatory tone, introduced the segment with a provocative statement: "Is Georgiy Garbuz's dream of space exploration really about humanity's future? Or is it just another ploy by the elites to consolidate their power?"

The screen shifted to footage of Garbuz's recent speech at the World Economic Forum, followed by sound bites of critics questioning his motives.

"This project sounds good on the surface," one pundit said, "but who really benefits? The billionaires backing Garbuz, or the ordinary citizens who are being crushed under the weight of this collapsing economy? Why should we trust a group of globalists who think space is the answer to the problems they created?"

The media assault was relentless. News outlets across the political spectrum began questioning whether the IISF was viable or even necessary. Garbuz's personal history was scrutinized, with headlines calling him "out of touch" and "an idealist who's disconnected from reality."

Back in Washington, Senator Michael Trent, one of the most vocal critics of the IISF, seized the moment to push his narrative.

"We need to invest in the American people," Trent said during a televised interview. "Not in some far-fetched space project that benefits only the ultra-wealthy. The IISF is a waste of taxpayer money, and I intend to make sure Congress doesn't fund it."

Trent's words carried weight. He represented a growing faction within the government that saw the IISF as a threat to national sovereignty, a way for Garbuz and his global coalition to usurp control of critical resources. This faction was becoming louder, more organized, and more dangerous.

As the media campaign against Garbuz intensified, his enemies struck again. This time, they targeted his allies.

In Berlin, just as the German Chancellor prepared to announce Germany's formal support for the IISF, an anonymous dossier was leaked to the press. It contained allegations of corruption within the Chancellor's administration, accusing key officials of accepting bribes from Garbuz-linked corporations in exchange for backing the IISF.

The scandal erupted across German media, casting a shadow over the Chancellor's government and forcing him to delay any public endorsement of the IISF. Though the allegations were largely unfounded, the damage was done. The political fallout shook Germany's leadership, weakening one of Garbuz's most critical alliances.

As Garbuz's enemies deployed their strategies of sabotage, subterfuge, and smear campaigns, the foundation of the IISF seemed to be cracking. The cyber-attacks, the media frenzy, and the political scandals were taking their toll, threatening to unravel everything he had worked for.

But Garbuz wasn't ready to give up. He had always known this path would be fraught with danger. And now, more than ever, he realized that the stakes were higher than just the future of the IISF—this was a battle for the future of humanity itself.

CHAPTER 8

INTERNAL STRUGGLES

The lights of Washington D.C. sparkled below as Garbuz stood in front of the wide windows of his penthouse office. The city had never looked more chaotic—both outside and within the halls of power. The escalating sabotage, the relentless media attacks, and the targeted disruption of his key alliances were weighing heavily on his shoulders. But it wasn't just the external forces that were closing in. Inside, Garbuz was beginning to feel the pressure—his internal struggle between visionary ambition and the harsh reality of opposition.

His phone vibrated on his desk, and when he glanced at the screen, he saw a name that gave him pause: Dmitry Volkov. He hadn't spoken to Volkov in years. The Russian scientist had been one of Garbuz's closest collaborators during the early days of the IISF project. Together, they had dreamed of a unified world exploring the stars. But as Garbuz's ambitions took off, their paths had diverged. Volkov remained in Russia, sidelined by Orlov's more immediate political and military ambitions.

Garbuz hesitated before answering the call. He had learned to be cautious—especially now, with tensions rising on all fronts. Still, curiosity got the better of him.

"Dmitry," Garbuz said as he picked up the phone. "It's been a long time."

"It has," came Volkov's deep, familiar voice, tinged with the same intensity Garbuz re-membered. "I've been following your progress, Georgiy. And your... struggles."

Garbuz's brow furrowed. "Struggles?"

"Let's not pretend," Volkov said with a slight chuckle. "The cyber-attacks. The media campaign. The political sabotage. Russia's fingerprints are all over it. You must know that."

Garbuz tightened his grip on the phone, but kept his voice steady. "And what do you want, Dmitry?"

"I want to help you, Georgiy," Volkov replied. "You and I once shared a vision. A united world reaching for the stars. But that vision is slipping away, and you're under siege. Orlov is playing a dangerous game. He's feeding the flames of opposition while keeping Russia in a position to swoop in and take over the IISF if it falters."

"I'm aware of Orlov's ambitions," Garbuz said flatly. "But what do you want from me?"

There was a pause on the line before Volkov responded, his tone more serious. "We both know the future is in space. Orlov and the other power players don't see it yet, but they will. And when they do, the IISF needs to be strong enough to withstand their interference. I'm offering you access to resources, connections, and information. But in return, I need a place at the table when the IISF is fully realized."

Garbuz turned away from the window, his mind racing. Volkov was no ordinary ally. He was brilliant, with connections to some of Russia's top scientists and technocrats. But he was also ambitious, perhaps too much so. Accepting his help could give the IISF the boost it needed, but it could also open the door to even more complications.

"I'll think about it," Garbuz said, his tone cautious.

"Don't think too long," Volkov warned. "You don't have much time."

The call ended, leaving Garbuz standing alone in the dim light of his office. The offer hung heavy in the air. He had always been wary of Volkov's opportunism, but now, with the walls closing in, the possibility of aligning with him was tempting. Garbuz knew that in order to win this battle, he might have to make compromises—even ones that left him vulnerable to future threats.

Later that evening, Garbuz met with his closest confidante and advisor, Elena Markov, in a private room of the Senate offices. Elena had been by his side from the beginning, helping him navigate the political labyrinth of Washington and Europe. A former intelligence officer with a sharp strategic mind, she had proven indispensable in guiding the IISF through its early stages. But now, even she was feeling the strain.

"We're losing control of the narrative," Elena said bluntly as she spread out the latest news clippings across the table. Headlines screamed about corruption scandals in Germany, financial mismanagement at the University of Minnesota, and rising skepticism over the viability of the IISF.

"They're targeting our allies, our research, and now our public image," Elena continued. "And it's working. Support for the IISF is waning. If we don't respond soon, we'll lose more than just credibility—we'll lose our funding."

Garbuz sat down, his head in his hands. "What do we do, Elena? I'm running out of options. The media is turning against us. Orlov is orchestrating attacks from the shadows. And now, Volkov is offering help—but I can't trust him."

Elena leaned forward, her eyes steely. "Volkov is dangerous, but we need to be smart. If we reject his offer, we risk losing valuable resources and intelligence. But if we accept, we have to make sure we control the terms. We use him, not the other way around."

"And the media?" Garbuz asked, his voice heavy with frustration.

"We fight fire with fire," Elena said. "We've been too reactive. It's time to go on the offensive. I've already started planting stories in more favorable outlets—highlighting the scientific advancements the IISF has made, the jobs it's creating, the long-term economic benefits. We need to take back the narrative and remind people why the IISF matters."

Garbuz nodded slowly, grateful for Elena's relentless focus. But beneath his appreciation was a deeper unease. He had always known that the path to realizing his dream would be fraught with challenges, but he hadn't anticipated how quickly the opposition would become personal. His reputation, his integrity, even his closest allies were now under attack. And it was only going to get worse.

As the night wore on, Garbuz found himself alone in his apartment, staring at the ceiling. His thoughts drifted back to the beginning, to the moment when he had first conceived of the IISF. It had been a dream born from necessity—a way to unite a fractured world under a common goal, to escape the petty squabbles over territory and resources that had plagued humanity for centuries.

He had believed that space was the answer. That by looking beyond Earth, humanity could find not only new resources but a new sense of purpose. But now, that dream felt more distant than ever. The very forces he had hoped to overcome—greed, fear, and power politics—were threatening to destroy everything he had built.

His phone buzzed again, breaking the silence. It was a message from Senator Elizabeth Warner:

Meeting confirmed. 9 AM tomorrow. We need a plan.

Garbuz exhaled, feeling the weight of tomorrow pressing down on him. The battle was far from over, but it was becoming clear that the fight for the IISF wouldn't be won with vision alone. It would require strategy, alliances, and perhaps, compromises he had never expected to make.

Chapter 9

The Confrontation at Court

The hearing chamber buzzed with anticipation. Journalists packed into the gallery, their cameras and microphones pointed at the raised dais where members of Congress prepared to grill Georgiy Garbuz. It wasn't just another routine hearing—it was a public showdown. The future of the *International Intergalactic Space Federation* (IISF) hung in the balance, and both Garbuz's allies and enemies were poised for battle.

Garbuz sat at a long table in the center of the room, flanked by Senator Elizabeth Warner and his legal counsel. He had faced challenges before, but this felt different. The stakes were higher, and the opposition was more organized than ever. Across the room, Senator Michael Trent, his chief antagonist, looked ready for a fight. Trent's faction had been hammering away at the IISF for weeks, and this was their opportunity to take it down publicly.

The room quieted as the chairman of the committee, a stern-faced man with graying hair, called the session to order. "We are here today to discuss the feasibility, funding, and national security implications of Mr. Georgiy Garbuz's International Intergalactic Space Federation proposal."

The chairman's voice echoed through the chamber, and Garbuz could feel the weight of the moment. Cameras zoomed in on his face, capturing every flicker of emotion. He knew the world was watching.

Senator Trent wasted no time. As soon as the floor was opened for questions, he leaned forward, his voice dripping with skepticism. "Mr. Garbuz, your proposal for the IISF is ambitious, to say the least. But what I—and many of my colleagues—fail to understand is why you believe that this project should take priority over addressing the crises we face right here on Earth."

Garbuz met Trent's gaze evenly, knowing this would be the first of many attacks. "Senator, I believe that space exploration is not just about curiosity or ambition. It's about survival. The crises we face on Earth—economic instability, resource scarcity, and geopolitical conflict—are symptoms of a larger problem. Our planet's resources are finite, and unless we expand beyond Earth, we will continue to face these challenges."

Trent raised an eyebrow, unimpressed. "So, let me get this straight. You want American taxpayers to fund a multi-trillion-dollar project to explore space when we can barely keep the lights on in parts of the country? How do you justify that?"

Garbuz leaned forward slightly, his voice calm but firm. "The IISF isn't just an exploration project, Senator. It's an investment in the future. The technologies we develop—whether it's asteroid mining, new energy sources, or medical advancements—will create industries that generate trillions in revenue. The jobs, the infrastructure, the scientific breakthroughs—all of that will directly benefit the American people."

Trent wasn't satisfied. "And what about national security? By inviting other nations—many of whom are our adversaries—into this so-called 'federation,' aren't you opening the door for them to gain access to sensitive space technologies? Technologies that could be used against us?"

Garbuz expected this line of attack. "The IISF is structured to ensure that no single nation, corporation, or entity can dominate its research or technologies. Every participant brings something to the table, and every nation benefits from the discoveries we make. But let's be clear: if America doesn't take the lead in space, someone else will. Whether it's Russia, China, or private corporations, we cannot afford to be left behind."

Senator Warner, who had been quietly observing the proceedings, finally spoke up. Her voice cut through the tension with a precision that commanded attention. "I think it's important to remember, Senator Trent, that space is no longer a theoretical concept. We're already seeing the commercialization of low-Earth orbit. Companies like SpaceX and Blue Origin are leading the way. But the IISF is about more than just space tourism or launching satellites. It's about building the infrastructure for the next phase of human civilization."

Trent shot her a pointed look. "And at what cost, Senator Warner? You're asking us to commit billions—possibly trillions—of taxpayer dollars to a project with no guarantees."

Warner didn't flinch. "There are never guarantees, Senator. But what we can guarantee is this: if we do nothing, we will face a future where other nations control the resources of space. They will dictate the terms of access to new technologies, new energy sources, and new industries. The cost of inaction is far greater than the cost of investment."

The hearing continued for hours, with Garbuz fielding questions from skeptical senators, some of whom were more interested in scoring political points than in understanding the true potential of the IISF. The media was having a field day, with pundits on both sides framing the hearing as either the last gasp of a doomed project or the dawn of a new era.

But Garbuz wasn't just fighting for his vision—he was fighting for the future of humanity. And he could feel the opposition mounting.

In the final round of questioning, Senator Trent leaned forward again, his voice lower but more deliberate. "Mr. Garbuz, I'm going to ask you something that I think a lot of Americans want to know. You've talked a lot about the benefits of the IISF. But what I want to know is: who are you really doing this for? Is this about helping humanity? Or is it about securing your own legacy, your own place in history?"

The question hung in the air, a thinly veiled accusation of vanity and self-interest. Garbuz felt the weight of every eye in the room on him, waiting for his response.

He took a breath before speaking. "Senator, I didn't start this project to make a name for myself. I started it because I saw a future that was coming, whether we were ready for it or not. I believe that the challenges we face today—on Earth—cannot be solved by looking inward. We have to look outward. We have to imagine a future where we are not bound by the limits of our planet. This isn't about me. It's about all of us."

The room fell silent as Garbuz's words resonated. Even those who had come to the hearing ready to tear him down seemed momentarily caught off guard by his sincerity. But Garbuz knew this wouldn't be enough to change their minds. He would need more than words—he would need action.

After the hearing, as Garbuz and Senator Warner left the chamber, they were swarmed by reporters shouting questions. Garbuz remained calm, answering briefly before slipping into the back of the waiting car with Warner by his side.

Once they were safely away from the press, Warner turned to him, her expression unreadable. "That was a tough session, but you handled it well. Trent's attacks were predictable, but the public reaction might be harder to control."

Garbuz nodded, his mind still racing from the events of the day. "I know. We need to move fast. We can't wait for them to come to us—we have to show the world why the IISF is necessary."

Warner glanced out the window, the city lights flashing by. "The hearing wasn't the end of it, Garbuz. The fight has just begun. We need to rally more allies, and quickly."

Garbuz's phone buzzed with a new message. He glanced at it and saw it was from Elena Markov:

We need to talk. New intel on Orlov.

Garbuz clenched his jaw. The Russian president had been pulling strings behind the scenes, working to undermine the IISF from the shadows. Now, with tensions rising, Garbuz knew he would need to confront Orlov directly—and soon.

Chapter 10

Divided Loyalties

The tension in the air was palpable as Georgiy Garbuz paced the length of his office, deep in thought. The congressional hearing had been bruising, but the real damage had come afterward. News of the cyber-attacks, the corruption scandal in Germany, and the wavering support from key allies had thrown the entire *International Intergalactic Space Federation*(IISF) into a state of uncertainty.

The IISF coalition, which had once seemed like a solid foundation for the future, was beginning to fracture. Now, Garbuz had to face the painful reality that some of his most trusted allies were wavering in their commitment. They were spooked by the relentless political and economic attacks, and without strong leadership, their support was slipping away.

The first blow came from Europe. In Berlin, the Chancellor sat behind his desk, his expression weary as he stared at the television screen displaying headlines about the corruption scandal. A high-ranking official in his administration had been accused of accepting bribes in exchange for backing the IISF, and while the accusations were largely unfounded, the damage was done. The Chancellor's political capital had taken a serious hit.

His advisor, a wiry man in his mid-50s with sharp features, stood nearby, his hands clasped behind his back. "Chancellor, we may need to distance ourselves from the IISF. Public opinion is turning against it, and the opposition is growing louder."

The Chancellor rubbed his temple, the pressure of the situation weighing on him. "We've invested a great deal into this project," he said slowly. "But you're right. If the public believes we're involved in corruption..."

His voice trailed off as the thought of losing Germany's hard-earned credibility weighed on him. For years, the Chancellor had pushed Germany to become a leader in Europe's scientific and technological development. Supporting the IISF was part of that vision, but now it felt like a political liability.

"What do we tell Garbuz?" the advisor asked.

The Chancellor sighed. "For now, we don't make any public statements. We quietly pull back our support, at least until this scandal blows over. We cannot afford to be seen as reckless, especially with elections coming up."

In Washington, Garbuz received the news through a late-night phone call from one of his European contacts. Germany was pulling back. He gripped his phone tightly, his knuckles white with tension. The Germans had been one of his strongest backers. If they faltered, others might follow.

"Do we know how long they'll stay silent?" Garbuz asked, his voice betraying his frustration.

"They're not saying," came the reply. "But the Chancellor is facing a lot of pressure. He's fighting for his political life right now."

Garbuz muttered a curse under his breath. "We need to stabilize this situation, fast. Keep me updated on any changes."

He hung up the phone and stood in silence for a moment, weighing his options. Germany's withdrawal—however temporary—could send ripples through the entire coalition. And the sabotage wasn't just coming from outside forces. Inside the U.S., political resistance was mounting, and some of his closest allies were starting to show cracks under the pressure.

In Senator Elizabeth Warner's office, the mood was equally tense. Warner sat at her desk, reviewing a growing pile of reports detailing the opposition's latest maneuvers. Across from her sat her chief of staff, an experienced political operator who had been with her through some of her toughest battles.

"Trent's faction is pushing hard," the chief of staff said. "They're gathering signatures for a bill that would block any federal funding for the IISF. If it passes, it'll cripple the project."

Warner's brow furrowed. "How many signatures do they have?"

"Too many," the chief of staff replied. "They're gaining traction with moderate Republicans and even a few Democrats. The attacks on the IISF are hitting home with voters—Trent's team is framing it as a waste of taxpayer money, and people are starting to listen."

Warner stood and began pacing, much like Garbuz had in his office. She had known from the beginning that this fight wouldn't be easy, but the ferocity of the opposition was staggering. She had been through political battles before, but this felt different. The IISF wasn't just a project—it was a vision for the future, one that transcended borders and national interests. But convincing the American public to see the bigger picture was proving more difficult than she had anticipated.

"We need to counter this," Warner said firmly. "We need to show the public that the IISF isn't a luxury—it's a necessity. Space isn't some distant dream anymore. It's the key to solving our problems here on Earth."

The chief of staff nodded. "I'll start working with our media contacts. But it's going to be tough. Trent has the media on his side, and his messaging is resonating. We'll need to push back hard."

Warner's mind was racing. The IISF couldn't afford to lose momentum now. They needed to win the narrative, and they needed to win it fast.

Meanwhile, halfway across the world in Beijing, President Zhang Wei was weighing his own options. China's role in the IISF had yet to be fully decided. While Zhang saw the long-term potential of the project, he was also aware of the risks. China's participation would provoke Russia and potentially strain its relationships within BRICS. But on the other hand, it was an opportunity to secure China's dominance in the space race and expand its influence beyond Earth.

Zhang's top advisor, Lin Cheng, stood across from him in the grand office of Zhongnan-hai. "We've received feelers from Garbuz's team," Lin said. "They're eager to begin formal talks with us. But if we align with the IISF, we'll need to negotiate from a position of strength."

Zhang nodded slowly. "We cannot rush this decision. China must enter the IISF on our terms, or not at all. I want Garbuz to understand that we will be equal partners—no more, no less."

"Agreed," Lin replied. "But we also need to consider the ramifications. Russia will not be pleased if we join."

Zhang smiled faintly. "Let Orlov fume. He's already undermining the IISF with his sabotage, but he cannot stop the future. If Garbuz's vision succeeds, space will belong to those who control its resources. And China must be part of that future."

Back in Washington, Garbuz was struggling to keep the coalition together. The withdrawal of Germany's public support, combined with the growing opposition in Congress, had shaken confidence in the IISF. Some of his most loyal backers were beginning to question whether the project could survive the relentless attacks.

As he reviewed the latest reports with Elena Markov, his security advisor, Garbuz couldn't shake the feeling that time was running out. He needed to shore up support—fast. But the pressure from all sides was mounting, and even his closest allies were beginning to feel the strain.

"How much more of this can we take?" Garbuz asked, rubbing his forehead in frustration.

Elena, always calm and calculating, studied him for a moment before answering. "We've been hit hard, but we're not finished. The opposition is gaining ground, but we can still turn this around. We just need a win—something big enough to shift the momentum back in our favor."

Garbuz nodded, though he wasn't sure what that win would look like. He had bet everything on the IISF, and now it felt like the project was teetering on the edge of collapse. But he knew one thing for certain: he wasn't going to give up. The future of the IISF, and perhaps humanity itself, depended on what he did next.

Chapter 11
Orlov's Counterattack

The heavy clouds that hung over Moscow seemed to mirror the mood inside the Kremlin. President Vasily Orlov stood at the head of a long, polished table, his gaze fixed on the detailed reports laid out before him. The cyber-attacks and media campaigns against Garbuz had succeeded in creating chaos, but the IISF had not yet crumbled. Garbuz was still pushing forward, and even worse, China was edging closer to supporting him. Orlov knew he had to act decisively before the momentum shifted completely in Garbuz's favor.

Viktor Karpov, Orlov's top advisor, sat across from him, his expression grim but composed. He had orchestrated the first wave of sabotage, targeting the IISF's infrastructure and corporate backers. But it wasn't enough. Garbuz was more resilient than they had anticipated, and his coalition—while weakened—was still holding on.

"China is about to make its move," Karpov began, breaking the tense silence. "If they join the IISF, it will solidify Garbuz's position. We need to hit them before that happens. Harder."

Orlov nodded slowly, his mind working through the possibilities. "We need something more aggressive, something that will send a clear message to the world—and to China—that the IISF is doomed to fail."

Karpov leaned forward, lowering his voice. "We've identified a new target. A European aerospace company—Astra Technologies. They're a key partner in the IISF's space propulsion research. Without their technology, Garbuz's plan for sustainable space travel would collapse."

Orlov's eyes gleamed with interest. "You're proposing we take them out?"

"Not directly," Karpov replied. "But we can sabotage their operations in a way that cripples their research and causes a ripple effect throughout the European tech sector. A cyber-attack that targets not only their data but their reputation. If they fall, Garbuz loses a critical piece of his coalition."

Orlov considered this for a moment, then nodded. "Make it happen. And ensure it's untraceable. The last thing we need is Europe uniting against us."

The following week, the CEO of Astra Technologies, Leonie Müller, sat in her Berlin office, scanning through reports with growing anxiety. The company's cutting-edge propulsion systems were at the heart of the IISF's space travel plans, and Astra was seen as a leader in the global aerospace industry. But now, strange anomalies were showing up in their systems. Data was being corrupted, files disappearing. At first, it seemed like a technical glitch, but it was quickly becoming clear that something far more sinister was happening.

Leonie frowned as she read the latest report from her IT security team. "Cyber-attack confirmed," the subject line read. The details were chilling—months of research, gone. Entire servers wiped clean. She picked up the phone and dialed her head of IT, her voice sharp.

"How bad is it?"

The response on the other end was grim. "Bad, Leonie. We're not sure how they got in, but it's a sophisticated attack. They knew exactly what to target—our most sensitive research on the IISF propulsion systems. We're trying to recover what we can, but it's going to take time."

Leonie leaned back in her chair, her mind racing. She knew what this meant. Without that data, Astra's involvement in the IISF was in jeopardy. The project was already facing intense scrutiny, and if word got out that their research had been compromised, the backlash would be severe.

"Keep this quiet," she ordered. "Don't release any information to the press yet. We need time to figure out what we've lost and how to recover."

But even as she gave the order, Leonie knew that it was only a matter of time before the news leaked. The attack wasn't just an attempt to cripple Astra—it was a message to the entire aerospace community. And Leonie feared that the damage might be irreparable.

Back in Washington, Garbuz received the news through an encrypted message from Leonie Müller herself. He read the report in silence, his face unreadable, but inside, he felt a cold surge of anger. The attack on Astra was a direct assault on the IISF, and Garbuz knew exactly who was behind it. Orlov's fingerprints were all over this.

"Elena," he called, summoning his chief security advisor. "We've been hit again. Astra Technologies was targeted—months of propulsion research, gone."

Elena Markov entered the room swiftly, her expression serious but not surprised. "Orlov is escalating. He knows the pressure is mounting on us, and he's trying to break our alliances before China makes a decision."

Garbuz clenched his fists, struggling to maintain his composure. "We can't afford to lose Astra. If we do, the entire propulsion initiative could collapse."

Elena nodded. "I've already put our cyber team on high alert. We need to fortify our systems and work with Astra to recover what we can. But I have to be honest, Garbuz—Orlov isn't just trying to sabotage the IISF. He's trying to make us look weak, vulnerable. If we don't respond, it'll embolden him."

Garbuz met her gaze, his mind racing through possible strategies. He had always known Orlov would be a formidable opponent, but the Russian president's willingness to use covert attacks on such a massive scale was becoming more dangerous by the day. The IISF was fighting a war on multiple fronts—political, corporate, and now, in the shadows.

"What do we do?" Garbuz asked, though he already had an idea forming in his mind.

"We hit back," Elena said without hesitation. "Not with a direct attack—that would be too risky. But we need to send a message that we're not backing down. Let's work through our allies in Europe and the U.S. to launch a counter-narrative. We'll frame this attack as an act of aggression, not just against the IISF, but against the global scientific community. We'll rally support by painting Orlov as a rogue actor, trying to stifle humanity's future in space."

Garbuz nodded slowly, the plan taking shape. "And what about China? If we can get them to commit publicly, it could change the game. Orlov would think twice before escalating further."

Elena agreed. "That's the key. We need to get China on our side, officially. Once they're in, the political landscape shifts dramatically in our favor."

Garbuz exhaled, the weight of the situation pressing down on him. "Reach out to China's emissary. Let's set up a meeting with President Zhang. It's time to finalize their role in the IISF."

As Garbuz prepared to rally his allies, President Orlov was already planning his next move. In the Kremlin, he sat with Karpov, reviewing the fallout from the Astra attack. The aerospace industry was in turmoil, and the European press was buzzing with speculation about who was behind the cyber-sabotage.

"They're shaken," Karpov said, a hint of satisfaction in his voice. "Astra's stock is plummeting, and their investors are getting cold feet. It'll be difficult for them to recover from this."

Orlov allowed himself a small smile, but it was fleeting. "Good. But this is just the beginning. Garbuz is resilient, and he'll try to spin this attack to his advantage. We need to stay ahead of him."

"What's next?" Karpov asked.

Orlov's smile faded, replaced by a steely resolve. "We target their funding. Garbuz is relying on corporate backers and financial institutions to keep the IISF afloat. We can't let that happen. Find out which companies are still supporting him—and hit them where it hurts."

Karpov nodded, already formulating the next phase of the attack. Orlov's strategy was simple but effective: weaken the IISF's foundation piece by piece, until the entire structure collapsed.

Chapter 12

Allies in the Shadows

The moonlight filtered through the tall windows of a private conference room in Geneva, casting long shadows across the room's minimalist furnishings. Georgiy Garbuz sat across from Dmitry Volkov, his former collaborator, whose expression was as guarded as ever. Volkov had come alone, just as they had agreed. No security detail, no assistants—only the two men, bound by their shared history and ambitions, though now separated by a widening gulf of mistrust.

Volkov leaned back in his chair, his fingers tapping softly on the armrest. "You're in trouble, Georgiy. Orlov is tightening the noose around your neck, and the attacks will only get worse. You need help. My help."

Garbuz remained silent for a moment, studying Volkov's face. They had once worked together, back when the dream of uniting the world in space exploration had seemed possible—before politics, power, and greed had twisted everything. Now, the man sitting across from him was as much a potential threat as he was an ally.

"You're offering help," Garbuz said finally, his tone cautious. "But at what cost?"

Volkov smiled faintly, though there was no warmth behind it. "I have no interest in seeing Orlov control the future of space. My loyalty is to science, not to any political regime. But you and I both know that this isn't just about technology or exploration anymore. It's about control. Whoever leads the IISF will shape the next century, and I intend to be part of that leadership."

Garbuz exhaled, leaning forward slightly. "So, you want a seat at the table. You want to help me, but you also want power."

Volkov's smile widened, but it was humorless. "Power is relative. What I want is to ensure that the IISF doesn't fall into the hands of those who will corrupt its mission. Orlov will stop at nothing to sabotage you—and if he wins, Russia will dominate space, and the rest of the world will be left behind. You need someone who understands how he operates, someone who can anticipate his next moves."

Garbuz weighed the proposition carefully. He didn't trust Volkov—not entirely—but there was truth in what he was saying. Orlov's attacks were growing more aggressive, and Garbuz was running out of time to secure the IISF's future. The recent cyber-assault on Astra Technologies had shaken his coalition, and more attacks were likely to come. Volkov's offer of help could turn the tide, but it came with significant risks.

"Orlov is planning another strike," Volkov continued, his voice lowering slightly. "He's targeting your funding sources. The European financial institutions that back the IISF—Orlov's agents are already working to disrupt their operations, spread rumors, and create instability. If you lose their support, the IISF will collapse before it even gets off the ground."

Garbuz's stomach tightened. He had feared this. Without the backing of key financial players, the IISF would be dead in the water.

"And you can stop this?" Garbuz asked, narrowing his eyes.

Volkov nodded. "I still have connections inside Russia. I can give you the information you need to stay ahead of Orlov's plans. But in return, I want a formal role in the IISF. Not just as a scientist, but as a strategic partner."

The room fell into a heavy silence as Garbuz considered the offer. He had always been wary of making deals with people like Volkov—those who played the game of power for personal gain. But the truth was, Garbuz needed allies. And if Volkov could help him protect the IISF from Orlov's sabotage, perhaps the risk was worth taking.

Finally, Garbuz nodded. "You'll have your role. But remember this, Dmitry—if you betray me, if you undermine the IISF for your own gain, you'll regret it."

Volkov raised an eyebrow, seemingly amused. "Understood. But let's focus on stopping Orlov first."

With the uneasy alliance formed, Garbuz wasted no time. That evening, he called Elena Markov to brief her on the situation. She wasn't happy about the deal with Volkov, but she understood the necessity.

"We can't afford to lose any more ground," Elena said, her voice tense over the phone. "Orlov's been systematically weakening our coalition. First Astra, now the financial backers. We need to go on the offensive."

"I agree," Garbuz replied, pacing his office as he spoke. "But we can't make any direct moves against Russia without escalating things too far. We need to outmaneuver them in the shadows, just as they've been doing to us."

Elena paused for a moment before speaking again. "I've already started working with our media contacts. We're going to shift the narrative. We'll position these attacks on Astra and our financial backers as an assault on scientific progress—on humanity's future. We'll frame Orlov as a rogue actor, someone willing to sabotage the next phase of human civilization for his own political gain."

Garbuz nodded. "Good. And what about China?"

"That's the key," Elena said. "If we can secure China's public support, Orlov will have no choice but to back down. But Zhang Wei is still holding back. They're waiting for the right moment."

Garbuz clenched his jaw, frustrated. He had been in negotiations with China for weeks, and while President Zhang seemed interested in the IISF, he was cautious—too cautious. The Chinese leader didn't want to anger Russia, but Garbuz knew that securing China's backing was the game-changing move that could shift the global power balance in favor of the IISF.

"Set up a meeting with Zhang's emissary," Garbuz said firmly. "We need to close this deal. If China joins, the entire world will take notice."

In the coming days, Garbuz and Elena worked around the clock to fortify their defenses. Volkov provided them with crucial intelligence, helping them anticipate Orlov's next moves and counter the financial disruption attempts before they could cause irreparable damage. Using this information, Garbuz shored up his alliances with European financial institutions, reassuring them that the IISF was still strong, despite the attacks.

Meanwhile, Elena's media campaign began to gain traction. News outlets across the world ran stories about the sabotage, framing Orlov as a villain who was standing in the way of humanity's future in space. Public opinion started to shift, and the narrative of the IISF being a target of political aggression resonated with both politicians and citizens alike.

But Garbuz knew that none of this would matter if they couldn't secure China's involvement.

Two weeks later, Garbuz found himself in a high-level meeting with President Zhang's emissary, Liang Chen, at a discreet location in Singapore. The room was quiet, with only the low hum of the air conditioner breaking the silence. Garbuz had prepared meticulously for this moment. China's participation in the IISF was the missing piece that could tilt the balance of power in his favor.

Liang was a calculating figure—polished, with sharp eyes that gave nothing away. He had been Zhang's right hand for years, trusted to handle delicate negotiations like these. Garbuz could sense that Liang wasn't just here to talk—he was here to assess whether Garbuz and the IISF were worth China's time.

"The IISF represents the future," Garbuz began, leaning forward slightly. "And China has always been a leader in scientific innovation. Joining the IISF will solidify your position as a global leader in space exploration. Together, we can build something that benefits all of humanity."

Liang listened intently but didn't react immediately. "China is interested," he said after a long pause. "But there are concerns. Russia will not take kindly to our involvement, and we cannot afford to provoke them too directly. We need assurances that the IISF will not be used as a tool of Western domination."

Garbuz nodded. He had anticipated this. "The IISF is an international project—there's no room for domination by any one nation. China will have an equal role, just as the U.S., Europe, and other nations do. We're building a new world order—one where the benefits of space exploration are shared."

Liang studied Garbuz carefully. "You make a compelling case. But understand this—if China joins the IISF, we will expect to have a say in its direction. We cannot be seen as secondary to anyone, especially not the West."

Garbuz smiled. "I wouldn't expect anything less."

As the meeting concluded, Garbuz left with a sense of cautious optimism. The talks with China were progressing, and if all went according to plan, they would soon make their support public. It was the breakthrough he had been waiting for.

But he knew better than to let his guard down. Orlov wouldn't give up easily, and there were still forces within his own ranks that could turn against him at any moment.

The battle for the IISF was far from over. But with Volkov's help and China's potential backing, Garbuz felt a renewed sense of hope. The future was still uncertain, but for the first time in weeks, it seemed within reach.

Chapter 13

The Betrayal Within

The corridors of the IISF's headquarters in Washington D.C. had never felt so quiet. Georgiy Garbuz sat in his office, a lingering sense of unease gnawing at the edges of his thoughts. The recent developments—the sabotage, the attacks on Astra, and the delicate negotiations with China—had pushed the IISF to the brink. But now, a new threat had surfaced, one that was far closer and more insidious than any external attack: betrayal from within.

Garbuz had always known that running a project as ambitious as the IISF would attract enemies. Orlov's sabotage had been expected, even if its scale had caught them off guard. But discovering that someone inside his own organization had been feeding sensitive information to Russia? That was something he hadn't prepared for. The revelation had come just days earlier, through a quiet investigation spearheaded by his trusted advisor, Elena Markov. She had uncovered evidence of a mole within the IISF—a high-ranking figure with access to classified information about the project's financial backers and future plans.

Now, as he waited for Elena's final report, Garbuz couldn't help but feel the weight of every decision he had made. The IISF had been built on trust, on the idea that humanity could unite to explore the stars. But trust, it seemed, was in short supply.

The door to his office opened quietly, and Elena stepped inside, her face grave. She held a tablet in one hand, and Garbuz could tell from her expression that the news wasn't good.

"We've confirmed it," Elena said, sitting across from him. "The mole has been feeding information to Orlov for months. Every move we've made, every plan we've discussed—he's known about it."

Garbuz leaned back in his chair, his face impassive but his mind racing. "Who is it?"

Elena hesitated for a moment before answering. "It's David Carlisle."

The name hit Garbuz like a punch to the gut. Carlisle had been one of his earliest supporters, a brilliant engineer and strategist who had helped shape the IISF from the ground up. He had been integral in securing corporate sponsorships and designing the propulsion systems. If Carlisle was the mole, it explained why Orlov's attacks had been so precisely targeted.

Garbuz exhaled slowly, his mind processing the implications. "Do we have proof?"

Elena nodded. "We intercepted communications between Carlisle and an intermediary working for Russia. He's been leaking information about our financial backers and our technological developments. He's also been giving them intel on our negotiations with China."

Garbuz felt a surge of anger rise in his chest. Carlisle had been there from the beginning, had shared the vision of a united humanity. To think that he had been undermining the IISF from within was almost too much to bear.

"Why?" Garbuz asked, though he wasn't sure he wanted to hear the answer.

Elena handed him the tablet, showing a series of encrypted messages. "It seems Carlisle has been in contact with Russian intelligence for over a year. They offered him significant financial incentives in exchange for his cooperation. But it's more than just money—Carlisle believes that Orlov's vision of a Russian-led space program is the future. He's convinced that the IISF is doomed to fail and that aligning with Russia is his best chance at survival."

Garbuz stared at the messages in disbelief. Carlisle, the man he had trusted with some of the IISF's most sensitive secrets, had been bought off by promises of wealth and power.

"What do we do?" Garbuz asked, his voice low but steady.

Elena's eyes were cold, calculating. "We can't let him know we're onto him—not yet. If we confront him, he'll flee, and Russia will tighten its grip on the information he's already given them. We need to use this to our advantage."

Garbuz raised an eyebrow. "How?"

"We feed him false information," Elena said. "We make it seem like the IISF is struggling, like we're on the verge of collapse. Carlisle will pass that intel to Russia, and Orlov will believe it. Meanwhile, we tighten our defenses, secure our backers, and finalize the deal with China. By the time Orlov realizes the truth, it'll be too late."

Garbuz considered the plan carefully. It was risky, but it could work. By feeding Carlisle false intel, they could buy themselves time to stabilize the IISF and rally their remaining allies.

"Do it," Garbuz said finally. "But keep a close eye on Carlisle. If he suspects anything, we'll have to act fast."

Elena nodded, rising from her chair. "I'll handle it. And Georgiy—be careful. Carlisle isn't the only one we need to worry about. Orlov has other agents out there. We're being watched."

Garbuz watched her leave, the weight of the situation pressing down on him. Trust had always been the foundation of the IISF, but now that foundation was crumbling. He had to wonder how many more betrayals lay in wait, hidden in the shadows.

Later that evening, Garbuz sat in a darkened conference room, reviewing the latest reports from their financial backers. The attacks on Astra Technologies had shaken confidence in the IISF, but Elena's media campaign had helped mitigate the damage. Still, the financial landscape was fragile, and Garbuz knew that Orlov's agents were working to destabilize it even further.

As he scanned through the documents, his phone buzzed with an incoming message. It was from Liang Chen, the emissary from China. Garbuz opened the message, his heart racing.

President Zhang has agreed to meet. Formal negotiations for China's involvement in the IISF can begin.

Garbuz's pulse quickened. This was the breakthrough he had been waiting for. If China committed to the IISF, it would change the entire global calculus. With China's backing, Orlov's influence would diminish, and the project would gain the momentum it needed to move forward.

But Garbuz couldn't afford to celebrate just yet. The betrayal by Carlisle had reminded him of how precarious the situation still was. The IISF was a battleground, and even as new alliances were being formed, old ones were breaking apart.

The next morning, Garbuz stood before his inner circle, the weight of recent events clear in his expression. Elena was there, along with several other high-ranking officials from the IISF. David Carlisle was also present, his face betraying no hint of guilt as he took his seat at the table.

"We're moving into the final phase of negotiations with China," Garbuz announced. "President Zhang has agreed to formal talks, and if all goes well, we'll have their support within the week. This is a critical moment for the IISF. With China on board, we'll have the strength to push back against Russia's attacks and solidify our position globally."

Carlisle nodded along with the others, his expression as calm as ever. But Garbuz couldn't shake the feeling of betrayal that lingered beneath the surface. He kept his tone steady, but every word felt like a test—waiting to see if Carlisle would betray any sign that he knew his deception had been uncovered.

"We need to be cautious," Elena added, her eyes briefly flicking to Carlisle. "Russia won't stop just because China is coming to the table. Orlov is preparing new attacks, and we need to stay vigilant."

The room buzzed with quiet agreement, but Garbuz's focus remained on Carlisle. He had to play this carefully. If Carlisle sensed that they were onto him, the mole could do even more damage before they had a chance to neutralize him.

As the meeting concluded, Garbuz watched Carlisle closely, his mind racing with questions. How long had Carlisle been playing this game? How much damage had already been done? And more importantly, when would be the right moment to confront him?

For now, the facade would remain intact. Garbuz would pretend that nothing had changed. But beneath the surface, the pieces were already in motion.

Chapter 14

The First Victory

T he weight of anticipation hung over the room as Georgiy Garbuz stepped into the conference hall in Beijing. The air was thick with the gravity of what was about to unfold. This meeting would define the future of the *International Intergalactic Space Federation* (IISF), perhaps even the future of humanity's reach into space. As Garbuz adjusted his tie, his eyes swept across the polished marble floors and the towering columns of the Great Hall, where China's most powerful leaders had gathered to negotiate.

The Chinese delegation sat at the far end of the long table, led by President Zhang Wei and his chief emissary, Liang Chen. Garbuz could feel the tension in the room as both sides prepared for what could be a historic agreement. Behind Garbuz stood his own team, including Senator Elizabeth Warner and Elena Markov, each of them poised, ready to make the final push to secure China's backing for the IISF.

The stakes could not have been higher. With China's support, the IISF would have the resources and international credibility it desperately needed. More importantly, it would send a signal to the world—and to President Orlov—that Garbuz's vision for the future could not be easily derailed.

President Zhang spoke first, his tone measured but his words laced with an underlying tension. "Mr. Garbuz, we have followed your progress with great interest. The *International Intergalactic Space Federation* is an ambitious project—one that aligns with China's long-term goals in space exploration. However, we must ensure that our participation is not merely symbolic. We expect a significant role in decision-making and strategic planning."

Garbuz nodded, fully prepared for Zhang's demands. China had been cautious throughout the negotiations, but now that they were ready to enter formal talks, Garbuz knew that securing their involvement would mean significant concessions.

"I understand, President Zhang," Garbuz replied, his voice steady. "The IISF is designed to be an equal partnership among nations. China's contributions—both technologically and financially—are critical to its success, and we are prepared to offer China a leading role in the development of our space propulsion systems, as well as the governance of future space colonies."

Zhang exchanged a glance with Liang Chen, who gave a subtle nod. The tension in the room seemed to ease ever so slightly.

"We are pleased with this proposal," Zhang said, his expression softening. "But there is another matter. China must be assured that the IISF will remain free from any single nation's dominance—especially Western influence."

Garbuz leaned forward slightly. "The IISF is not an extension of Western powers. It is an international initiative, and every member nation will have equal standing. We have safeguards in place to ensure that no single country or corporation can control the project. This is a new frontier for humanity—one that must belong to all of us."

Zhang considered this for a moment, and then, to Garbuz's relief, gave a slow nod. "Very well. China will officially join the IISF as a founding member. We look forward to working together to build the future of space exploration."

A sense of triumph surged through Garbuz as the agreement was formalized. The room buzzed with the sound of official documents being passed back and forth, signed by both sides. As the ink dried on the papers, Garbuz couldn't help but feel that they had crossed a major threshold. China's participation was the breakthrough the IISF needed. With their resources, technological expertise, and global influence, the project now had the backing to counter Orlov's aggressive sabotage.

Senator Warner leaned over, her voice barely above a whisper. "This changes everything. Orlov won't be able to ignore this."

Garbuz nodded, his thoughts already moving toward the next phase. "Orlov's playing a dangerous game. This will force him to recalibrate."

But even as Garbuz allowed himself a moment of victory, a part of him remained cautious. The battle for control over the IISF was far from over. Orlov had already proven that he was willing to use underhanded tactics to undermine the project, and there was no doubt that Russia would respond to China's involvement.

Back in Moscow, President Orlov received the news with thinly veiled fury. His intelligence officers had briefed him on China's decision within hours of the signing. The announcement that China had formally joined the IISF was a seismic shift in the geopolitical landscape. It was exactly what Orlov had feared.

Sitting across from Viktor Karpov, Orlov's jaw tightened as he processed the implications.

"This is a disaster," Orlov said, his voice cold and restrained. "China was supposed to remain neutral—now they've thrown their lot in with Garbuz."

Karpov remained composed, but the tension in the room was unmistakable. "Zhang made his move sooner than we expected, but this doesn't mean we've lost. We still have leverage."

Orlov's eyes narrowed. "What leverage?"

"We've weakened their financial infrastructure," Karpov said. "And we still have a mole inside the IISF. Carlisle can continue feeding us valuable information. They won't see the next strike coming."

Orlov nodded slowly, though his frustration simmered beneath the surface. He had known from the beginning that Garbuz's project would be difficult to kill. The man was a visionary—driven, relentless—but Orlov had no intention of letting the IISF succeed. His goal was simple: to ensure that Russia dominated space, and that any other nation attempting to challenge that supremacy would be crushed.

"If China is backing Garbuz, then we hit them harder," Orlov said, his voice dropping to a dangerous whisper. "I want another cyber-attack—this time on a critical component of their infrastructure. Something that will cripple their operations, but without leaving any trace back to us."

Karpov nodded, already formulating the plan in his mind. "I'll mobilize our cyber units immediately. We'll target their energy systems. A well-timed blackout could disrupt their operations for weeks."

Orlov allowed himself a faint smile. "Good. And ensure that Carlisle continues to believe he's safe. He's still useful to us."

As the days passed, the IISF began to feel the impact of China's involvement. Financial institutions that had once been on the fence now expressed renewed confidence in the project. Investors from both the public and private sectors poured resources into the initiative, and the media began to shift the narrative. Where once the IISF had been portrayed as an overambitious, fragile endeavor, it was now being hailed as the future of global cooperation in space.

Garbuz could feel the momentum shifting in his favor. He had scored a major victory, but he remained vigilant. The IISF was still vulnerable, and with Carlisle's betrayal still hidden, the threat of another attack from Russia loomed large.

One evening, as Garbuz sat reviewing the latest reports in his office, Elena Markov entered, her expression serious.

"We have a problem," she said quietly.

Garbuz looked up, immediately on alert. "What is it?"

Elena handed him a file. "We've intercepted new communications from Carlisle. He's still feeding information to Orlov, and they're planning something big. A cyber-attack—targeting our energy grid."

Garbuz's pulse quickened as he flipped through the file, scanning the details. If Orlov managed to pull off another attack, it could cripple the IISF's operations, just as they were gaining momentum. The entire project could be brought to its knees.

"We need to stop this," Garbuz said, his voice resolute. "And we need to take Carlisle down."

Elena nodded. "I've already begun laying the groundwork. But we'll need to act carefully. Carlisle doesn't know we're onto him, and we can use that to our advantage. If we play this right, we can not only stop the attack but turn the tables on Orlov."

Garbuz leaned back in his chair, the weight of the coming confrontation settling over him. The stakes had never been higher, but this time, he had an advantage. He knew the enemy's next move—and he was ready to strike back.

Chapter 15
The Turning Point

The air in the IISF headquarters was unusually still, as if the entire building was holding its breath in anticipation. Georgiy Garbuz sat at the head of the long conference table, staring at the reports scattered in front of him. They had waited long enough. The final piece of evidence had been collected, and the time had come to expose the mole within their ranks.

Across from him, Elena Markov was calm but focused, her fingers tapping lightly on the tablet that displayed Carlisle's encrypted communications with Orlov's agents. Everything was in place. Their cybersecurity team had laid the trap, feeding David Carlisle false information about an upcoming IISF operation. The moment Carlisle passed that data to Orlov, they had their proof.

Garbuz had spent days preparing for this moment. Carlisle had been a trusted advisor, an integral part of the IISF's leadership. He had helped secure corporate sponsorships, shaped strategy, and contributed to some of the most critical technological developments. And yet, all the while, he had been feeding information to Russia, undermining everything Garbuz and his team had worked so hard to build.

"Are we ready?" Garbuz asked, breaking the silence.

Elena nodded. "We're ready. Carlisle's in his office. As soon as he transmits the false data, we'll move in."

Garbuz's jaw tightened. He hated the thought of betrayal, especially from someone so close. But this wasn't about personal feelings—this was about the survival of the IISF. If they didn't deal with Carlisle now, the project could be irreparably damaged. Orlov's next attack could be devastating if they didn't cut off his source inside the organization.

Elena's tablet pinged with a soft notification. She glanced down, then looked up at Garbuz, her eyes sharp.

"He's transmitting the data now."

David Carlisle sat in his sleek, modern office on the top floor of the IISF headquarters, completely unaware that his every move was being monitored. The faint hum of the air conditioning was the only sound as his fingers tapped out the final few keystrokes, sending the latest round of intel directly to his contact within Russian intelligence.

He felt a small sense of satisfaction as he leaned back in his chair, glancing out the large windows at the Washington D.C. skyline. Orlov had promised him safety, wealth, and a place in Russia's new space initiative—an offer Carlisle couldn't refuse. He had been convinced for months that the IISF was doomed to fail. In his eyes, aligning with Russia was his best chance to ensure his own future.

The message sent, Carlisle closed his laptop and stood, stretching his arms. He had no idea that the trap was already closing in on him.

Back in the main conference room, Garbuz's voice was cold and measured. "It's time."

Elena nodded and signaled the security team, who were already waiting outside Carlisle's office. They moved swiftly and silently, their steps echoing through the quiet halls as they approached.

Within minutes, they reached Carlisle's door. The team leader, a tall man with a military bearing, knocked sharply. "Mr. Carlisle, we need you to come with us."

There was a brief pause before the door opened. Carlisle's face was calm, though confusion flickered in his eyes. "What's going on?"

"You're needed for an urgent meeting with Mr. Garbuz," the team leader said, his tone neutral. "Please follow us."

Carlisle hesitated for a moment but nodded, grabbing his jacket from the back of his chair. As he stepped into the hallway, the security team flanked him, guiding him toward the conference room where Garbuz and Elena were waiting.

The room felt cold as Carlisle stepped inside, the door clicking shut behind him. He saw Garbuz seated at the head of the table, his expression unreadable, while Elena stood off to the side, her arms crossed. The tension in the room was palpable.

"What's this about?" Carlisle asked, trying to sound casual, though a sliver of doubt crept into his voice.

Garbuz didn't answer right away. Instead, he motioned to Elena, who brought up a series of encrypted messages on the screen at the front of the room. Carlisle's face paled slightly as he recognized the communications—the same ones he had been sending to Orlov's agents over the past several months.

"We know everything, David," Garbuz said, his voice low but steady. "We've been monitoring your communications with Russia. Every bit of information you've passed on, every move you've made—it's all here."

Carlisle's heart pounded in his chest, but he tried to maintain his composure. "I don't know what you're talking about," he said, though the denial sounded hollow even to his own ears.

Garbuz's eyes darkened. "Don't insult me by lying. We have the proof. We know you've been working for Orlov. The false information you just sent him—it's part of the trap we set to catch you. It's over, David."

For a moment, there was silence. Carlisle's mind raced, searching for an escape, for a way to turn the situation to his advantage. But there was no way out. The betrayal had been laid bare, and there was nothing he could say to change it.

Finally, Carlisle exhaled, the last of his defiance draining away. "I did what I had to do," he said, his voice flat. "The IISF is doomed, Garbuz. You know it, I know it. Orlov's vision is the only future that matters. He'll control space, whether you like it or not. I was just ensuring my own survival."

Garbuz's expression didn't change, though inside, he felt a surge of disgust. "You sold out the future of humanity for your own selfish gain," he said quietly. "You betrayed everything we were building."

Carlisle shrugged, his face a mask of indifference. "Survival is all that matters in the end."

Elena stepped forward, her voice cold. "You're finished here, Carlisle. You've been removed from all IISF operations, effective immediately. Security will escort you off the premises, and if you attempt to contact anyone within the organization, we'll press charges for espionage."

Carlisle's face tightened, but he remained silent. There was nothing left for him here. He had played his part, and now he would face the consequences.

Garbuz watched as Carlisle was led out of the room, his mind still reeling from the betrayal. But there was no time to dwell on it. They had exposed the mole, but the real battle was just beginning.

As the door closed behind Carlisle, Garbuz turned to Elena. "Is the information he passed to Orlov being fed through the decoy system?"

Elena nodded. "Yes. The Russians think they've intercepted critical intel about our financial situation and upcoming operations, but it's all false. It'll buy us time to reinforce our defenses and mislead Orlov's next move."

Garbuz exhaled slowly, feeling a small sense of relief. "Good. But we need to stay vigilant. Orlov isn't going to stop, and now that Carlisle's been exposed, we'll need to move quickly before they launch their next attack."

Elena nodded in agreement. "I'll double our cybersecurity measures and brief the team. We need to be ready for anything."

Garbuz glanced at the empty chair where Carlisle had just been sitting, the weight of the betrayal still lingering. But now was not the time for hesitation. The future of the IISF depended on their next moves, and Garbuz knew that every decision from here on out would shape the fate of the project—and possibly the future of space exploration itself.

Chapter 16

The Cyber-Attack

The atmosphere in the IISF control center was tense, the quiet hum of machines and the rapid typing of keyboards the only sounds. Everyone was on edge. The trap they had set for Carlisle had worked—he had fed false information to Orlov, just as planned. But Garbuz and his team knew the Russians wouldn't wait long to strike back.

Suddenly, alarms blared through the control room. Screens flickered, and critical systems began to glitch. Elena Markov immediately moved to the central console, her fingers flying over the keyboard as she accessed the system's diagnostics.

"It's happening," she said sharply, her voice tense. "We're under attack."

The cyber-offensive had begun.

Garbuz moved to Elena's side, his face grim. He watched as the monitors showed the first signs of a massive, coordinated cyber-attack. The Russians had launched their assault—targeting the IISF's energy grid and core infrastructure, just as Carlisle's intercepted messages had warned.

Across the room, the cybersecurity team was working frantically to defend the organization's systems, but the scale of the attack was overwhelming. It wasn't just a single hack—it was a wave of penetrations hitting multiple entry points simultaneously. Firewalls were crumbling, systems were shutting down, and key infrastructure was being compromised.

"They're targeting the grid," one of the technicians called out. "If they breach it, they could knock out power to our main facilities."

Elena's fingers moved rapidly across the screen as she pulled up the energy grid's defenses. "We need to isolate the grid. Shut down all non-essential systems, divert power to critical infrastructure."

"On it," the technician replied, his voice strained as he worked to reroute the power.

Garbuz turned to Elena, his expression hard. "Can we hold them off?"

Elena didn't look up from the screen, her voice clipped. "We have a chance, but it's going to be close. They're using sophisticated malware—this isn't an ordinary hack. Orlov's pulling out all the stops."

Garbuz's jaw tightened. He had expected Orlov to retaliate, but the sheer scale of the attack was staggering. If the Russians succeeded in taking down the IISF's energy grid, it wouldn't just cripple the project—it could destroy it.

As the attack intensified, chaos began to spread throughout the IISF's operations. Communications with several satellite facilities were cut off, and the internal network was compromised. Engineers in the propulsion research labs reported critical systems failures, and several departments were forced to shut down to prevent further breaches.

Elena's voice was sharp as she barked orders to her team. "We need to isolate each sector. Cut them off from the main network. If we can't keep the grid protected, we'll lose everything."

A technician looked up from his terminal, panic in his voice. "They're hitting the financial system too! They're trying to lock us out of our funding sources."

Garbuz felt a knot form in his stomach. The financial systems were the lifeblood of the IISF—without access to funds, they couldn't pay their staff, continue research, or maintain partnerships. Orlov was targeting every weak point, trying to suffocate the project.

"Can you stop it?" Garbuz asked, his voice urgent.

Elena's face was a mask of concentration as she worked furiously to block the breach. "I can slow them down, but they're using advanced tools. We need more time."

Garbuz turned to the cybersecurity lead. "What about the decoy system we set up?"

"We're using it to funnel some of their attacks into dead ends, but they're adapting fast," the lead replied, sweat beading on his forehead. "We can't keep them distracted forever."

As the attack wore on, Garbuz realized the battle wasn't just about technology—it was about time. They needed to outlast the assault, to keep their systems alive long enough to repel the Russian hackers. But with every passing minute, the damage mounted. Entire departments had gone offline, and even the most secure systems were under threat.

"Elena," Garbuz said quietly, "we need to make a decision. If we can't stop this, we have to protect the core systems. Whatever it takes."

Elena's eyes flicked to him, understanding the gravity of his words. The IISF's core systems held the most valuable research and data—the foundation of their entire operation. If they lost that, the project would be set back by years, if not destroyed entirely.

"I can isolate the core," Elena said, her voice tense. "But it means cutting off most of our external systems. We'll lose communication with the outside world, and the rest of the network will be vulnerable."

Garbuz's mind raced. If they cut themselves off, they would be isolated, blind to the outside world. But if they didn't, Orlov could break through and devastate the entire project.

"Do it," Garbuz said firmly. "We protect the core at all costs."

Elena nodded, immediately typing commands into the system. "Shutting down non-essential systems. Diverting all resources to the core."

As the external systems went dark, the tension in the room grew even thicker. The IISF had effectively gone into lockdown, sealing off its most vital systems from the outside world. Garbuz felt the weight of his decision, knowing that this was a temporary solution—a last resort. If the Russians found a way through the core defenses, there would be no coming back.

Minutes passed like hours as the attack continued to rage. The team worked relentlessly, blocking breaches, rerouting power, and keeping the critical systems alive. Garbuz stood at the center of it all, directing the effort with cold determination. There was no room for error.

"They're pulling back," Elena said suddenly, her voice cutting through the tension. "We've blocked most of their access points. They're still trying, but we've got control of the grid again."

A collective sigh of relief swept through the room, but it was short-lived. The damage had been done. Communications were down, systems were compromised, and parts of the IISF's infrastructure were in disarray. But the core remained intact. The project had survived, for now.

Garbuz turned to Elena, his face still set in a grim expression. "What's the status?"

Elena scanned the readouts on her console. "We've held them off for now. But the damage is extensive. We'll need days—maybe weeks—to fully repair the breaches. We were lucky this time, but we can't withstand another attack like that."

Garbuz nodded slowly. "Then we need to make sure there isn't one. Orlov has played his hand, and now it's our turn. We need to go on the offensive."

Elena looked at him, understanding dawning in her eyes. "You want to strike back."

Garbuz's expression hardened. "We can't just keep defending ourselves. Orlov's not going to stop. We need to take the fight to him."

As the team began the process of stabilizing their systems, Garbuz's mind was already working through the next steps. The cyber-attack had been a devastating blow, but they had survived. Now, it was time to shift the balance of power.

The battle for the future of space wasn't just being fought in boardrooms or laboratories—it was being fought in the shadows, in the digital battlefield where nations vied for control. And Garbuz was ready to push back.

But even as the immediate crisis passed, Garbuz knew that Orlov wouldn't rest. The next attack could come from anywhere, at any time. The stakes were rising, and the survival of the IISF depended on their ability to adapt, to strike before they were struck down.

The war for control of space had only just begun.

Chapter 17

Carlisle's Betrayal

The chill of betrayal lingered in the air as David Carlisle was escorted out of the IISF headquarters under the watchful eyes of security. His face, once so assured, was now a mask of stoic defeat, though Garbuz doubted the man felt any true remorse for his actions. Carlisle had made his choice—siding with Orlov and selling out everything the *International Intergalactic Space Federation* stood for. Now, he would face the consequences.

Garbuz stood in silence at the window of his office, watching as the vehicle carrying Carlisle disappeared down the street. He could still feel the tension from the cyber-attack that had rocked the IISF just hours ago. Though they had managed to repel Orlov's forces and protect their core systems, the damage was done. Communications were down, resources were strained, and morale had taken a heavy blow. But the biggest wound of all was the trust that had been shattered.

"You made the right call," Elena Markov said as she stepped into the room, her tone reassuring but edged with gravity. "Carlisle was a threat from the moment he started working with Orlov. We had to remove him before he caused more damage."

Garbuz turned to face her, his expression conflicted. "I know. But knowing doesn't make it any easier. He was one of us, Elena. He helped build this project, and now he's nearly destroyed it."

Elena approached the desk, her eyes sharp with determination. "The damage he's done is significant, but it's not fatal. We've already started repairs, and most of our critical systems are back online. The real problem is Orlov. He's not going to stop—this attack was just the beginning."

Garbuz nodded, pacing the length of the room. "Carlisle was just a pawn. Orlov's playing a larger game, and as long as he's out there, the IISF will never be safe."

Elena folded her arms. "We've neutralized Carlisle, but we need to turn this situation to our advantage. Orlov thinks he has the upper hand, but we can use that against him. The false information Carlisle fed to the Russians has already thrown them off course. They believe we're more vulnerable than we really are."

Garbuz's eyes narrowed. "So, we keep playing the part. Make them believe we're still on the ropes."

Elena smiled, a small, cold smile. "Exactly. Let Orlov think we're weak, and while he's busy planning his next move, we'll be ready to strike back."

As they solidified their plans, Garbuz and Elena began preparing for the inevitable fallout from Carlisle's betrayal. Though the immediate crisis had been contained, the repercussions would ripple through the organization. The team needed to be informed, and more importantly, reassured.

Garbuz gathered his senior staff in the main conference room. The mood was somber, the weight of the attack and the betrayal heavy on everyone's shoulders. Engineers, scientists, strategists—all of them looked to Garbuz for leadership in this critical moment.

He stood at the head of the table, his voice steady but firm. "You've all seen the damage from the cyber-attack. It was severe, but we held our ground. We've identified the source of the breach—David Carlisle. He was working with Orlov to sabotage the IISF from within."

There was a murmur of shock from the group. Carlisle had been a respected figure among them, and the revelation of his betrayal hit hard.

"He's been removed," Garbuz continued. "And the information he leaked to Orlov was carefully controlled. They think we're on the verge of collapse, but we're not. We're going to rebuild, and we're going to use this moment to strengthen our defenses and rally our allies."

Elena stepped forward to brief the team on the specifics of the damage control efforts. "We've isolated the systems they targeted, and while it will take time to fully recover, we've secured our core infrastructure. But we need everyone on high alert—Orlov won't stop with one attack."

The room fell silent again, but Garbuz could sense a renewed determination in his team. They were shaken, yes, but they weren't broken. The IISF had weathered the storm, and now it was time to prepare for the next phase.

As the meeting broke up, Garbuz and Elena retreated to the secure command center to oversee the final steps of their counteroffensive. Carlisle's betrayal had shaken the foundation of trust within the organization, but now they had an opportunity to turn the tables on Orlov.

Elena pulled up the latest intelligence reports on her screen. "We've tracked the flow of information that Carlisle sent to Russia. The decoy system worked perfectly—Orlov's agents think they've gotten hold of key financial data, but it's all fabricated. If they act on it, it'll lead them into a trap."

Garbuz studied the reports, his mind racing through the possibilities. "And what about the core systems? Are we secure?"

Elena nodded. "We've fortified our defenses and set up additional layers of encryption. It'll be much harder for Orlov to break through next time. But we can't get complacent. This was a close call."

Garbuz knew she was right. Orlov had played his hand, but it was only a matter of time before he struck again. The next attack could come from any direction, and Garbuz needed to stay one step ahead.

"We need to think long-term," Garbuz said, his voice low but firm. "Orlov's not going to stop with cyber-attacks. We need to prepare for something bigger—something more direct."

Elena glanced at him, her brow furrowed. "What are you thinking?"

Garbuz crossed his arms, staring at the map of global IISF operations on the screen. "Orlov's next move won't just be digital. He's losing control of the space race, and he knows it. His next attack could be physical—an attempt to sabotage our facilities or disrupt our space missions."

Elena's eyes narrowed. "You think he'd go that far?"

"I know he will," Garbuz replied grimly. "And we need to be ready for it."

As Garbuz and Elena plotted their next moves, the wheels were already turning in Moscow. President Vasily Orlov sat in his darkened office, reviewing the latest reports from his intelligence officers. The cyber-attack had failed to cripple the IISF, but that didn't mean the war was over. Far from it.

Viktor Karpov, Orlov's top advisor, stood at the window, gazing out at the Kremlin's snow-dusted courtyard. "The information Carlisle sent us was a dead end. Garbuz played us."

Orlov's lips pressed into a thin line. "Garbuz is clever, but he's not invincible. We've weakened him, and now we press the advantage."

Karpov turned to face Orlov, his expression cautious. "How far do you want to take this?"

Orlov's gaze darkened. "As far as it takes. If Garbuz thinks he's safe behind his firewalls and his international partnerships, he's mistaken. I want a direct strike—something that will send a message to the entire world."

Karpov hesitated. "You mean... a physical attack?"

Orlov nodded slowly. "Yes. It's time we reminded the IISF—and the world—that space is not theirs to control. We will cripple their operations before they have a chance to recover."

Karpov's face remained unreadable, but he nodded. "I'll begin making the arrangements."

Orlov leaned back in his chair, his mind racing with the possibilities. Garbuz had survived the first round, but this was far from over. The next move would be decisive, and when it came, the IISF wouldn't see it coming.

Chapter 18
The Last Defense

The weight of the attack still hung over the IISF headquarters like a storm cloud, its aftershocks rippling through every department. Repairs were underway, but the organization was still vulnerable. The Russian cyber-attack had exposed weaknesses, and though the immediate threat had been repelled, Garbuz knew they weren't out of danger yet. The next blow would come soon, and this time, it wouldn't just be digital.

Garbuz stood in the heart of the IISF command center, surrounded by rows of monitors and technicians, their fingers flying over keyboards as they scrambled to bring their systems back online. He exchanged a glance with Elena Markov, who was standing beside him, reviewing the latest intelligence.

"Orlov's next move is coming," Garbuz said quietly, his voice filled with a cold certainty. "We have to be ready."

Elena's eyes were focused on the display in front of her. "We've stabilized the core systems and restored most of the internal communications. But if Orlov shifts to a physical attack, we'll need to prepare for a much more dangerous confrontation."

Garbuz nodded, his jaw set in determination. The idea of a physical strike was no longer just a theory—it was a looming threat. Orlov was becoming increasingly desperate, and there were whispers from their intelligence contacts that the Russians were planning something far more aggressive. Whether it was sabotage, an assault on IISF facilities, or even an attack on one of their early space missions, Garbuz knew they needed to act fast.

"Any word from our contacts in Moscow?" Garbuz asked, glancing at Elena.

Elena shook her head, frustration flickering in her eyes. "Nothing concrete yet. We know Orlov's planning something, but he's keeping it tightly controlled. Our best chance is to anticipate his next move before it happens."

Garbuz's mind raced as he considered the possibilities. They needed to fortify their defenses—both physical and digital—before Orlov's forces could make their move. But there was also an opportunity here. If they could preempt Orlov's attack, they might be able to turn the tables on him once and for all.

Later that evening, Garbuz called a meeting with his senior staff in a secure room deep within the IISF's headquarters. The team gathered around a circular table, their faces grim but focused. Each one of them had been shaken by the cyber-attack, but there was a shared sense of determination in the room. They all knew that the IISF was under siege, and now it was time to fight back.

"Orlov's next strike will be physical," Garbuz said, wasting no time. "We've intercepted enough chatter to know that much. He's desperate to cripple us before we recover from the cyber-attack."

Elena pulled up a series of blueprints on the display behind her, highlighting key IISF facilities across the globe. "Our main vulnerabilities are the propulsion research labs in Germany and the spaceport in French Guiana. Both are critical to our upcoming missions, and if Orlov targets them, it could set us back months—maybe longer."

Garbuz studied the maps, weighing their options. "We need to increase security at both locations. Double the staff, bring in military advisors if we have to. We can't afford to leave any opening for sabotage."

"Already in motion," Elena confirmed. "But there's more. Our sources in China have picked up increased activity near our joint research facility in Beijing. It's possible Orlov could target one of our international partnerships, trying to drive a wedge between us and our allies."

Garbuz clenched his fists, feeling the pressure mounting. Orlov wasn't just aiming to cripple the IISF—he was trying to unravel the international coalition that supported it. If he succeeded, Garbuz's vision for a united future in space could collapse before it ever truly began.

"We can't defend everywhere at once," Garbuz said after a long pause. "But we need to make it clear that we're prepared. Orlov is counting on us being reactive—let's show him we're ahead of the game."

Elena nodded. "We'll set up countermeasures at all critical points, increase surveillance, and coordinate with local governments. If Orlov tries anything, we'll be ready."

As Garbuz's team worked to strengthen their defenses, Orlov was already moving forward with his plans in Moscow. In a hidden operations center deep within the Russian military complex, Orlov sat at the head of a table, surrounded by his top advisors. His mood was dark, but his determination remained unwavering.

"The cyber-attack didn't break them," Orlov said, his voice like ice. "But it weakened them. The IISF is vulnerable right now, and this is our opportunity to deliver a final blow."

Karpov, his chief advisor, leaned forward, the light from the overhead projector casting harsh shadows across his face. "We have several options. A direct assault on their facilities would cripple their operations, but it carries significant risk. They've increased security since the attack."

Orlov considered the options. "What about their spaceport in French Guiana? If we can sabotage their next mission, it would send a message to the entire world that the IISF isn't invincible."

Karpov nodded. "We have agents in place who could infiltrate the spaceport. The upcoming launch is critical to their operations. If we can delay it—or destroy key components—we'll set them back months."

Orlov's eyes gleamed with cold satisfaction. "Do it. I want this mission to fail, publicly and spectacularly. Garbuz may have survived the first round, but he won't survive this."

Back at the IISF headquarters, preparations were already underway. Garbuz had doubled security at the spaceport and deployed additional teams to the research labs in Germany and the facility in Beijing. They were fortifying their defenses, but Garbuz knew that defense alone wouldn't be enough. They needed to be proactive.

Elena entered Garbuz's office, her face set with determination. "We've put everything in place, but there's still a chance we're missing something. Orlov's agents are good. If they get inside, it could be catastrophic."

Garbuz nodded, staring out the window into the dark night. "That's why we're going to beat him to the punch. I want our own teams embedded at the spaceport and the labs—people we trust, people who can move quickly if things go wrong."

Elena raised an eyebrow. "You're talking about counter-sabotage?"

Garbuz's gaze hardened. "We've been on the defensive long enough. Orlov thinks he can walk all over us, but it's time we hit back. If his agents make a move, I want them neutralized before they can do any damage."

Elena smiled faintly, a glint of approval in her eyes. "I'll make the arrangements."

The tension only grew as the launch date for the IISF's next major space mission drew closer. The French Guiana spaceport buzzed with activity, engineers and technicians working around the clock to prepare for the mission. But beneath the surface, there was a constant undercurrent of anxiety. Security had been ramped up, but the threat of sabotage loomed over everything.

Garbuz monitored the situation from the IISF command center, watching live feeds from the spaceport. His team had done everything possible to secure the site, but the unknown variables still gnawed at him. Orlov's forces were out there, somewhere, waiting for the right moment to strike.

"Elena," Garbuz said quietly, his eyes on the screens. "How are our agents holding up?"

"They're in position," Elena replied. "No signs of infiltration yet, but we're keeping a close watch. If Orlov's agents try to breach the facility, we'll know."

Garbuz nodded, but his mind raced. They were prepared, but there was no guarantee they could prevent an attack. Orlov had shown that he was willing to do whatever it took to sabotage the IISF, and Garbuz had no illusions about the stakes.

Suddenly, one of the technicians called out from across the room. "We've got movement near the west perimeter!"

Garbuz's heart pounded as he moved to the screen. On the live feed, shadows moved near the edge of the spaceport's restricted zone, figures barely visible in the dim light.

"Is it them?" Garbuz asked, his voice tense.

Elena stepped forward, her eyes narrowing as she studied the screen. "It's hard to tell, but we can't take any chances. I'll alert the security teams."

As Elena made the call, Garbuz watched the figures on the screen with growing dread. This was it. The final move in Orlov's game was about to play out—and everything depended on how they responded.

Chapter 19

The Aftermath

The tension in the control room was thick as Garbuz watched the security feed from the French Guiana spaceport. Shadows moved along the perimeter, barely distinguishable from the darkness that stretched across the jungle. Elena was by his side, coordinating with the on-site security teams, her voice calm but firm as she relayed instructions.

"They're closing in," Elena said, her eyes glued to the screen. "We need to move now."

Garbuz nodded. "Send in the teams. Neutralize any threats before they get close to the launch pad."

The room burst into activity as the security teams on the ground received their orders. Armed personnel moved swiftly through the complex, their night-vision goggles cutting through the darkness as they searched for intruders. Every second counted—the upcoming launch was critical to the IISF's future, and if Orlov's agents managed to sabotage it, the consequences would be catastrophic.

On the ground at the spaceport, the security forces fanned out, moving with precision through the various sectors of the facility. The site, usually buzzing with engineers and technicians, was now on high alert, its lights dimmed to avoid detection. The launch was only hours away, and the tension was palpable.

Suddenly, movement was detected near one of the fuel storage depots—a critical point that, if attacked, could halt the entire mission. The security teams closed in, their weapons raised, and the situation escalated quickly.

"There! On the south side!" one of the security officers shouted into his comms.

The figures in the shadows scattered, but one was apprehended before they could escape. The rest of the intruders vanished into the dense jungle, but it was clear—they were operatives working for Orlov, attempting to sabotage the launch.

In the control room, Garbuz watched the scene unfold, his heart pounding. Elena turned to him, her voice steady but urgent. "We've got one of them. We're sweeping the perimeter to make sure there aren't any more."

"Good," Garbuz replied, though he remained tense. "We can't let them delay the launch. Keep sweeping until we're certain the site is secure."

Hours later, with the perimeter secured and the intruders dealt with, Garbuz's team made final preparations for the mission. The launch was back on schedule, but the lingering threat of sabotage was still fresh in everyone's minds. The sense of urgency hadn't disappeared—it had only deepened.

The mission itself was crucial for the IISF, symbolizing their ability to move forward despite the attacks. It wasn't just a launch—it was a statement to the world, especially to Orlov, that the IISF would not be broken.

"Everything is set," Elena reported, her voice steady over the comms. "The launch window is clear, and the rocket is fueled. We're ready to go."

Garbuz exhaled, feeling the weight of the past few days bear down on him. "Let's make this happen."

As the countdown began, the IISF command center was filled with a charged silence. Every eye was on the live feed from the French Guiana spaceport, where the massive rocket sat on the launch pad, its engines ready to ignite.

The seconds ticked down, and Garbuz's pulse quickened. He knew the stakes—this launch had to succeed. It was the culmination of months of work and a demonstration that the IISF was still standing, despite everything Orlov had thrown at them.

"Ten... nine... eight..."

The room seemed to hold its breath.

"Seven... six... five..."

Garbuz could almost hear the pounding of his own heart.

"Four... three... two..."

The engines roared to life, sending vibrations through the ground. The rocket lifted off in a fiery blaze, streaking into the sky, cutting through the night like a beacon of hope.

"Liftoff," Elena said, a hint of relief in her voice.

Cheers erupted in the control room, and Garbuz felt a wave of emotion wash over him. Against all odds, they had done it. The mission was a success. The IISF was still in the game.

Later, as the adrenaline began to fade, Garbuz stood alone in his office, staring out at the night sky. The launch had gone off without a hitch, but the battle was far from over. They had survived Orlov's latest assault, but the war for control of space was still raging.

Elena entered the room, her expression a mixture of exhaustion and triumph. "The rocket is on course. We've received confirmation from the mission control team. Everything is going smoothly."

Garbuz nodded, but he didn't turn away from the window. "We won this round," he said quietly. "But Orlov's not going to stop. He'll come at us again—and next time, he won't be as subtle."

Elena stepped closer, her tone more serious. "He'll escalate. Now that he knows we're not easily beaten, he'll try something more direct. We need to be ready for anything."

Garbuz sighed, the weight of leadership pressing down on him. "I know. And we will be. But this—" he gestured toward the sky, where the rocket had disappeared moments earlier—"this shows that we're capable of more than just defending ourselves. We can move forward."

Elena's eyes softened for a moment. "This was a victory, Georgiy. Don't lose sight of that."

Garbuz nodded, though his mind was already turning to the next challenge. "We've bought ourselves time. Now, we need to solidify our alliances. If Orlov thinks we're weak, he'll keep pushing. We need to show him—and the world—that the IISF isn't just a project. It's the future."

Across the world in Moscow, Orlov was seething. His operatives had failed to stop the IISF's launch, and the mission had been a public success. He sat in his darkened office, the anger radiating from him like a storm cloud.

Karpov, his top advisor, stood by the window, watching the snowfall outside. "Garbuz played us," Karpov said, his voice calm but cold. "The sabotage didn't work, and now he looks stronger than ever."

Orlov's fist slammed down on the desk. "This isn't over. We lost this battle, but we haven't lost the war. Garbuz is getting too bold—he's showing the world that he can stand up to us. That ends now."

Karpov nodded. "What's the next move?"

Orlov's eyes burned with fury. "We hit them harder. No more games. Garbuz wants to push humanity into space? Fine. But we'll make sure he doesn't get there first."

Back at IISF headquarters, Garbuz and Elena continued to discuss the future. The successful launch had given them a crucial win, but they both knew it was only the beginning. Orlov would come at them again—stronger, more determined, and more dangerous.

Elena pulled up a new report on her tablet. "We've received word that Orlov's agents are regrouping. He's not backing down."

Garbuz's expression was grim. "I didn't expect him to. We'll have to be ready. But we've proven something tonight."

"What's that?" Elena asked.

Garbuz turned to her, his gaze steely. "That no matter how hard he hits us, we're still standing. And now, it's our turn to hit back."

Chapter 20

A Fragile Victory

The mood in the IISF headquarters was tense but cautiously optimistic. The successful rocket launch had been a crucial victory, a demonstration to the world—and to Orlov—that the IISF wasn't about to crumble under pressure. But even as the mission progressed smoothly, the reality of the situation hung heavy over the team. They had barely survived the last sabotage attempt, and there was no question that Orlov would strike again. The sense of relief that had followed the launch was already being replaced by a growing sense of unease.

Georgiy Garbuz stood in front of a large screen in the IISF command center, the after-action report from the launch displayed in crisp, glowing text. Engineers and analysts scurried around him, finalizing their assessments of the mission, but his mind was already elsewhere—thinking of the next challenge.

Elena Markov entered the room, her steps quick and purposeful. She approached Garbuz, a tablet in hand, and handed it to him without a word. He glanced down at the display and frowned.

"This is the full damage report?" Garbuz asked, scrolling through the information. The screen showed a detailed breakdown of the sabotage attempt at the French Guiana spaceport. Though the launch had been a success, the report detailed how close they had come to disaster. Several of Orlov's agents had been apprehended, but a few had managed to slip away, vanishing into the jungle before security could close in.

"Everything we have so far," Elena replied, her voice low but steady. "We caught most of the intruders, but we didn't get all of them. Our people are still sweeping the area, but it's clear Orlov was behind this."

Garbuz's face tightened as he studied the report. He had anticipated sabotage, but the speed and precision of the attack were unsettling. Orlov was no longer playing games—he was escalating, pushing the conflict into dangerous territory. The agents they had captured had been highly trained, moving with the efficiency of military operatives.

"How close did we come to losing the launch?" Garbuz asked, his voice edged with concern.

Elena hesitated for a moment. "Too close. If they had gotten to the fuel depot, the entire mission would've been scrapped. The damage would have been catastrophic."

Garbuz nodded grimly, feeling the weight of the near-disaster settle in his chest. They had won this round, but it had been by the slimmest of margins. One mistake, one misstep, and Orlov would have dealt a serious blow to the IISF's future.

"We need to tighten security across all our sites," Garbuz said, his tone firm. "Orlov's moving fast, and we can't afford to be one step behind him. Every facility, every mission—we need to be prepared."

Elena nodded, her expression resolute. "Already in motion. I've doubled the security teams at the propulsion research labs in Germany and the Beijing facility. We're also reviewing our protocols for the upcoming satellite network mission. But Georgiy, this attack was different. It wasn't just sabotage—it was a coordinated military operation."

Garbuz looked up sharply, meeting Elena's gaze. "What do you mean?"

"The operatives we captured weren't amateurs," Elena explained. "These weren't just mercenaries hired to cause chaos. They were trained, professional agents. Whoever orchestrated this wanted to do more than just delay the launch—they wanted to cripple us. Orlov's moving to a more direct approach."

The realization hit Garbuz hard. The conflict had escalated beyond cyber-attacks and covert sabotage. Orlov was willing to use force, and that meant the stakes were higher than ever. If Orlov succeeded in striking at their facilities, it could set the IISF back by years, maybe even destroy their chances of achieving their vision for space exploration.

Garbuz's mind raced as he processed the information. "We need to take this seriously. If Orlov's moving to physical attacks, it's only a matter of time before he hits us again. We need to stay ahead of him."

Elena leaned in slightly, lowering her voice. "And we can't rely on defense alone, Georgiy. We need to consider a counteroffensive. If we keep letting him dictate the terms of this conflict, we'll always be reacting, always one step behind."

Garbuz paused, considering her words. He had always been careful about escalating the conflict with Orlov, knowing that any overt action could have massive geopolitical consequences. But Elena was right—they couldn't afford to stay on the defensive forever. Orlov had already crossed a line, and it was only a matter of time before the situation spiraled further out of control.

"Let's not rush," Garbuz said cautiously. "We need to be smart about this. We'll start by reinforcing our security and shoring up our defenses. But I want options on the table for a counterstrike. If Orlov keeps pushing, we need to be ready to push back."

Elena gave a small nod, her eyes flashing with approval. "I'll start putting together a plan. But Georgiy, we can't wait too long. If we don't act soon, Orlov will keep gaining ground."

Garbuz turned back to the report, the weight of the moment pressing down on him. The successful launch had bought them time, but it wasn't enough. Orlov was escalating, and the future of the IISF—and humanity's expansion into space—was more uncertain than ever.

Meanwhile, the aftermath of the launch and the sabotage attempt was playing out in the global media. News outlets from every major nation were covering the story, some praising the IISF's resilience, while others raised concerns about the organization's security vulnerabilities.

Senator Warner was on a media blitz, giving interviews and making statements in support of the IISF. She stood before a group of reporters outside the U.S. Capitol, her voice firm as she defended the organization.

"The IISF has shown incredible fortitude in the face of these threats," Warner said, the cameras flashing around her. "What we're seeing is not just about space exploration—it's about the future of international cooperation and human advancement. The recent sabotage attempts are a clear sign that certain actors fear this progress, but I have full confidence in Mr. Garbuz and his team to lead us through this crisis."

But not everyone shared Warner's optimism. A growing faction within the U.S. Congress, led by Senator Trent, was calling for a deeper investigation into the IISF's operations and security practices. Trent's rhetoric painted the IISF as an organization that was becoming too dangerous, too vulnerable to foreign interference.

"We cannot afford to pour billions into an initiative that is consistently under attack," Trent declared in a televised statement. "The risks are too high. We need to reconsider our role in the IISF before we become collateral damage in a geopolitical war."

The media coverage was mixed, with some outlets focusing on the IISF's accomplishments and others questioning whether the project was sustainable under the constant threat of sabotage.

Chapter 21

Orlov's Escalation

In Moscow, the air was thick with tension. President Vasily Orlov sat in the dimly lit briefing room deep within the Kremlin, his expression cold as he stared at the reports spread out in front of him. His plans to sabotage the IISF's recent rocket launch had failed, and Garbuz's space program was still advancing—gaining not just technical ground but global support. That infuriated him.

Orlov's jaw tightened as he received the update: the IISF crew had overcome the first of his carefully planned sabotage measures. His grip on the glass in his hand tightened.

"Prepare to increase our military presence along the Ukrainian border," he said sharply to his advisor. "If the West sees this as an open challenge, we will show them our resolve."

The advisor hesitated but nodded, knowing better than to question Orlov's authority. Viktor Karpov, Orlov's chief advisor and a man known for his icy pragmatism, stood across from him, his face calm despite the president's rage. "They underestimated the IISF's security. The agents we sent to French Guiana did everything they could, but Garbuz's team was prepared. Their response was quicker than we anticipated."

Orlov's eyes flashed with anger. "Being prepared isn't enough. We need to send a message that the IISF will not succeed—no matter what. It's time we escalate. Enough playing in the shadows."

Karpov raised an eyebrow. "You mean a direct strike?"

Orlov leaned back in his chair, his gaze sharp. "Yes. Garbuz thinks he can push forward, build his little coalition, and challenge Russia's dominance in space. But we will show him that space is ours, not his. We will hit him where it hurts."

Karpov nodded, understanding where this was heading. "The propulsion research labs in Germany are a vital part of the IISF's infrastructure. If we take them out, Garbuz will lose months of research. His next missions will be delayed—possibly canceled. It will be a devastating blow to his program."

Orlov smiled, but it was a smile without warmth. "That's exactly what we need. Disrupt his operations. Delay his progress. Make his allies question whether they want to stay on board with a program that's constantly under attack."

Karpov stepped forward, activating a holographic display of the German propulsion research lab. "We have mercenaries on standby—operatives who can carry out the mission without it being traced back to us. They'll strike fast, sabotage the core systems, and disappear before anyone realizes what's happened."

Orlov studied the display, his expression unreadable. "When can they move?"

Karpov glanced at his watch. "Within 48 hours. They're already in position, just waiting for the go-ahead."

Orlov nodded slowly. "Then do it. But make sure there are no loose ends this time. I want this operation to succeed."

Karpov turned and left the room, leaving Orlov alone with his thoughts. The failure of the previous sabotage attempt had left him angry, but this plan—this direct strike—would be different. If the IISF's propulsion lab was destroyed, Garbuz would have no choice but to delay his next mission, and the international support for the IISF would begin to falter.

Orlov's grip tightened on the arm of his chair. He wouldn't allow Garbuz to succeed. Space belonged to Russia, and Orlov intended to keep it that way.

"Inform our field commanders along the Ukrainian border to initiate intensified strikes," he ordered. "Let the world see that while the IISF may escape us for now, there will be consequences. Prepare for retaliation, and make sure it's clear who's responsible for this."

***

Two days later, in a remote industrial park on the outskirts of Berlin, the German propulsion research lab was bustling with activity. Engineers and scientists moved between the sterile corridors, focusing on their work. The lab was critical to the IISF's upcoming mission, working on advanced propulsion systems that would enable longer and more efficient space travel. The success of the next stage of Garbuz's plan depended on it.

But as the sun dipped below the horizon, unnoticed by the busy staff, shadows moved along the perimeter of the facility. A small team of mercenaries, dressed in black tactical gear, advanced silently through the darkness, their movements precise and rehearsed. They had been briefed on their objective: infiltrate the lab, disable the propulsion systems, and disappear before anyone realized what had happened.

Inside, the night shift engineers were largely unaware of the impending danger. They were deep into their work, running simulations, fine-tuning engine designs, and preparing reports for the following day. The hum of machinery filled the air, blending into the background of their routine.

The mercenaries moved closer, bypassing the outer security systems with ease. Orlov's intelligence had provided them with detailed schematics of the facility, and they knew exactly where to strike. They split into two teams—one targeting the propulsion testing chambers, the other heading for the control center to plant a virus that would wipe the lab's data and cause a systems failure.

The leader of the group gestured silently to his team, and they moved into position. The plan was running smoothly—too smoothly, in fact. The lab's security seemed minimal for such a vital facility. But they didn't question it. They had their orders.

In the control center of the lab, a single security monitor flickered, briefly showing a group of figures moving through the shadows before the screen went black. The night shift security guard, barely awake, missed the signal entirely.

Back at IISF headquarters, Garbuz was reviewing final reports on the next mission when a warning light flashed on one of the main monitors. It was a security breach alert—coming from the propulsion lab in Germany. His heart sank as he immediately realized what it meant.

"Elena!" he called sharply, as she was already on her way to him. "We've got trouble. Security breach at the propulsion lab."

Elena quickly accessed the system, her fingers flying across the keyboard. "We're getting reports of unauthorized access to the testing chambers. Looks like multiple intruders—armed. They're targeting the propulsion systems."

Garbuz's mind raced. The propulsion systems were the backbone of their next mission. If Orlov's agents destroyed them, the entire project would be delayed—potentially crippled.

"Do we have anyone on the ground who can stop them?" Garbuz asked, his voice tense.

Elena scanned the readouts. "The on-site security team is small. We can alert local authorities, but it'll take time for them to respond."

Garbuz clenched his fists. Time was the one thing they didn't have. If the mercenaries succeeded, Orlov would have dealt a massive blow to the IISF's operations—and Garbuz couldn't let that happen.

"Send the alert," Garbuz ordered. "Get everyone we can on the ground, now. We can't afford to lose the lab."

Inside the propulsion testing chamber, the mercenaries moved swiftly. They planted explosive charges at key points in the propulsion systems, aiming to disable the engines beyond repair. The leader of the group signaled his team to move out, but as they turned to leave, the first sirens blared through the facility.

"Security's been alerted," one of the mercenaries muttered.

The leader scowled. "Finish the job. We're not leaving until those engines are down."

As the lab's security forces scrambled to respond, a firefight broke out in the control center. The small security team did their best to hold off the attackers, but they were outmatched, and the mercenaries pushed further into the facility, determined to complete their mission.

Meanwhile, local authorities were en route, but Garbuz knew it might be too late. He watched the security feed from the lab, his mind racing. If the propulsion systems were destroyed, it would be a devastating setback.

"Elena," Garbuz said, his voice filled with resolve. "Get in touch with the German authorities and our partners. We need to secure the lab, and we need to do it now."

Chapter 22

A New Front

The sounds of gunfire echoed through the corridors of the German propulsion research lab. The facility, usually humming with the quiet of innovation, had been transformed into a battlefield. The mercenaries moved with deadly efficiency, their weapons aimed at the few security officers who remained in their way. They were just moments from completing their mission—planting the final explosive charges that would cripple the IISF's most critical research.

In the control room, the head of the on-site security, Klaus Bauer, barked orders into his radio, desperately trying to organize a response to the invasion. "We need backup in the propulsion testing chamber! Get those doors locked down!"

But it was chaos. The security team had been caught off guard by the precision of the attack, and now they were scrambling just to keep control of the situation.

Meanwhile, Garbuz stood tensely in the IISF command center, watching the live feed as the mercenaries pushed deeper into the facility. His fingers tapped against the edge of the console, his face grim with worry. The German facility wasn't just another lab—it was the heart of their next space mission. If the propulsion systems were destroyed, the IISF's future would be in jeopardy.

"Elena, where are the authorities?" Garbuz asked sharply, his eyes never leaving the screen.

Elena glanced at her monitor, frustration evident in her expression. "They're on their way, but traffic and local security protocols are slowing them down. The police response unit will be there in five minutes, but…" She hesitated, not needing to finish the sentence.

Five minutes was too long. The intruders had already made it into the most sensitive areas of the lab, and with each second that passed, the chances of catastrophic damage increased.

"We can't wait," Garbuz muttered under his breath. "Can we access the internal security systems remotely? Seal off the testing chambers?"

Elena quickly scanned the options. "I'm trying, but the internal network's been compromised. They've taken control of some systems. It's going to take time to override."

Time. That was the one thing they didn't have.

In the propulsion testing chamber, the leader of the mercenary team knelt beside one of the engines, setting the final charge. The red light on the detonator blinked ominously, counting down the seconds until it would blow. His team had worked swiftly, methodically. They were trained for this—sabotage missions that would leave no trace of their employer's involvement.

"We're set," he said into his earpiece. "Moving to extraction."

But just as they rose to leave, the door at the far end of the chamber slid open with a screech. Two IISF security guards rushed in, weapons drawn.

"Stop!" one of them shouted, aiming his rifle at the mercenaries.

The lead mercenary didn't hesitate. He drew his sidearm in a single motion, firing two precise shots that dropped the guards to the floor. The others in his team moved to cover the exits, ensuring no more surprises would interfere.

"Let's move. We're out of time."

Back in the IISF command center, Garbuz's heart sank as he saw the guards fall. His frustration turned to anger. Orlov had gone too far this time. This wasn't just an attack on infrastructure—it was a war for the future of space, and Garbuz knew it.

"We need to shut this down," Garbuz said to Elena, his voice tense. "I don't care what we have to do—shut down that facility."

Elena, her face set in determination, nodded. "I'll take the facility offline remotely. It'll stall their progress, but the explosives..." Her voice trailed off. Even if they could shut down the lab's systems, the explosives that had already been planted would still go off.

Garbuz's mind raced. They were running out of options. If the propulsion systems were destroyed, the IISF would be crippled for months. And if they lost their technological edge, Orlov would gain the upper hand in the race for space dominance.

"Get me Bauer," Garbuz ordered. "If there's any way to stop this, we need him to do it."

In the lab, Klaus Bauer was pinned down behind a reinforced steel door, his pulse racing as he listened to the chaos unfolding over the radio. He had been head of security for the facility for five years and had never seen anything like this. His men were outgunned, and the mercenaries had already taken control of the critical areas of the lab.

Suddenly, his radio crackled to life. "Bauer, this is Garbuz."

Bauer pressed the receiver to his ear, a wave of relief washing over him. "Sir, we've got a full-scale breach here. They're targeting the propulsion systems."

"I know," Garbuz's voice came through, calm but urgent. "We're seeing it on the live feed. What's your status?"

"We've locked down the outer areas, but they've breached the testing chamber. I've only got a few men left. We're outnumbered."

Garbuz took a breath, his mind racing. "Listen to me, Klaus. They've planted explosives. If those go off, the entire propulsion project is gone. We need to stop them—now."

Bauer grimaced, glancing at his remaining men. "Understood. I'll do what I can, but we need backup. Where are the authorities?"

"They're on their way, but you don't have time to wait for them," Garbuz replied. "I need you to act now."

Bauer's jaw clenched. He didn't hesitate. "We'll move in."

As Bauer and his remaining team prepared for a last-ditch effort to stop the mercenaries, the tension in the control room at the IISF headquarters reached a breaking point. Elena worked feverishly to regain control of the facility's systems, her fingers flying across the console as she attempted to cut the power to the testing chambers.

"We're running out of time," Elena said, her voice tight. "If Bauer can't stop them, those engines are gone."

Garbuz stood behind her, his mind racing with possibilities. They had anticipated sabotage, but not like this—not with such precision and force. Orlov was pushing the conflict beyond what Garbuz had ever expected. This wasn't just a battle for control of space technology—it was becoming something far more dangerous.

"Elena," Garbuz said, his voice low, "if this fails, we need to have a backup plan in place."

Elena glanced up at him, her expression serious. "You're talking about retaliation?"

Garbuz nodded slowly. "If Orlov is willing to go this far, we need to be ready to hit back. Hard."

Elena didn't flinch. "I'll start drawing up contingency plans."

In the propulsion chamber, Bauer and his men burst through the door, weapons drawn. The mercenaries were startled, but quickly responded, firing back as Bauer's team moved in. The firefight was brutal, with sparks flying from control panels and ricocheting bullets pinging off the walls.

Bauer took cover behind a massive engine, his heart pounding. The mercenaries had the upper hand, but he couldn't afford to back down. They had to stop the explosives—no matter the cost.

Suddenly, he spotted the lead mercenary near the control panel, where the detonator for the charges was wired. If he could take him down, maybe—just maybe—they could disarm the explosives in time.

Bauer nodded to his remaining men, signaling them to cover him. He broke from his cover, moving swiftly toward the detonator, his weapon raised.

The lead mercenary spotted him, raising his gun, but before he could fire, Bauer squeezed off two shots. The mercenary staggered back, clutching his chest before collapsing to the ground. Bauer sprinted forward, his heart pounding, and grabbed the detonator.

His hand hovered over the disarm switch, his breath coming in short gasps. Sweat dripped down his forehead as the countdown on the detonator continued to blink.

"Come on," Bauer muttered, his fingers trembling as he input the code to stop the timer.

For a brief, agonizing moment, the screen blinked red. Then, with a beep, the countdown stopped.

The explosives were disarmed.

At IISF headquarters, Garbuz and Elena stared at the monitor as the screen showed the mercenaries being subdued and Bauer's team securing the propulsion systems.

"We did it," Elena said, a note of disbelief in her voice.

Garbuz exhaled, relief washing over him. "This time."

Chapter 23

Rallying Allies

The tension in the IISF command center had finally eased, but only slightly. The German propulsion lab was secure for now, thanks to Bauer's quick thinking and decisive action. Yet the victory felt fragile, as though it could be snatched away at any moment. Garbuz knew the truth—Orlov wasn't done. This was just the beginning of an all-out assault on the IISF.

Garbuz leaned against his desk, his eyes fixed on the latest reports from the German authorities. The mercenaries had been apprehended, but they weren't talking, which wasn't a surprise. The damage to the lab had been minimal, but the psychological toll on the IISF staff was heavy. Many felt exposed and vulnerable, knowing the lengths Orlov was willing to go.

Elena entered the room, her usual calm exterior replaced by a look of determination. "We got lucky tonight," she said, crossing her arms. "If it weren't for Bauer, we'd be dealing with a major disaster. But we can't keep relying on luck. We need to take action."

Garbuz nodded, his mind already working through the next steps. "I agree. Orlov won't stop until we've been completely dismantled. But we can't face him alone—we need our allies more than ever."

Elena raised an eyebrow. "Are you thinking about China?"

"Yes," Garbuz replied. "China, Europe, and the U.S. We need to solidify their support. If Orlov's willing to sabotage our operations, there's no telling what he'll do next. We need to make sure our coalition stays strong."

Elena nodded, moving to the holographic display that showed key IISF partners. "China has been watching the situation closely. President Zhang has already expressed concern over the escalation. But if Orlov continues these attacks, China might hesitate to stay involved."

Garbuz frowned, knowing that Elena was right. China's involvement was crucial to the IISF's success, but their government would only remain supportive as long as the project didn't devolve into an international conflict. Orlov's strategy was clear—create chaos, weaken the coalition, and isolate the IISF until it crumbled from within.

"We need to reassure Zhang," Garbuz said, pacing the room. "I'll call him personally. We have to convince him that the IISF is still strong and that pulling out now would only hand the future of space to Russia."

Elena's expression softened. "And Europe?"

Garbuz sighed. "The German lab attack has shaken our European allies. They've been some of our strongest supporters, but this attack on their soil will make them question how vulnerable we are. I'll speak with them too. We need to rally them around the idea that the future of space isn't just about exploration—it's about security."

Hours later, Garbuz sat in a secure communications room, the dim light casting shadows over his face as he waited for the connection to China to be established. The line crackled to life, and the face of President Zhang Wei appeared on the screen, his sharp eyes studying Garbuz carefully.

"Mr. Garbuz," Zhang began, his voice cool and measured, "I've been following the events in Germany closely. It seems that your program is under considerable threat."

Garbuz inclined his head in acknowledgement. "That's true, President Zhang. The attack on the propulsion lab was a serious escalation by our adversaries, but we managed to secure the facility in time."

Zhang's expression didn't change. "Orlov is growing bolder. If Russia is willing to attack your research facilities so openly, it raises questions about how long this conflict can remain confined to the shadows."

Garbuz leaned forward, his voice steady but urgent. "You're right. Orlov has escalated this beyond sabotage. But that's precisely why we need to stand together. The IISF isn't just a space program—it's the future of international cooperation in space. If Orlov succeeds in undermining it, he won't just stop with us. He'll dominate space, and the rest of the world will be left behind."

Zhang remained silent for a moment, considering Garbuz's words. "China is committed to the future of space exploration. But we cannot afford to be drawn into a conflict that threatens global stability. My government needs reassurances that the IISF can defend itself—and that this won't become a proxy war with Russia."

Garbuz's mind raced. He knew that Zhang was concerned about China's diplomatic position—if China was seen as supporting a Western-led initiative against Russia, it could have serious geopolitical consequences. But he also knew that losing China's backing would be a disaster for the IISF.

"I understand your concerns," Garbuz said, his voice calm. "And we're doing everything we can to strengthen our defenses. But this isn't just about the West versus Russia. The IISF is a global initiative, and China is a key part of that. By standing together, we can ensure that no single nation controls the future of space."

Zhang's eyes narrowed slightly. "You speak of cooperation, Mr. Garbuz, but your adversaries are playing a different game. I will discuss this with my advisors, but know that China will not be dragged into a conflict that does not serve our long-term interests."

Garbuz nodded, though his heart sank. Zhang's support wasn't guaranteed, but the fact that he was willing to listen was a small victory. For now, China remained a tenuous ally, but Garbuz knew that any further attacks would push them closer to pulling out.

The next morning, Garbuz turned his attention to Europe. He contacted President Johann Ritter of Germany, whose government had been deeply shaken by the attack on the propulsion lab.

The holographic screen flickered to life, and Ritter's stern face appeared. There was no warmth in his expression, only the look of a leader forced to deal with a crisis on his own soil.

"Mr. Garbuz," Ritter began, his voice clipped, "I've just been briefed on the full extent of the attack. This could have been a disaster for my country."

Garbuz nodded solemnly. "I understand, President Ritter. The IISF deeply regrets that the German propulsion lab was targeted. We're taking every measure to ensure that this doesn't happen again."

Ritter raised an eyebrow. "And how exactly do you plan to do that? Your program has been a constant target of sabotage, and now armed operatives are attacking your facilities. Germany is one of your strongest supporters, but we cannot continue to back a program that puts our own security at risk."

Garbuz took a deep breath. He knew Ritter's concerns were valid, but losing European support would be a devastating blow to the IISF.

"President Ritter," Garbuz said, his voice firm, "we are implementing new security measures at every facility. We've learned from this attack, and we're taking steps to prevent it from happening again. But pulling out now would only embolden Orlov. He wants to weaken our coalition—to divide us. If we let him succeed, we're handing him control of space."

Ritter's expression softened slightly, but the tension in his voice remained. "Germany stands for progress in space, Mr. Garbuz. But we also stand for security. You need to prove that the IISF can protect its assets—because if we face another attack like this, my government will be forced to reconsider our involvement."

Garbuz nodded, knowing that Ritter's words were a warning. The attack had shaken Europe's confidence in the IISF, and they were teetering on the edge of pulling out. It was now up to Garbuz to show that they could defend themselves and continue pushing forward.

As Garbuz worked to secure the international coalition, tensions were brewing within the IISF itself. The constant threat of sabotage, the increasing attacks, and the growing pressure from their allies were taking a toll on the organization's leadership.

In a private meeting room, Garbuz met with several senior scientists and engineers. Their faces were drawn with fatigue, and some of them looked more frustrated than afraid.

"Georgiy, we can't keep working like this," Dr. Andrei Volkov, one of the senior propulsion scientists, said, his voice tinged with exhaustion. "We're engineers, not soldiers. Our people are scared. They're worried that the next attack could be worse—that we could lose everything."

Garbuz leaned against the table, his expression sympathetic but firm. "I understand, Andrei. But the work we're doing is too important to stop now. We're on the verge of breakthroughs that could change the future of space exploration."

Volkov shook his head. "It's not just about the science anymore. This is becoming a war, and we didn't sign up for that. Some of our engineers are already talking about leaving the program if the situation doesn't stabilize soon."

Garbuz's heart sank. He had been so focused on external threats—Orlov's sabotage, the international coalition—that he hadn't fully realized how much strain the conflict was putting on his own team. If the IISF's best minds began to leave, the program would fall apart from the inside.

"We'll address the security concerns," Garbuz said, his voice steady. "I'll do everything I can to make sure you and your teams are protected. But we need to stay united. The future of space depends on it."

Volkov hesitated, but after a moment, he nodded. "We trust you, Georgiy. Just make sure we're not left vulnerable."

Chapter 24

The Counterstrike

The fallout from the sabotage attempt had shaken the IISF to its core. While Garbuz worked tirelessly to keep international support intact, the internal fractures within his team had started to widen. Trust was fragile, and fear lingered in the halls of the organization's headquarters. But one thing had become clear to Garbuz—defense wasn't enough. If they continued to react to Orlov's strikes without making a bold move of their own, they would eventually be overwhelmed.

Now, as Garbuz stood alone in his office, the lights dimmed and the city beyond his window glowing faintly, he made a decision. The IISF couldn't afford to remain on the defensive. It was time to hit back.

The door opened, and Elena Markov entered. She could tell by the look on Garbuz's face that something had shifted in his thinking. She closed the door behind her, her expression curious and cautious.

"You're thinking about a counterstrike," Elena said, more a statement than a question.

Garbuz nodded, his eyes hard with resolve. "Orlov has gone too far. If we keep playing this game his way, he'll keep escalating until we have nothing left. We need to show him that we're not just here to defend ourselves. We're ready to fight back."

Elena crossed her arms, her gaze intense. "I agree. But you know what that means, Georgiy. Once we cross that line, it'll change everything. This won't just be sabotage and shadow games anymore. It could turn into open conflict."

Garbuz stared at the holographic display on his desk, the map of Russia's secret space facilities glowing softly in the dark. "I know. But we don't have a choice. We need to cripple Orlov's space program before he has a chance to recover from his own failures."

Elena pulled up a detailed map of the facility they had been monitoring for weeks. It was located deep in Siberia, a research base that was critical to Russia's next-generation propulsion systems. The IISF's intelligence sources had confirmed that Orlov was pouring resources into the site, developing technology that could give Russia a significant edge in space exploration and militarization.

"This facility is the key," Elena said, her voice steady. "If we hit them here, we'll delay Orlov's next move by months, maybe even years. But we have to be careful. Russia has the resources to retaliate if they trace this back to us."

Garbuz sat down, his fingers tracing the lines of the facility's layout on the hologram. "We'll have to use a third-party team. Mercenaries, the same way Orlov used them against us. It can't come back to the IISF."

Elena nodded, already considering the logistics. "I'll contact the right people. This needs to be clean, quick, and leave no trace."

For a moment, they sat in silence, the enormity of what they were about to do weighing on them. This counterstrike would change the nature of the conflict—moving it from sabotage and defense into something more dangerous. But Garbuz knew that it was the only way forward. If Orlov believed that the IISF was content to simply defend itself, he would continue his relentless assault.

"Let's do it," Garbuz said quietly, his voice filled with determination. "We strike first."

The next morning, the wheels were set in motion. Elena contacted an elite mercenary group through a series of secure channels, ensuring that their connection to the IISF would remain hidden. The team was highly trained, specializing in covert operations and sabotage, with a reputation for working in the shadows. They had no allegiance other than to their paycheck, and that's exactly what Garbuz needed—deniability.

The target was simple: infiltrate the Siberian facility, disrupt its propulsion research, and leave behind just enough destruction to set back Orlov's plans without triggering an international incident. The mission had to be surgical—there was no room for error.

Elena coordinated with the mercenary leader, a former special forces operative known only as Kiril, to outline the plan. They would strike at night, using the cover of the harsh Siberian winter to mask their approach. The facility was heavily guarded, but the mercenaries had the skills to get in and out without being detected. That was the theory, at least.

Garbuz watched from the sidelines as the plan was finalized. Though he trusted Elena's judgment, the weight of the decision pressed heavily on him. This wasn't just about sabotage—it was a turning point. If the mission succeeded, it would cripple Orlov's ability to advance his space program. If it failed, the repercussions could be catastrophic.

In Moscow, Orlov sat in a high-level meeting with his military advisors. The failure to destroy the German propulsion lab had left him furious, and he knew that Garbuz was becoming bolder. The IISF had survived one attack, and it would only embolden them to push further.

Karpov, his ever-loyal chief advisor, stood by his side, reviewing the latest reports. "We need to step up our efforts," Karpov said, his voice calm but firm. "The IISF is gaining too much momentum. If we don't cripple them soon, they'll pull ahead in this race."

Orlov clenched his fists, his temper barely under control. "What's the status of our research facility in Siberia?"

"It's progressing well," Karpov replied. "But we need more time. The propulsion technology being developed there will give us a significant edge, but it's not ready yet."

Orlov's eyes narrowed. "Then make it ready. Garbuz is getting bolder, and we need to stay ahead of him."

Karpov hesitated. "We've received intelligence that the IISF may be planning a counter-strike."

Orlov's expression darkened. "Let them try. If they think they can outmaneuver us, they're sorely mistaken. But double the security at all our facilities. I want nothing left to chance."

Under the cover of night, the mercenary team led by Kiril made their way toward the Siberian research facility. The biting cold of the Siberian winter worked in their favor, masking their approach as they moved silently through the snow-covered landscape. The facility was a massive industrial complex, its towering structures lit dimly by spotlights that cast long shadows across the snow.

Kiril signaled his team to stop just outside the perimeter. He checked the coordinates on his wrist display, confirming that they were in the right place. The facility's security systems were top-of-the-line, but they had already neutralized most of the surveillance with a cyber-attack coordinated by Elena's team back at IISF headquarters.

"We move in quiet, plant the charges, and get out," Kiril whispered into his comms. "No mistakes."

The team moved swiftly, scaling the outer walls and slipping into the complex. They made their way toward the propulsion labs, where the core research was being conducted. Inside, Russian scientists worked late into the night, unaware of the threat creeping toward them.

Kiril reached the lab's main control room and planted the first of several explosives, designed to destroy the delicate propulsion engines and wipe out months of research. His team moved through the facility, planting charges at key points, ensuring that the damage would be total.

Suddenly, a door opened nearby, and a guard stepped into the hallway, his eyes widening as he spotted the intruders. Before he could sound the alarm, Kiril's silenced pistol fired twice, dropping the guard to the ground. But the noise had been enough to alert the rest of the facility.

"Move!" Kiril barked into his comms. "We've been spotted."

Back at IISF headquarters, Garbuz and Elena monitored the operation in real-time, watching the feed from Kiril's team. Elena's fingers flew across the console, trying to ensure that the facility's security systems remained offline long enough for the mercenaries to escape.

"They're cutting it close," Garbuz muttered, his eyes glued to the screen.

Elena didn't respond, her focus entirely on the operation. The explosives had been planted, but the alarm had been triggered. Russian guards were now swarming the facility, and Kiril's team was running out of time.

Inside the Siberian lab, Kiril led his team toward the extraction point, but the sound of boots on metal grated through the air as Russian soldiers closed in. They had minutes, maybe seconds, before they were surrounded.

"Detonate the charges!" Kiril shouted into his comms.

Elena's hand hovered over the control panel, ready to give the command. She looked to Garbuz, her expression tense. "We're out of time. Do we blow it?"

Garbuz stared at the screen, knowing that the decision would change the course of the conflict. He nodded.

"Blow it."

A series of explosions rocked the facility as the charges detonated, fire and smoke billowing out from the propulsion labs. Alarms blared as chaos erupted inside the complex, the Russian soldiers scrambling to contain the disaster. Kiril's team slipped away into the night, their mission complete.

Back at IISF headquarters, Garbuz and Elena watched as the feed from the facility went dark, the flames consuming the research complex.

"It's done," Elena said quietly.

Garbuz sat back, the weight of his decision settling in. The counterstrike had been a success, but the consequences were yet to unfold. They had struck a blow against Orlov's space program, but the retaliation was sure to follow. The battle for the future of space had only just begun.

Chapter 25

Aftermath of the Counterstrike

The cold, quiet air in the IISF command center contrasted sharply with the intensity of the debriefing session taking place. Garbuz sat at the head of the table, his eyes fixed on the holographic display in the middle of the room, where a detailed map of the Siberian facility flickered in front of him. The strike had been a success. Orlov's propulsion research facility lay in ruins, its critical systems disabled, and his space program set back by months—perhaps even longer. But the tension in the room told Garbuz that the victory was not without consequences.

Elena Markov stood next to him, her arms folded across her chest as she reviewed the final report. The mission had gone as planned—the mercenaries had planted the charges, destroyed the engines and research labs, and escaped before Russian security could mobilize. Orlov's facility was crippled.

"Initial intel suggests they'll need at least six months to recover," Elena said, her voice steady but filled with a cautious undertone. "Maybe longer, depending on how well they manage the fallout. This was a significant blow to their propulsion program."

Garbuz nodded, though his expression remained guarded. "Good. That buys us time."

But even as he said the words, the weight of what they had done pressed heavily on his mind. The mission had been a necessary move, but one that had crossed a line. For months, the IISF had operated in the shadows, reacting to Orlov's sabotage and attacks.

This was their first offensive strike—a direct blow to Russia's space ambitions. And now, the clock was ticking on when and how Orlov would respond.

Elena lowered her tablet and met Garbuz's gaze. "You know what's coming, don't you?"

Garbuz exhaled slowly, leaning back in his chair. "He's going to retaliate. And when he does, it's not going to be subtle."

The room was silent for a moment, the tension thick. Garbuz glanced around at his senior team, all of them processing the enormity of the situation. They had struck first, and in doing so, they had escalated the conflict. The space race between the IISF and Russia was no longer just about innovation or exploration—it was becoming a war of attrition.

"Elena," Garbuz continued, his voice firm, "we need to prepare for a counter-response. Orlov won't wait long before he hits us back. I want all of our facilities on high alert. Double the security at the propulsion labs and the launch sites. If Orlov's next move is physical, we need to be ready."

Elena nodded, already typing commands into her tablet. "I'll make sure everything is in place."

As the debriefing continued, Elena pulled up another report on her screen, this one detailing the status of the mercenaries who had carried out the strike. Garbuz glanced at the file, his eyes narrowing as he scanned the details.

"They're back in hiding," Elena explained. "No one was caught. The Russian authorities are still investigating, but there's nothing to trace back to us. For now, we're in the clear."

Garbuz nodded but didn't feel reassured. The mercenaries had done their job well, but the risk remained. If Russia ever connected the dots, if Orlov found a way to prove the IISF's involvement, the fallout could be catastrophic. Garbuz knew they were walking a fine line—balancing their need to strike back with the danger of being exposed.

"Keep them safe," Garbuz said quietly. "If anything goes wrong, we need to make sure this operation stays buried."

Elena didn't need to be told twice. She knew how dangerous the situation had become and the lengths Orlov would go to if he found out who was responsible for the attack.

After the debriefing, Garbuz made his way back to his office, but he didn't have a moment to settle before Dr. Andrei Volkov entered the room. Volkov was one of the IISF's senior propulsion scientists—a brilliant mind, but not one prone to rash decisions. His expression was serious, his usual calm replaced by concern.

"Georgiy, we need to talk," Volkov said, his tone sharp.

Garbuz sighed, knowing this conversation was coming. He gestured for Volkov to sit. "I'm guessing you're not here to congratulate us on a successful mission."

Volkov sat but didn't relax. "Successful? Maybe. But I'm not sure that's the right word for it."

Garbuz raised an eyebrow. "Go on."

Volkov leaned forward, his hands clasped tightly together. "We're scientists, Georgiy. Engineers. Our job is to push the boundaries of what humanity can achieve in space, not to get involved in these... these games of sabotage and retaliation. This isn't what the IISF was meant to be."

Garbuz leaned back in his chair, his face impassive. "You think I don't know that? You think I enjoy what we've been forced to do?"

"I'm not questioning your intentions," Volkov replied, though his frustration was evident. "But this isn't a battle we should be fighting. We're supposed to be advancing humanity's reach into space, not escalating geopolitical conflicts."

Garbuz's expression hardened. "And if we don't fight back, what happens? Orlov keeps sabotaging our operations, setting us back every chance he gets. We wouldn't be advancing anything. We'd be crushed before we even had a chance to launch."

Volkov looked down for a moment, his voice quieter. "I understand that. But we're losing sight of our mission. Some of the scientists and engineers... they're starting to question whether this is what they signed up for. They're worried, Georgiy. If this escalates any further, we could start losing people."

Garbuz's heart sank. He had been so focused on keeping the IISF moving forward, on surviving Orlov's attacks, that he hadn't realized how much strain the conflict was putting on his own team.

"I hear you," Garbuz said after a long pause. "And I'll address it. But for now, we have to be ready for whatever comes next. We can't afford to let Orlov think we're weak."

Volkov nodded reluctantly, though it was clear the conversation wasn't over. He stood to leave, but before he did, he gave Garbuz one last look.

"Just remember what we're doing this for. We're supposed to be building a future—one that's bigger than all of this."

Garbuz didn't respond, but the weight of Volkov's words lingered long after he left the room.

Chapter 26

Orlov's Retaliation

The heavy drumming of rain echoed off the windows of the Kremlin, but inside the war room, the tension was palpable. President Vasily Orlov sat at the head of the long table, his eyes narrowing as he studied the intelligence reports in front of him. The Siberian facility lay in ruins, its propulsion research set back by months, maybe longer. The room was filled with advisors, military officers, and key figures from the Russian space program, all anxiously awaiting Orlov's response.

At his side, Viktor Karpov stood silently, his calm demeanor betraying none of the urgency of the situation. He had been the first to brief Orlov on the attack, delivering the news that the IISF had struck first. The failure at the Siberian facility had enraged Orlov, but now it was time to channel that fury into action.

Orlov's fingers tapped against the polished wood of the table, his mind racing through possibilities. "They think they can strike us and get away with it," he muttered, almost to himself.

Karpov, ever composed, leaned forward slightly. "They've become bold. Garbuz knows the IISF is vulnerable, but he's also willing to push the boundaries. He's no longer just reacting—he's taking the initiative."

Orlov's lips curled into a snarl. "That ends now. We'll remind Garbuz that space is not his to control."

Karpov nodded. "We need to respond, decisively and publicly. The world needs to see that we're still in control. A failure at this level cannot go unanswered."

Orlov's gaze flicked to the holographic display that showed the IISF's upcoming missions. One particular mission caught his eye—a high-profile satellite launch scheduled for the next month. The mission was designed to deploy the first phase of a satellite network that would serve as the backbone for future deep-space exploration. The launch was crucial for the IISF, and it would be broadcast live to the world as a symbol of their progress.

"That launch," Orlov said, pointing at the display. "We destroy it."

Karpov's eyes gleamed with approval. "Sabotaging the launch would be a crippling blow. If we can sabotage the satellite deployment in a public way, it will do more than set them back—it will humiliate them. Garbuz will be seen as reckless, and the world will question his ability to lead."

Orlov leaned back, the wheels in his mind turning. "Make it happen. I want that launch to fail—spectacularly."

Karpov immediately began outlining the plan. Orlov's agents, already embedded in various locations around the world, would infiltrate the IISF's primary launch site. They would plant explosives in key locations, ensuring that the mission would end in disaster.

"The media will be watching closely," Karpov continued. "If we time this right, the entire world will see the IISF fail."

Orlov's smile was cold. "Good. Let's show Garbuz what happens when you play with fire."

While Orlov and his team set the sabotage plan into motion, Russian intelligence also began a covert campaign of media manipulation. They leaked stories to the press, suggesting that the IISF had been involved in a clandestine operation to destroy the Siberian facility. News outlets across the globe picked up on the story, speculating on whether Garbuz's organization had crossed a dangerous line.

Within hours, the narrative shifted. What had been a quiet victory for the IISF turned into a political storm. Headlines around the world questioned the morality and legality of the IISF's actions: *"Did the IISF Sabotage Russia's Space Program?" "Shadow Games: Is the IISF Becoming a Global Threat?" "Geopolitical Conflict in Space: Are We on the Brink of a New Cold War?"*

The reports fueled growing skepticism about the IISF's mission. Many began to wonder whether Garbuz had lost control, pushing the organization into dangerous territory that could lead to international conflict.

At IISF headquarters, Garbuz watched the media frenzy unfold on his screen. The attack on the Siberian facility had been planned carefully, with no trace left behind, but Orlov's media campaign was creating a narrative that they were involved.

Elena stood by his side, her arms crossed. "They're trying to turn the world against us," she said, her voice filled with frustration.

Garbuz clenched his fists. "And it's working."

The pressure was mounting. Garbuz knew that if the IISF's reputation continued to erode, they would lose support from their international partners—and without that support, the future of the organization was in jeopardy.

The phone rang in Garbuz's office later that day, and he answered it with a sense of dread. On the other end of the line was Senator Warner, the IISF's strongest ally in the U.S. government.

"Georgiy," Warner began, her voice firm but laced with concern, "we need to talk."

"I've seen the reports," Garbuz said, cutting straight to the point. "It's all lies."

"Maybe, but that's not how it's being perceived," Warner replied. "Several members of Congress are starting to ask questions about what really happened in Siberia. Senator Trent is leading the charge. He's calling for an investigation into the IISF's activities."

Garbuz's pulse quickened. "An investigation? Trent's been trying to undermine the IISF for months. He'll use this as an excuse to pull U.S. support."

Warner's silence was all the confirmation Garbuz needed.

"Look," Warner finally said, "I'll do what I can to keep this contained, but you need to address the media. Right now, the world is starting to think that the IISF is engaging in dangerous games, and it's making our allies nervous. You have to get ahead of this."

Garbuz rubbed his temples, feeling the weight of the situation pressing down on him. "I understand. I'll handle it."

But even as he said the words, Garbuz knew that the media narrative was slipping out of his control. Orlov's manipulation had turned the world against them, and the IISF's carefully cultivated image as a beacon of international cooperation was being eroded.

As Garbuz hung up the phone with Warner, a message flashed on his console. It was from President Zhang Wei of China, one of the IISF's most critical partners. Garbuz immediately opened the secure line, knowing that Zhang's involvement was crucial to keeping the organization afloat.

"Mr. Garbuz," Zhang began, his tone measured, "I've been following the media reports. There are growing concerns here about the IISF's role in the recent events."

Garbuz's heart sank. He had feared this call.

"I assure you, President Zhang, the IISF is not involved in any illegal or military actions," Garbuz said firmly. "These are fabrications designed to undermine us."

Zhang remained silent for a moment, his expression unreadable. "Be that as it may, the optics are concerning. China has invested heavily in the IISF, but if this situation escalates into an open conflict with Russia, we may need to reconsider our position."

Garbuz could feel the ground shifting beneath him. Losing China's support would be disastrous. "I understand your concerns, but pulling out now would only play into Russia's hands. Orlov wants to isolate the IISF, and we cannot let him succeed."

Zhang nodded slightly. "We will continue to monitor the situation closely. But be aware, Mr. Garbuz, that China will not be dragged into a conflict that threatens global stability."

The line went dead, leaving Garbuz staring at the screen in silence. The pressure was mounting from all sides—international fallout, media backlash, and the growing threat of Orlov's retaliation. The stakes had never been higher, and Garbuz knew that the next move could determine the future of the IISF.

Chapter 27
The Rising Political Pressure

The following day, the tension at IISF headquarters was palpable. The media storm swirling around the organization was gaining momentum, and political pressure was coming from all directions. The once-unstoppable momentum of the IISF's mission to push humanity into the stars was being overshadowed by allegations of recklessness and political intrigue. For Garbuz, it was no longer just about securing space—it was about defending the very existence of the IISF.

In Washington, Senator Warner was working tirelessly to contain the situation. She had been the IISF's most vocal advocate, ensuring that U.S. support for the program remained strong. But now, her position was being threatened by growing opposition, particularly from Senator Trent, who had seized the opportunity to cast doubt on the IISF's mission.

The secure line connecting Garbuz to Warner buzzed again, and this time, the senator's tone was more urgent than before. The usual pleasantries were dispensed with as soon as the call connected.

"Georgiy, it's getting worse," Warner said, her voice clipped and direct. "Senator Trent is pushing for a full congressional investigation into the IISF. He's already garnered significant support from both sides of the aisle. If this goes through, it could jeopardize the entire program."

Garbuz's chest tightened. "What exactly are they investigating? The IISF hasn't broken any laws. The attack on the Siberian facility has nothing to do with us."

Warner sighed heavily. "That doesn't matter. Perception is everything in politics. Trent and his allies are framing this as an issue of national security. They're claiming that the IISF's actions could provoke an international conflict with Russia—and with Orlov stirring the pot in the media, people are buying it."

Garbuz could feel the walls closing in. "What are our options? Can we stop this before it becomes a full-blown investigation?"

"I'll do what I can to delay it," Warner replied, "but I can't make any promises. You need to get ahead of this, Georgiy. You need to address the media, make a public statement, and reassure everyone that the IISF is still a peaceful, international initiative. If you stay silent, Trent will control the narrative, and that'll be the end of us."

"I understand," Garbuz said, his voice tense. "I'll make a statement. But I'm telling you, we need to act fast. Orlov isn't going to stop at manipulating the media. He's planning something bigger, and we're running out of time."

Warner paused for a moment before responding, her voice softened. "I know. Just be careful, Georgiy. One wrong move, and everything we've built could come crashing down."

As the call ended, Garbuz sat back in his chair, rubbing his temples. The IISF was being attacked on all sides—by the media, by politicians, and by Orlov himself. And the worst part was that their enemies weren't just using weapons or technology; they were using perception and fear to undermine everything the IISF stood for.

Just as Garbuz finished his call with Warner, another alert came through—this time from President Johann Ritter of Germany. Germany had been one of the IISF's strongest backers, hosting some of its most important research facilities. But after the attack on the Siberian propulsion lab, Germany's confidence in the IISF had been shaken.

The holographic display in Garbuz's office flickered to life, revealing President Ritter's somber expression. There was no pleasantry this time, no warm greeting—just a cold, hard reality.

"Mr. Garbuz," Ritter began, "we need to discuss the recent developments. Germany has been a staunch supporter of the IISF, but the recent attack on Russian soil has caused great concern here in Berlin. The media narrative, whether true or not, is that your organization is involved in dangerous covert operations. This is not what we signed up for."

Garbuz took a deep breath, choosing his words carefully. "President Ritter, I understand your concerns, but I want to be clear—the IISF had nothing to do with the attack on Russia's facility. Orlov is orchestrating these rumors to undermine our mission and turn our allies against us. The IISF remains committed to peaceful space exploration."

Ritter's eyes narrowed. "Whether the IISF is directly responsible or not is no longer the issue. The perception is that your organization is entangled in a geopolitical conflict, and that is damaging. We cannot afford to be seen as complicit in an international escalation."

Garbuz leaned forward, his voice calm but firm. "If we let Orlov dictate the narrative, if we back down now, we'll be handing the future of space over to him. He wants us divided and weak. This is exactly what he planned."

Ritter sighed, his face softening slightly. "I don't disagree with you, Mr. Garbuz, but you need to understand the political realities here. My government is under immense pressure to reconsider its support for the IISF. If this situation continues to spiral, we may be forced to withdraw our involvement."

Garbuz felt a chill run down his spine. Losing Germany's support would be a catastrophic blow. The IISF was already on shaky ground, and if Europe began to pull out, the entire project could unravel.

"Give me time, President Ritter," Garbuz said, his tone urgent. "I'm going to make a public statement. We'll reassure the world that the IISF is still dedicated to its original mission. Please, don't pull out now."

Ritter was silent for a moment, then nodded slowly. "I'll give you time, Mr. Garbuz. But know this—my government will not wait forever. We need to see decisive action."

The hologram faded, leaving Garbuz alone once more. The pressure from Europe, from the U.S., from China—it was all building toward a breaking point.

Later that evening, Garbuz convened with his senior team, including Elena Markov and the IISF's head of communications, Sophia Arlen, to craft a public statement. The media had been hounding the IISF for days, and every delay in their response only made the situation worse.

Garbuz stood at the front of the room, the stress of the past few days evident on his face. "We need to take control of the narrative. Orlov's manipulating the media, making us look like the aggressors. That stops now."

Sophia, a sharp and experienced PR strategist, nodded. "We need to emphasize that the IISF is still committed to peaceful, international space exploration. We'll distance ourselves from the rumors of sabotage and focus on our core mission. The public needs to see that we're not involved in any kind of military conflict."

Elena stepped forward, her arms crossed. "But we also need to be careful. If we come off as too defensive, it'll look like we're hiding something. We have to be firm but transparent. This isn't just about the media—it's about regaining the trust of our allies."

Garbuz nodded. "Exactly. We can't just dismiss the allegations—we need to confront them head-on. We'll issue a public statement and hold a press conference. I'll address the media myself."

The room went quiet for a moment. The decision to put Garbuz front and center was risky, but it was necessary. He was the face of the IISF, and if they were going to regain control of the narrative, it had to come from him.

"Let's draft the statement," Garbuz said, his voice steady. "This is our chance to show the world that we're still united, still committed to pushing the boundaries of space."

As the team prepared the media response, the internal divide within the IISF continued to grow. Scientists like Dr. Andrei Volkov had voiced their concerns about the organization's direction, and now, more members of the engineering and research teams were beginning to question the IISF's future.

In a private meeting later that evening, Garbuz met with Volkov once again, this time joined by several other senior scientists. Their faces were tired, their expressions uncertain.

"We've heard about the press conference," Volkov began, his tone calm but firm. "But many of us are still concerned, Georgiy. The IISF's mission was supposed to be about exploration, about pushing humanity forward. But now... it feels like we're getting drawn into a conflict we never intended to be part of."

Garbuz leaned forward, his hands clasped on the table. "I understand your concerns. But you need to trust me on this—if we don't push back against Orlov, if we let him dictate the terms of this conflict, we'll lose everything. The future of space exploration will be controlled by a single nation, and we'll be left behind."

Volkov's expression softened, but the uncertainty remained. "I trust you, Georgiy. We all do. But the longer this drags on, the more we risk losing what makes the IISF special. We can't let this turn into a war."

Garbuz met Volkov's gaze, his voice quiet but resolute. "It already is."

Chapter 28

Sabotage at the Launch Site

The next morning, the mood at IISF headquarters was tense. Garbuz had spent the night preparing for his upcoming media address, but there was little time to dwell on it. The countdown to the IISF's next major mission—launching the first phase of their satellite network—had already begun. This launch was more than just another mission; it was a statement. Success would reaffirm the IISF's capabilities, restoring confidence after weeks of turmoil. But failure would be catastrophic, not just for their technical ambitions but for their public image as well.

The launch was scheduled to be broadcast live across the globe. Garbuz knew that the world's eyes would be on them, watching closely for any sign of weakness or error. What he didn't know was that Orlov's retaliation was already in motion, and it was aimed directly at this high-profile mission.

At the IISF's primary launch site in South America, preparations for the satellite launch were well underway. Engineers, scientists, and technicians moved with purpose, running final diagnostics on the rocket that would carry the critical payload into space. The atmosphere was electric with anticipation. Everything had to go perfectly.

Unbeknownst to them, Orlov's agents had already infiltrated the site. Disguised as contractors and technicians, they moved through the facility with practiced ease, avoiding suspicion as they made their way to the rocket's launch platform. Their goal was simple but devastating: plant explosives at key points within the rocket's structure, ensuring that the launch would end in failure.

Nikolai, the leader of the sabotage team, gestured for his men to follow as they approached the restricted area where the fuel cells were housed. They had rehearsed this operation a dozen times—every step, every move—calculated to be swift and undetectable.

"We'll plant the charges here," Nikolai whispered, crouching down beside the rocket's exterior. "Set the timer for five minutes after launch. That way, it will look like a technical failure. The IISF won't know what hit them."

One of his men pulled a small, cylindrical device from his tool bag and began attaching it to the rocket's fuel line, careful not to trigger any alarms. They had managed to bypass most of the security systems already, thanks to Orlov's cyber team, who had hacked into the facility's surveillance network, temporarily disabling key cameras.

As they worked, the countdown to launch continued ticking away. Everything was set for a seamless sabotage, but Orlov's team hadn't accounted for one thing: Elena Markov's suspicion.

Back at IISF headquarters, Elena sat in the control room, monitoring security feeds from the launch site. It was a routine task she had overseen many times before, but something about today felt different. She couldn't shake the sense that something was off.

As she scanned the feeds, her eyes landed on one particular camera angle near the rocket platform. For a split second, she thought she saw a figure moving through a restricted area—an area that should have been empty until final checks were complete. The figure disappeared from view almost as quickly as they appeared, but Elena's gut told her something wasn't right.

"Elena," one of the security officers called out from across the room, "we're getting some interference on the launch site's surveillance feeds. Could be the storm rolling in."

But Elena wasn't convinced. "Check it again," she ordered, pulling up the feed herself. The interference wasn't random—it was too specific, too targeted.

She tapped her earpiece, connecting directly to Garbuz, who was in his office preparing for the press conference. "Georgiy, we might have a problem," she said, her voice low but urgent.

Garbuz, already on edge from the pressure of the upcoming media statement, immediately shifted his focus. "What kind of problem?"

"I'm seeing some strange activity on the feeds from the launch site. I don't want to jump to conclusions, but something doesn't feel right. I think we need to check for unauthorized personnel near the rocket."

Garbuz's expression darkened. After everything they had been through, the last thing they needed was a security breach at the launch site. "Send a team to investigate, but keep it quiet. If there's something going on, I don't want to cause a panic. And if you find anything—shut it down."

On the ground, Nikolai and his team were just finishing planting the last of the charges when they heard the faint sound of footsteps approaching. Nikolai froze, signaling for silence. They were still in the restricted area, and getting caught now would mean failure.

But it was too late. The IISF security team, led by Captain Martinez, had been dispatched by Elena and was closing in on the launch platform. Martinez, a no-nonsense veteran, had been briefed on the possibility of unauthorized personnel, and he wasn't taking any chances.

"Check every corner," Martinez ordered his team as they spread out, moving through the restricted zones. As they approached the fuel cells, one of the guards spotted movement.

"Over here!" the guard shouted, drawing his weapon.

Nikolai's team sprang into action, realizing they had been compromised. Shots rang out as the saboteurs attempted to flee, but Martinez's team was well-trained and quickly moved to intercept. Nikolai barely managed to avoid the gunfire as he and his team scrambled to escape, but the charges had already been set.

Martinez moved swiftly to secure the area, but the countdown on the explosives had already begun.

Elena's heart raced as she watched the situation unfold on the live feed from the launch site. The saboteurs had been stopped, but the real danger remained—the explosives attached to the rocket were still active.

"We have to stop those charges from going off," Elena said, her fingers flying across her console as she accessed the remote systems for the launch platform. "If those bombs detonate, we'll lose the rocket, and the entire mission will be compromised."

Garbuz joined her in the control room, his face set in a grim expression. "What are our options?"

"We can try to remotely disable the charges," Elena replied, "but there's no guarantee it'll work. Orlov's agents knew what they were doing. They've likely put in failsafes to prevent remote disarming."

Garbuz stared at the clock on the screen, watching the minutes tick down. They were running out of time. "Do whatever you can, but if that fails, we need a backup plan."

Elena nodded, already working on a solution. She had managed to access the explosives' interface remotely, but just as she suspected, the system was encrypted. There was no way to disarm the charges remotely without triggering them.

"We're going to need to send someone in to manually disarm the bombs," Elena said, her voice steady but urgent. "It's the only way."

On the ground, Captain Martinez received the order to manually disarm the explosives. He and his team moved quickly, securing the area around the rocket and assessing the situation. The charges were small but placed in critical locations—if they went off, the rocket would be rendered useless, and the launch would fail in spectacular fashion.

Martinez crouched beside one of the charges, his hands steady as he examined the device. It was sophisticated—far more advanced than anything he had seen before. He radioed Elena for guidance.

"Martinez here. We've found the charges, but these aren't standard explosives. Any guidance on disarming them?"

Elena's voice came through his earpiece. "I'm looking at the schematics now. It looks like there's a fail-safe built into the detonation system. You'll need to disable the main trigger before you attempt to cut the wires. If you cut the wrong one, it could set them all off."

Martinez took a deep breath, his fingers moving carefully over the device. The pressure was immense—one mistake, and the entire mission would be lost. Slowly, methodically, he worked to disable the trigger, his eyes never leaving the timer as the seconds ticked down.

"Come on," Martinez muttered under his breath, sweat dripping down his forehead as he worked. "Just a little more…"

Finally, with a soft click, the trigger disengaged. Martinez exhaled in relief as the countdown on the explosives stopped.

"Charges disarmed," he reported into his radio. "The rocket is secure."

Back in the IISF control room, Elena and Garbuz watched the live feed from the launch site, the tension in the room finally easing as the situation was brought under control. The saboteurs had been captured, and the charges had been disarmed. But the close call weighed heavily on everyone involved.

"Restart the countdown," Garbuz ordered, his voice calm but firm. "We're still going forward with this launch."

The countdown resumed, and moments later, the rocket engines roared to life. The satellite launch proceeded as planned, the rocket soaring into the sky as the world watched. It was a success—a much-needed victory for the IISF after weeks of turmoil.

But even as the cheers erupted in the control room, Garbuz knew this was just the beginning. Orlov's agents had nearly succeeded in sabotaging the mission, and the political fallout from the attack was far from over.

Chapter 29
The Public Relations Nightmare

The satellite launch had been saved, the explosives disarmed in the final moments, and the mission had gone off without a hitch—at least, from the outside. The world saw the rocket take off into the sky, a fiery plume behind it, marking a significant step forward for the IISF's ambitions. But inside IISF headquarters, the atmosphere remained tense, overshadowed by the fact that they had just barely averted disaster. Orlov's attempt to sabotage the launch had come dangerously close to succeeding, and now Garbuz and his team were left dealing with the aftermath.

Just hours after the launch, Garbuz sat at the head of a conference table in the IISF communications center, surrounded by his senior team. Screens on the walls displayed headlines from around the world, as news outlets broadcast coverage of the satellite deployment.

At first glance, the news seemed positive—articles praised the successful launch, celebrating the technological leap the IISF had made by deploying the first phase of their satellite network. But underneath the praise, there was an undercurrent of doubt. Some reporters speculated about the security breach at the launch site, while others questioned whether the IISF had been fully transparent about the situation.

On one screen, a news anchor spoke gravely: "There are growing concerns about the vulnerability of the IISF's operations, as reports surface that a potential sabotage attempt was thwarted just before today's launch. This raises questions about whether the organization can ensure the safety and success of future missions in the face of increasing geopolitical tensions."

Elena, seated beside Garbuz, shook her head as she read the headlines. "Orlov didn't need the charges to go off. He just needed the world to know how close we came to disaster."

Garbuz rubbed his temples, feeling the pressure mounting. "It doesn't matter that the launch was successful. All anyone will focus on is the fact that we almost lost it."

Sophia Arlen, the head of communications, leaned forward. "We need to get ahead of this narrative. Right now, there's a lot of speculation about the breach. If we don't release a statement soon, the rumors will spiral out of control, and Orlov's disinformation campaign will dominate the news cycle."

Garbuz nodded. "We can't afford to look weak or unprepared, especially after everything that's happened."

Sophia pulled up a draft of a public statement on her tablet. "We'll emphasize that our security measures worked. We detected the breach, neutralized the threat, and completed the mission successfully. We'll turn this into a story about resilience, not vulnerability."

Elena glanced at Garbuz. "And the media? Are we holding a press conference?"

Garbuz thought for a moment. "Yes, but we need to be careful. I don't want to downplay the seriousness of the breach, but we can't let it overshadow the launch either. We need to walk a fine line."

Sophia made a note on her tablet. "We'll prepare the key talking points. You'll need to reassure the public, and more importantly, our allies, that this was an isolated incident, and we're taking every step to prevent future threats."

Later that afternoon, Garbuz stood at a podium in the IISF's press room, facing a sea of reporters and flashing cameras. The tension in the room was palpable. This was Garbuz's first public appearance since the rumors of the Siberian facility attack had surfaced, and now, in the wake of the attempted sabotage, the world was watching even more closely.

Elena and Sophia stood nearby, their eyes fixed on Garbuz, as he prepared to deliver his statement. Taking a deep breath, he began.

"Today, we witnessed a remarkable achievement. The successful launch of the first phase of our satellite network marks a significant step forward in the IISF's mission to expand humanity's reach into space. This deployment will lay the groundwork for future exploration, creating a platform that will enable us to push further than ever before."

The reporters waited, pens poised, knowing that the more pressing issue hadn't been addressed yet. Garbuz continued, his tone steady but serious.

"However, I also want to address the reports of an attempted security breach during today's launch. While our mission was a success, we did face an attempted sabotage. Thanks to the swift action of our security teams, the threat was neutralized, and the launch proceeded as planned. I want to assure everyone watching that the safety and integrity of the IISF's operations are our top priorities. We are conducting a full investigation into the breach, and we are taking immediate steps to strengthen security at all of our facilities."

A murmur went through the room as the reporters processed his words. The acknowledgment of the breach was bold, but Garbuz knew they couldn't afford to hide the truth—not when Orlov's propaganda machine was already working overtime.

One reporter raised her hand. "Mr. Garbuz, can you comment on the reports suggesting that this breach may be part of a larger pattern of attacks on the IISF, including the recent sabotage attempt at the Siberian facility?"

Garbuz had expected the question, but that didn't make answering it any easier. "Let me be clear: the IISF has faced challenges, as any organization of this scale inevitably does. But we remain focused on our mission of peaceful space exploration. Any attempts to undermine that mission will be met with resilience and resolve. We will not be deterred by those who seek to slow our progress."

Another reporter jumped in. "Do you believe Russia is behind the sabotage attempts? And if so, how does the IISF plan to respond?"

This was the tightrope Garbuz had to walk. Accusing Russia outright could escalate the situation further, but ignoring the clear involvement of Orlov's forces would make the IISF look naive.

"We are not in the business of assigning blame without evidence," Garbuz said carefully. "Our focus is on ensuring the success of our missions and the safety of our people. We are working with our international partners to investigate the source of these attacks, and we will take appropriate action once we have all the facts."

The press conference continued for another half hour, with Garbuz fielding questions about the security breach, the IISF's future missions, and the ongoing media speculation about the organization's role in the broader geopolitical conflict. By the time it ended, Garbuz felt drained, but he knew that the message had been delivered: the IISF was still standing, still pushing forward.

Back in his office, Garbuz sat down heavily in his chair, exhausted from the press conference. Elena and Sophia joined him, both looking equally weary but satisfied that the message had been well-received.

"You handled it well," Elena said, taking a seat across from him. "The press seemed to buy it."

Garbuz rubbed his temples, still feeling the weight of everything that had happened in the past few days. "For now. But we both know Orlov isn't going to stop. He's coming at us from every angle—sabotage, media manipulation, political pressure. This was just a taste of what's coming."

Sophia crossed her arms, leaning against the wall. "We've bought ourselves time, but we need to stay ahead of the narrative. The public is watching every move we make, and if Orlov strikes again, we need to be prepared."

Garbuz nodded, his mind already racing with the next steps. The IISF had survived the sabotage attempt, but the real battle was still unfolding—one that wasn't just being fought with rockets and satellites, but with perception, influence, and power.

"Elena," he said, his voice quiet but determined, "we need to find out what Orlov's planning next. He's not going to wait long before he hits us again. And next time, we need to be ready."

Meanwhile, within the IISF itself, the internal tensions continued to simmer. In the days following the launch, more scientists and engineers began voicing their concerns. While the organization had technically succeeded in its mission, the near-disaster had shaken their confidence.

Dr. Andrei Volkov led a quiet meeting with several other senior scientists, many of whom had grown increasingly uneasy with the direction the IISF was heading. They gathered in a small conference room, their faces grim as they discussed the latest developments.

"We're not just explorers anymore," Volkov said, his voice laced with frustration. "We're being drawn into a geopolitical conflict that we never signed up for. The IISF was supposed to be about pushing the boundaries of space—not playing chess with world powers."

Dr. Liang Zhao, one of the lead engineers, nodded in agreement. "I've heard some of our people talking about leaving. They don't want to be part of this anymore if it's going to turn into a war."

Volkov sighed, leaning back in his chair. "We need to make a decision soon. If Garbuz keeps pushing in this direction, we may have no choice but to walk away."

The group sat in silence, knowing that their internal struggle was just as important as the external threats the IISF faced. The organization's future was on a knife's edge, and one misstep could send it spiraling into chaos.

Chapter 30

The Calm Before the Storm

The low hum of machinery filled the quiet of the IISF headquarters as Garbuz stood alone in his office, bathed in the soft glow of the city lights outside. The success of the satellite launch should have been a moment of celebration, but the weight of what had almost happened—the near disaster, the sabotage attempt—pressed heavily on his shoulders. His team had narrowly averted catastrophe, but the battle was far from over.

He walked slowly toward the floor-to-ceiling window that overlooked the sprawling complex. Below, scientists, engineers, and staff moved about, their focus already shifting to the next mission. To them, the launch was a success, another victory for the IISF. But Garbuz knew better. He knew just how fragile that success had been.

His reflection stared back at him from the glass, and in that moment, Garbuz felt the years of strain catching up with him. Leading the IISF had always been a monumental task, but now, with Orlov's shadow looming over every move they made, it was something else entirely. It wasn't just about exploration anymore. It was about survival.

In the early days of the IISF, there had been a purity to their mission. They had united nations under a shared vision, pushed the boundaries of human capability, and dared to dream of a future where humanity could reach the stars. But now, that vision felt distant, almost naïve. The realities of geopolitics had crept in, and instead of uniting the world, the IISF found itself at the center of a growing conflict—one that threatened to tear everything apart.

A knock on the door pulled Garbuz from his thoughts. He turned to see Elena Markov standing in the doorway, her face etched with the same weariness he felt.

"Georgiy," she said softly, stepping inside. "The board is meeting tomorrow to discuss the next phase of the satellite program."

Garbuz nodded, though his thoughts were elsewhere. He appreciated Elena's dedication. She had been by his side from the very beginning, a constant source of strength. But even she was starting to show signs of strain.

"Are you all right?" she asked, noticing the distant look in his eyes.

"I'm fine," he replied, though they both knew it wasn't entirely true. "Just thinking about how close we came to losing everything today."

Elena crossed the room and stood beside him, looking out at the city below. "We stopped Orlov this time. We'll stop him again."

Garbuz nodded slowly. "For now. But the cracks are starting to show, Elena. Inside the IISF, outside of it... I can feel it. We're holding things together, but barely."

Elena frowned, her sharp gaze scanning his face. "Are you worried about Volkov and the others?"

"Among other things," Garbuz admitted. "They're growing restless. They think we've lost our way—that we're becoming something we never intended to be."

"And what do you think?" she asked, her voice soft but probing.

Garbuz turned back to the window, the weight of the question heavy in his mind. "I think they're right. In some ways, we have lost our way. But it wasn't by choice. Orlov's forced our hand. If we don't fight back, we'll lose everything we've built."

Elena stayed quiet for a moment before responding. "Then remind them of that. Remind them why we're here. They may not agree with everything we've done, but they believe in the IISF. You've built something incredible, Georgiy. Don't let them forget that."

Garbuz smiled faintly at her words, though the concern didn't leave his eyes. He knew that things were fragile—more fragile than anyone realized. The threat wasn't just external anymore. It was inside, growing among his own people. And it was only a matter of time before something broke.

"I'll talk to Volkov," he said finally. "We can't afford to let this divide us."

Elena nodded, but her expression remained worried. "You know he's not alone in his doubts. There are others—people who might not speak up, but they're watching. Waiting to see what happens next."

"I know," Garbuz replied. "But I'm not giving up on them. Not yet."

Elena placed a hand on his shoulder before turning to leave. "Just be careful, Georgiy. We can't afford to lose you too."

After Elena left, Garbuz returned to his desk and opened a drawer, pulling out an old, worn notebook. Inside were the original sketches and notes he had made during the earliest days of the IISF's creation. Back then, it had been just a dream—an impossible idea to unite nations in the pursuit of something greater than themselves. But somehow, against all odds, they had made it real.

He flipped through the pages, his eyes scanning the sketches of spacecraft, the early mission outlines, and the notes on potential partnerships with international governments. Each page represented a different phase of the IISF's development, from those first hesitant meetings with diplomats to the groundbreaking moments of technological innovation that had pushed humanity further into space than ever before.

There had been setbacks, of course. There had always been setbacks. But the core vision had never wavered. Until now.

Orlov's attacks, the sabotage, the political pressure—it was all eroding the foundation they had built. And now, with Volkov and others beginning to question his leadership, Garbuz could feel the walls closing in.

He stared down at the final page of the notebook, where he had written a simple but profound statement years ago: *For the future of humanity, not just for nations.*

That was what had driven him all these years—the belief that the IISF was about more than politics, more than power. It was about pushing humanity forward, about ensuring a future where space exploration was not the domain of a single nation but a shared goal for all.

But as he closed the notebook and set it aside, Garbuz couldn't help but wonder if that vision was slipping away. He wasn't sure how much longer he could hold on to it, especially with the growing pressure from all sides.

He sighed deeply and looked toward the door. Tomorrow, he would face Volkov and the others. He would remind them of why they had joined the IISF in the first place. But in the back of his mind, he knew that it might not be enough. The storm was coming—and he wasn't sure if they were ready for it.

Chapter 31

Orlov's New Plan

In Moscow, the lights of the Kremlin flickered against the night sky as a storm gathered above the city. Inside the heavily fortified walls, President Vasily Orlov sat at the head of a long, dimly lit table, surrounded by his most trusted advisors. His cold gaze was fixed on the holographic display in front of him, which showed live footage from the IISF's recent satellite launch—images of the rocket soaring into the sky, a beacon of success for Garbuz and his team.

Orlov's fingers drummed against the table, the rhythm matching the sound of the rain tapping on the windows. He had come so close to bringing the IISF to its knees. His agents had infiltrated the launch site, planted the explosives, and almost succeeded in turning Garbuz's triumph into a disaster. Almost.

But Garbuz had slipped through his fingers once again. The IISF had weathered the storm, for now.

Karpov, Orlov's chief advisor, stood nearby, watching his leader's silence with measured patience. He knew better than to speak before Orlov was ready. The president's temper was infamous, and Karpov could sense the fury simmering beneath his calm exterior.

"Garbuz should have failed," Orlov muttered at last, his voice low and filled with venom. "We gave him every opportunity to collapse, and yet he stands."

Karpov nodded, stepping forward into the glow of the holographic display. "The sabotage was close to succeeding. But their security was more resilient than anticipated. Elena Markov's quick thinking saved them."

Orlov clenched his jaw, his grip on the armrest of his chair tightening. "It's not enough to attack them from the outside anymore. Garbuz is stronger than we expected. We need to destabilize them from within."

Karpov's lips curled into a slight smile. He had been waiting for this moment, knowing that Orlov's frustration would lead him here. "I agree. The IISF's greatest weakness isn't just Garbuz—it's the people around him. There are cracks in their foundation. People who doubt him, who question his decisions. We've already planted the seeds of dissent. Now we nurture them."

Orlov leaned forward, his eyes narrowing. "Volkov."

Karpov nodded. "Yes. Dr. Andrei Volkov. He's been vocal in his opposition to Garbuz's leadership, and his influence is growing. If we can turn him, the rest will follow. Volkov could be the key to fracturing the IISF from within."

Orlov stared at the display, his mind working through the possibilities. He had always known that brute force alone wouldn't be enough to destroy the IISF. Garbuz had built something resilient, something capable of withstanding external pressure. But from the inside? That was a different story.

"If Volkov can be persuaded," Orlov mused, "we could force Garbuz's hand. Create chaos, mistrust, weaken the leadership. It would cripple their organization."

Karpov stepped closer, his voice soft but insidious. "We've been monitoring Volkov and his inner circle. He's already questioning Garbuz's decisions—questioning whether the IISF has strayed too far from its original mission. We need to push him further. Give him the right nudge, and he'll take the rest of the scientists with him."

Orlov smirked, the glimmer of a new plan forming in his mind. "Volkov thinks he's acting in the best interest of the IISF. Let him believe that. We'll manipulate him from the shadows, make him think he's saving the organization when, in reality, he's doing exactly what we want."

Karpov nodded, pleased with the direction this was taking. "We'll initiate the next phase immediately. I'll send word to our agent within the IISF—our sleeper. They'll make sure Volkov stays on the path we've set for him."

Before Karpov could leave, Orlov spoke again, his voice cold and sharp. "What about the saboteurs?"

Karpov paused, knowing the subject would come up. "They've maintained their silence, as expected. The IISF hasn't been able to extract any useful information from them. For now, they remain in custody."

Orlov's eyes darkened. "For now? That's not good enough, Karpov. I don't want them to remain in IISF custody at all. They're a liability."

Karpov nodded in agreement. "I've already put plans in motion to retrieve them or eliminate them, whichever is necessary. We can't afford any loose ends."

Orlov leaned back in his chair, his fingers steepled in front of him. "Make sure it's done quickly. I don't want Garbuz learning anything from those men. They know too much."

Karpov gave a short nod. "It will be done."

As Karpov left the room, Orlov sat in silence, his mind churning with new possibilities. He had played this game for years, manipulating world leaders, crushing opposition, ensuring that Russia remained a dominant force on the world stage. But Garbuz and the IISF were different. They represented more than just a rival—they were a symbol of something Orlov despised. A symbol of international cooperation, of a world where Russia wasn't the sole power in space.

And that was something he could not allow.

Later that night, Karpov met in a dark, nondescript building on the outskirts of Moscow with a contact he trusted implicitly—one of Orlov's best operatives, tasked with infiltrating the IISF from the beginning. The operative, known only by their codename Sable, had been working undercover within the IISF for years, embedded deep within the scientific community.

Sable had been in place for a long time, waiting for the right moment to strike. And now, with Volkov's growing dissent, that moment had arrived.

"Karpov," Sable greeted with a curt nod as they entered the room.

Karpov returned the nod, stepping into the dimly lit space. "The time has come to push Volkov further. He's already leaning toward breaking away from Garbuz. Your task is to ensure that break happens—and that when it does, it shatters the IISF."

Sable smirked, clearly pleased that the plan was finally moving forward. "Volkov is already teetering on the edge. He's frustrated with Garbuz and feels like the IISF has lost its purpose. I can push him further. Make him think he's saving the organization."

"Good," Karpov replied, his tone cold. "But remember, this must be done carefully. Garbuz can't suspect external interference. Volkov needs to believe that this is his own decision. Once he moves against Garbuz, the rest will follow."

Sable nodded. "I'll make sure of it. When the time comes, Volkov won't be able to tell the difference between his doubts and the ones I've planted."

Karpov's eyes gleamed with satisfaction. "Make sure he takes as many with him as possible. The more fractured the IISF, the better for us. We'll pick up the pieces when Garbuz falls."

Sable gave a final nod before slipping back into the shadows, ready to set the plan in motion.

Chapter 32

Cracks in the Foundation

The following day, the atmosphere at IISF headquarters was charged with a tension that had been building for weeks. The successful launch had temporarily buoyed spirits, but the close call with sabotage had left a lingering unease. Beneath the surface, doubt simmered—not just about the security of their missions but about the leadership itself. Garbuz had fought to hold the organization together, but the cracks were starting to show.

In a quiet corner of the IISF complex, Dr. Andrei Volkov sat with a small group of senior scientists. The group had been meeting in secret more frequently in recent days, their conversations shifting from academic discussions about propulsion systems and satellite orbits to something more dangerous: the future of the IISF under Garbuz's leadership.

Volkov's face was grim as he spoke to the group, his hands resting on the table in front of him. Dr. Liang Zhao and Dr. Marta Novak, two of the most respected figures in the IISF's scientific community, sat beside him, their expressions mirroring his unease.

"This is not what we signed up for," Volkov said quietly, but with a conviction that made the others lean in. "We're not soldiers or politicians. We're scientists. Our mission was to push the boundaries of space exploration, to advance humanity's reach into the stars—not to engage in this political and military conflict."

Dr. Zhao nodded in agreement, his brow furrowed. "It's true. Every day, it feels like we're drifting further from our original mission. The IISF was supposed to be about cooperation, about bringing the world together to explore space. But now... it feels like we're being dragged into a war."

Dr. Novak, normally more reserved in these discussions, spoke up. "And Garbuz—he's leading us into that conflict, whether he admits it or not. Every move we make now seems to be in response to Orlov. We've become reactive, not proactive. I'm starting to wonder if we've lost our way."

Volkov leaned forward, his voice dropping to a near-whisper. "Exactly. And that's why I'm starting to think that maybe Garbuz isn't the leader we need right now. Maybe he's too entrenched in this fight to see that he's endangering everything we've built."

The room fell silent. The thought of removing Garbuz—of forcing him to step down—had been unthinkable just months ago. But now, with the escalating tensions, the doubts about his leadership were creeping into even the most loyal members of the team.

Dr. Zhao looked around the table, gauging the mood. "Are you suggesting... we ask him to step aside?"

Volkov hesitated, but only for a moment. "I'm saying that we need to consider all our options. The IISF is bigger than any one person. If Garbuz can't lead us without pulling us into this conflict with Orlov, then maybe we need to think about what's best for the organization. For the future."

Dr. Novak exchanged a glance with Zhao, uncertainty flickering in her eyes. "But if we do that, we risk fracturing the organization. There are still plenty of people who support Garbuz—people who believe in him."

Volkov sighed, leaning back in his chair. "I know. And I'm not saying we make any rash decisions. But we need to start thinking about what comes next. We can't let the IISF be dragged down by this fight. If Garbuz continues down this path, it may be too late to save the organization."

The weight of his words settled over the room, and for a long moment, no one spoke.

Unbeknownst to Volkov and the others, one of the scientists present in the room was not there by chance. Sable, Orlov's sleeper agent, had embedded themselves within the IISF years ago, blending seamlessly into the organization's ranks. Quiet, efficient, and always just a bit in the background, Sable had built a reputation for being competent but unobtrusive—exactly what was needed for deep-cover infiltration.

As Volkov and his colleagues discussed their growing dissatisfaction with Garbuz's leadership, Sable remained outwardly neutral, taking in every word. Orlov's plan was working. The seeds of doubt had been planted, and now they were beginning to bear fruit. Sable's job was to ensure those doubts blossomed into full-blown rebellion.

When the meeting ended, and the scientists began to disperse, Sable quietly approached Volkov, offering a sympathetic smile. "It's not easy, is it?"

Volkov looked at Sable, surprised by the comment. The two hadn't spoken much outside of professional settings, but there was something in Sable's demeanor—an understanding, a shared frustration—that made Volkov pause.

"No," Volkov replied after a moment. "It's not. We're in a difficult position."

Sable nodded. "I've heard a lot of people talking, and I know you're not the only one who's worried. It's just... I think a lot of people feel the same way, but they don't know what to do."

Volkov frowned, intrigued. "What do you mean?"

Sable hesitated, as if choosing their words carefully. "I just think that if there were a way to get the organization back on track—to refocus on the mission we all signed up for—people would follow you. You have the respect of the scientific community. If you lead, others will follow."

Volkov studied Sable for a moment, a flicker of uncertainty in his eyes. "That's a dangerous line of thinking."

Sable shrugged, maintaining their calm demeanor. "Maybe. But it's something worth considering. The IISF can't afford to be reactive anymore. We need leadership that's focused on the mission, not on this conflict with Orlov."

Volkov didn't respond immediately, but the seed had been planted. As Sable walked away, they knew they had done their job. Volkov's doubts were deepening, and with a little more pressure, he would be pushed toward making the move Orlov needed.

While the meeting between Volkov and the other scientists took place in secret, word of the growing dissent was beginning to reach Garbuz. Elena Markov entered his office later that evening, her expression serious as she sat down across from him.

"We have a problem," she said, her voice low.

Garbuz raised an eyebrow. "What is it?"

Elena hesitated before continuing. "It's Volkov. I've been hearing rumors that he's been meeting with other senior scientists—people like Zhao and Novak. They're questioning your leadership."

Garbuz leaned back in his chair, rubbing his temples. He had suspected as much, but hearing it confirmed was like a punch to the gut. Volkov had always been a key figure in the IISF's scientific community, a brilliant mind who had helped shape many of their most important projects. The thought of him leading a faction against Garbuz was unsettling.

"What exactly are they saying?" Garbuz asked, his voice tense.

"They're worried that the IISF has lost its way," Elena replied. "That we're becoming too entangled in the geopolitical conflict with Orlov. Volkov thinks we need to refocus on our original mission. And... from what I've heard, he's considering asking you to step down."

Garbuz's eyes flashed with anger. "Step down? He thinks that's the solution?"

Elena shook her head. "I don't think it's that simple. Volkov's frustrated, but he's not an enemy. He genuinely believes that the IISF is veering off course. I think he feels like he's trying to save the organization."

Garbuz stood up, pacing the room as he processed the information. "We're in the middle of a war with Orlov, and Volkov thinks now is the time to start questioning leadership? He doesn't understand what's at stake."

Elena watched him for a moment, then spoke quietly. "I think he does, Georgiy. But his idea of what's at stake is different from yours. He's thinking about the IISF's long-term future. You're thinking about the immediate threat."

Garbuz stopped pacing, his frustration boiling just beneath the surface. "What am I supposed to do, Elena? If I back down now, if I step aside, Orlov wins. He wants us divided, and that's exactly what's happening."

Elena stood and approached him, her expression calm but firm. "Then don't let him divide us. You need to talk to Volkov. Find common ground before this turns into something worse."

Garbuz exhaled slowly, his anger giving way to a deep sense of weariness. "You're right. I'll talk to him. But if he thinks I'm just going to walk away from this fight, he's wrong."

Elena nodded, though her concern remained. "Just be careful. The organization is more fragile than you realize."

Chapter 33

Diplomatic Crisis

The diplomatic fallout from the near-disastrous sabotage attempt at the IISF satellite launch was spreading faster than Garbuz had anticipated. Despite the success of the launch itself, the cracks were beginning to show, and key allies were starting to waver. Sitting in his office late at night, Garbuz stared at the screen in front of him, where a live feed of international news broadcasts displayed headlines that made his stomach churn.

"Growing Concerns Over IISF Stability"
"Has Garbuz Lost Control?"
"Space Sabotage Sparks Political Firestorm"

Each headline was a reminder that the battle with Orlov wasn't just being fought with technology and intelligence—it was a war of perception. And right now, the perception was that the IISF was a powder keg on the verge of exploding.

A knock on the door broke his concentration. Without waiting for a response, Elena Markov stepped inside, her face grim.

"You need to take this call, Georgiy," she said, holding out a secure line tablet. "It's President Zhang."

Garbuz's stomach tightened. President Zhang Wei of China had been one of the IISF's strongest allies, not only offering financial support but also critical technological collaboration. If Zhang was calling, it wasn't good news.

Garbuz accepted the tablet and took a deep breath before initiating the call. Zhang's face appeared on the screen, his expression as unreadable as ever. His eyes, however, conveyed a seriousness that Garbuz had only seen once before—during the initial discussions about bringing China into the IISF coalition.

"President Zhang," Garbuz began, forcing a smile. "Thank you for reaching out."

Zhang didn't return the pleasantries. He got straight to the point. "Mr. Garbuz, we need to talk about the direction of the IISF. I've been following the recent developments, and I must tell you that many in my government are concerned. The sabotage attempt at the satellite launch has raised questions about the organization's security, and now... there are rumors of internal dissent."

Garbuz felt the weight of those words hit him harder than any accusation from the media. Zhang was known for his calm, pragmatic approach to politics, but if he was concerned enough to mention internal dissent, then things were worse than Garbuz had realized.

"I understand your concerns, Mr. President," Garbuz replied carefully. "The sabotage was a close call, but we neutralized the threat. Our security protocols are being strengthened, and we've launched a full investigation into how the breach happened."

Zhang nodded slightly, but his expression didn't soften. "And what of the rumors about your leadership? About members of your senior team questioning your direction?"

Garbuz hesitated. He hadn't expected Zhang to be so direct about the internal tensions within the IISF. Clearly, the situation had reached international ears faster than he had anticipated.

"There are always differences of opinion in an organization of this size," Garbuz said, trying to sound measured. "But I assure you, the IISF is united in its mission to push forward with space exploration. We remain committed to our core principles."

Zhang's eyes narrowed. "That may be, but perception matters, Mr. Garbuz. If the international community begins to see the IISF as a fractured organization, it will undermine all of our efforts. China has invested heavily in this project, but if your leadership cannot hold the organization together, my government may have no choice but to reconsider its role in the IISF."

The words landed like a punch to the gut. Losing China's support would be catastrophic. Not only were they one of the biggest financial contributors, but they were also crucial in the technological developments needed for future deep-space missions. Garbuz's mind raced as he struggled to find the right response.

"I understand, President Zhang," Garbuz said, his voice steady but strained. "But I ask for your patience. The IISF is going through a challenging time, but we are addressing these issues head-on. The organization remains strong, and with your continued support, we can weather this storm."

Zhang remained silent for a moment, his sharp gaze locked on Garbuz. Then, with a nod, he replied, "I hope you are right, Mr. Garbuz. China remains committed to the vision of the IISF, but we cannot afford to be dragged into a conflict that jeopardizes global stability. If you cannot resolve these issues, we will need to reassess our involvement."

The line went dead before Garbuz could respond. He set the tablet down, his hands trembling slightly. Elena, who had been standing nearby, gave him a concerned look.

"What did he say?" she asked softly.

"He said we have to resolve the internal dissent, or we lose China," Garbuz replied, his voice flat.

No sooner had the conversation with President Zhang ended than another alert flashed on Garbuz's console. This time, it was President Johann Ritter of Germany, another key ally in the IISF coalition. Germany had hosted some of the IISF's most important research facilities, and they had been instrumental in securing European support for the organization's initiatives.

Garbuz initiated the call, bracing himself for what was coming next.

"Mr. Garbuz," Ritter said, his tone formal and a little cold. "I'll get straight to the point. The sabotage at your satellite launch has raised alarms here in Europe. There are serious concerns about the IISF's ability to safeguard its assets and maintain control. The media coverage has been relentless, and I've been fielding calls from several European leaders questioning whether we should continue our partnership with the IISF."

Garbuz felt the knot in his stomach tighten further. "I understand, President Ritter. The situation at the launch was a close call, but we've already taken steps to ensure it won't happen again. Security is our top priority, and we're addressing the root causes of the breach."

Ritter raised a hand, cutting him off. "It's not just the breach, Mr. Garbuz. It's everything else. The reports of internal conflict within your leadership team, the doubts being raised about your direction. We are in a difficult position. Europe has invested heavily in the IISF, but there are those in my government who are beginning to question whether this investment is worth the risk."

Garbuz's mind raced, trying to find a way to salvage the situation. "President Ritter, I assure you, the IISF remains committed to its original mission. Yes, we are facing challenges, but this is an organization built on cooperation, on the idea that we can achieve more together than we can apart. I need you to trust that we will overcome these obstacles."

Ritter sighed, his face softening slightly. "I do not doubt your commitment, Mr. Garbuz. But trust is fragile, and the cracks in the IISF are becoming more visible by the day. You need to present a clear path forward, or the support of the European Union may waver."

"We're already working on that path," Garbuz said, his voice firm. "I'm addressing the internal issues. The IISF will emerge from this stronger, I promise you."

Ritter looked unconvinced but nodded. "I hope so. Because if you don't, the consequences will be severe."

The call ended, and Garbuz felt the full weight of the situation pressing down on him. Two of his most important allies—China and Europe—were questioning the stability of the IISF. And behind all of it was Orlov, orchestrating the chaos from the shadows.

The final blow of the day came from Washington. Senator Warner, who had long been the IISF's strongest ally in the U.S. government, called Garbuz with an even more direct warning.

"Georgiy," Warner began, her voice tight with frustration, "I'm doing everything I can to keep Senator Trent and his cronies from launching a full-scale investigation into the IISF. But the rumors about internal strife and security breaches are making it hard to keep people in line. Trent is pushing for a congressional hearing, and if this gets any more public, I won't be able to stop him."

Garbuz rubbed his temples, the pressure mounting with every call. "I understand, Senator. We're dealing with the internal issues, but Orlov's sabotage is making it difficult to control the narrative."

Warner sighed. "You don't have much time. You need to get your house in order, fast. If this investigation goes public, it could lead to the U.S. withdrawing support. And once that happens, it'll be a domino effect. You know how this works."

Garbuz nodded, though inside he was spiraling. "I'll do what I can, Senator. But you have to give me more time."

Warner's voice softened slightly. "I'll do my best to buy you some time. But you need to fix this, Georgiy. The IISF is too important to let it fall apart now."

Chapter 34

The Betrayal Unfolds

Tension was thick in the air as Garbuz made his way through the corridors of IISF headquarters. The calls from President Zhang, President Ritter, and Senator Warner had left him shaken. The international support that had once been the foundation of the IISF was beginning to crumble beneath the weight of doubt and dissent. And now, Garbuz had to face the source of that dissent head-on.

He had arranged a private meeting with Dr. Andrei Volkov, the man who had once been one of the most respected voices within the IISF and now, the one who posed the greatest threat to its stability. Volkov's influence over the scientific community had only grown in recent weeks, and the quiet murmurs of discontent were no longer just whispers in the halls—they were becoming louder, more dangerous.

As Garbuz entered the conference room, Volkov was already there, seated at the long table, his expression unreadable. Dr. Liang Zhao and Dr. Marta Novak were with him, both of them silent but watchful, as though waiting to see how this confrontation would unfold.

Garbuz could feel the weight of their gazes as he took his seat across from them. He didn't waste time with pleasantries.

"Andrei," Garbuz began, keeping his voice calm but firm. "I've heard that you've been meeting with others, discussing the future of the IISF. I thought it was time we had an honest conversation about where we stand."

Volkov didn't flinch. He met Garbuz's gaze steadily, though there was a tension in his posture that hadn't been there before. "I think it's long overdue."

Garbuz nodded, folding his hands on the table. "I understand that you and others have concerns about the direction the IISF is heading. I'm not blind to the challenges we've faced, and I know that Orlov's attacks have put us in a difficult position. But the mission hasn't changed. We are still pushing the boundaries of space exploration. We're still fighting for a future where humanity can reach beyond this planet. We just have to adapt to the threats we're facing."

Volkov leaned forward slightly, his voice cool but charged with emotion. "Adapt? Is that what you call this? Adapting to sabotage, to political maneuvering, to turning the IISF into something it was never meant to be? We were supposed to be explorers, Georgiy. Innovators. But now we're fighting a war—one that we never agreed to fight."

Dr. Zhao nodded in agreement, speaking up for the first time. "We've lost sight of the mission, Georgiy. The original mission. Every decision we make now is in response to Orlov's moves. We've become reactive, not proactive. The focus is no longer on the stars—it's on survival."

Garbuz sighed, leaning back in his chair as he considered their words. He understood their frustration. He had felt it too—the weight of every decision dragging them further into a conflict they hadn't anticipated. But this was the reality they lived in now, and Garbuz knew there was no way to avoid it.

"We're in a war, whether we want to admit it or not," Garbuz said quietly. "Orlov has made sure of that. If we don't fight back, we'll be crushed. The IISF won't exist in a year if we pretend this conflict isn't happening."

Volkov's eyes flashed with anger. "But at what cost? At the cost of the organization's soul? At the cost of everything we stood for? You're driving us down a path that leads to militarization, to political entanglement. That's not why we joined this mission."

Garbuz could feel the weight of the room shifting against him. Volkov's words had struck a nerve, not just with the other scientists but with a part of himself that wondered if there was truth in what Volkov was saying.

"And what's your solution, Andrei?" Garbuz asked, his voice sharp now. "Step back? Give Orlov what he wants? Let him destroy everything we've built? Because that's what will happen if we don't push back."

Volkov didn't hesitate. "My solution is leadership that remembers what this organization was founded for. Leadership that doesn't lose sight of the mission, even in the face of external threats. If you can't steer us back on course, then maybe you're not the leader the IISF needs right now."

The words hung in the air like a bomb. Garbuz's jaw clenched as the realization of what Volkov was saying truly set in.

"You're suggesting I step down," Garbuz said, his voice low and dangerous.

Volkov's expression remained resolute. "I'm suggesting that the IISF can't survive under your leadership if you continue down this path. There are those of us who believe in the mission—who believe we can salvage what we've lost. But not if you keep treating this like a battlefield."

Dr. Novak, who had been quiet until now, spoke up, her voice hesitant but firm. "Georgiy, none of us want to see you fail. We're here because we care about the IISF. But the path we're on... it's dangerous. Volkov is right. If we don't course-correct, we'll lose everything we've worked for."

Garbuz felt the weight of their words, but more than that, he felt the threat behind them. Volkov wasn't just offering an opinion—he was offering an ultimatum. Either Garbuz changed course, or the senior scientific team would withdraw their support, leaving the IISF crippled from within.

He stood slowly, his eyes locked on Volkov. "You think you're saving the IISF, but you're playing into Orlov's hands. He wants us divided. He wants to weaken us from within. And if you walk away, you'll be giving him exactly what he wants."

Volkov stood as well, his expression hard. "I'm not walking away, Georgiy. I'm offering you a chance to save this organization. But if you can't see that, then maybe it's time for a change."

The two men stood in silence for a long moment, the tension between them thick and suffocating. Garbuz knew that Volkov wasn't bluffing. The scientist had built a quiet following within the IISF, and if he turned against Garbuz, others would follow. The internal dissent would tear the organization apart.

But Garbuz wasn't ready to give up—not yet.

"You want a change, Andrei?" Garbuz said finally, his voice cold. "You'll have it. But I'm not stepping down. This organization is too important to let personal grievances tear it apart. If you want to challenge my leadership, you'll have to do better than vague threats."

Volkov's jaw tightened, but he said nothing.

"I'll call an emergency meeting of the senior staff," Garbuz continued. "We'll address these concerns directly, in front of the entire leadership team. If there's to be a decision about the future of the IISF, it won't be made behind closed doors."

Dr. Zhao glanced nervously at Volkov, but Volkov nodded slowly, his eyes narrowing. "Fine. But be careful, Georgiy. You may not like the outcome."

As Volkov and the other scientists left the room, a shadow lingered behind—the silent presence of Sable, Orlov's sleeper agent. They had watched the confrontation unfold from a distance, their eyes carefully noting every word exchanged between Garbuz and Volkov. Sable knew that the moment was fast approaching when the dissent would reach its breaking point.

In the hallway, Sable caught up with Volkov, offering him a quiet word of support. "You did the right thing, Andrei. You're fighting for the future of the IISF."

Volkov sighed, the weight of the confrontation still heavy on his shoulders. "I hope so. But I'm not sure how much longer I can do this."

Sable smiled softly, laying a hand on Volkov's arm. "You're stronger than you think. And you're not alone. There are others who believe in your vision. When the time comes, we'll stand with you."

Volkov nodded, grateful for the support, unaware that he was being played by Orlov's agent, who was subtly guiding him toward open rebellion.

Chapter 35
A Decision Is Made

The next morning, the atmosphere at IISF headquarters was electric with tension. Word had spread quickly about the confrontation between Garbuz and Volkov, and now, an emergency meeting of the senior staff was set to take place. It was no longer just a disagreement between colleagues; it was a battle for the very future of the IISF.

In the main conference room, the most powerful figures within the organization had gathered. Around the long, polished table sat scientists, engineers, diplomats, and security personnel, all of them acutely aware that this meeting could change the course of the IISF—and their careers—forever. At the head of the table stood Georgiy Garbuz, his expression stony as he waited for the room to settle. Across from him sat Dr. Andrei Volkov, his closest allies Dr. Liang Zhao and Dr. Marta Novak by his side.

As the last of the senior staff took their seats, a tense silence filled the room. Everyone knew what was coming.

Garbuz was the first to speak, his voice steady but laced with frustration. "We're here today to address the growing concerns about the direction of the IISF. I've heard the rumors. I know some of you believe that the organization is straying too far from its original mission, that we're becoming reactive to external threats. And I understand those concerns. But let me be clear—the IISF is under attack. We didn't choose this fight. Orlov did. And if we don't defend ourselves, we will not survive."

There was a murmur of agreement from a few members of the room, but it was muted, hesitant. The scientists and engineers who had once supported Garbuz without question were now looking to Volkov for guidance.

Volkov cleared his throat and leaned forward, his voice calm but filled with conviction. "Georgiy, no one here doubts that Orlov poses a threat. We all understand the risks. But what we're questioning is how you've chosen to respond. The IISF was founded on principles of exploration and international cooperation. It wasn't meant to become a battleground for geopolitical conflict."

He gestured to the others around the table. "We've spoken to many of our colleagues—people who have dedicated their lives to this mission—and they're all saying the same thing. We're losing sight of what we're here to do. Every decision we make now is in reaction to Orlov's provocations. We're no longer leading. We're no longer innovating. We're just trying to survive."

There was a ripple of agreement from around the room. Dr. Novak nodded in support of Volkov, her voice steady as she added, "The sabotage attempt at the satellite launch—it was a wake-up call for all of us. We came so close to losing everything. And instead of reassessing our strategy, we doubled down. We're putting everything we've built at risk."

Garbuz clenched his jaw, his frustration rising. "We've survived because we've adapted. Yes, we're under pressure, but that's what makes us stronger. The world is watching us, and we're proving that the IISF can weather any storm. This organization was built to push the boundaries of space exploration, and that's exactly what we're doing."

Volkov leaned back in his chair, his expression thoughtful. "But at what cost, Georgiy? How long can we keep this up before we lose ourselves? Before the IISF becomes something unrecognizable—something we never intended?"

Garbuz's eyes flashed with anger, but before he could respond, Elena Markov spoke up. She had been quietly observing the exchange, but now her voice cut through the tension like a knife.

"We're at a crossroads," Elena said, her tone measured but firm. "We can't pretend that we're still the same organization we were when we started. The world has changed, and so have the stakes. But Volkov has a point. We need to find a balance between defending ourselves and staying true to our mission. If we lose sight of that, we risk losing everything."

Her words hung in the air, resonating with both sides. Garbuz felt a flash of gratitude for Elena's diplomacy, even though he knew that she, too, had her concerns. He had called this meeting to unite the IISF, but the room felt more divided than ever.

As the debate continued, Sable, Orlov's sleeper agent, quietly observed from their seat, watching the room with a calm, analytical gaze. Sable had done their work well—Volkov and his faction were pushing Garbuz into a corner, and the tension in the room was palpable. Now, all that remained was to push things a little further.

At a subtle nod from Sable, Dr. Novak spoke again, this time directing her words at Garbuz. "Georgiy, no one here wants to see the IISF fail. But we can't deny that there are fractures within this organization. If we don't address them now, they'll only get worse. You've been a strong leader, but maybe it's time to consider bringing more voices into the decision-making process. Let us share the responsibility. It doesn't have to fall on your shoulders alone."

It was a gentle suggestion, but it was exactly what Sable needed. A power shift within the IISF would weaken Garbuz's control, leaving room for Orlov to exploit the resulting instability.

Garbuz could feel the pressure mounting. He had expected a challenge from Volkov, but not from this many voices. He had spent years building this organization, turning it into a symbol of international cooperation, a beacon of hope for the future of space exploration. And now, in this room, it felt like it was slipping through his fingers.

But he wasn't ready to give up.

Taking a deep breath, Garbuz rose to his feet. His voice, though calm, carried the weight of his conviction. "I understand the fears that you all have. I understand the desire to turn away from conflict and focus on the stars. But if we don't face the reality of the situation, there won't be an IISF left to carry out that mission."

He looked directly at Volkov, then at each person in the room. "I've given everything to this organization. We all have. We've built something incredible—something that can change the future of humanity. But that future is under threat. Orlov won't stop, and we can't pretend that standing down will make him go away."

Garbuz's voice grew stronger, more resolute. "I won't step down. I won't hand over leadership when the stakes are higher than they've ever been. But I will listen. I will take your concerns seriously. I will make sure that the decisions we make reflect the mission we set out to achieve. But we cannot afford to be divided right now. If we fracture, Orlov wins. And that is something I will not allow."

The room was silent, the weight of his words hanging in the air. Volkov studied Garbuz for a long moment, the anger and frustration in his eyes tempered by something else—reluctant respect.

After what felt like an eternity, Volkov nodded slowly. "We don't want to see the IISF fall apart, either. We'll stand with you, Georgiy. But we need to make sure that we're not just reacting to Orlov. We need to be proactive again. Focused on the future."

Garbuz nodded in return. "Agreed. And we will. Together."

Far from the conference room, in Moscow, President Orlov received a report from Karpov about the outcome of the emergency meeting. The news was not what Orlov had hoped for.

"They're still united," Karpov reported, his voice laced with frustration. "Volkov and his faction haven't broken away. Garbuz managed to hold them together."

Orlov's jaw tightened, his eyes narrowing as he stared out the window of his office. "For now. But they're weaker than they were before. The fractures are still there. And when the next strike comes, they won't be able to recover."

Karpov nodded. "What are your orders?"

Orlov turned away from the window, his expression cold and calculating. "We push harder. We hit them where it hurts. Next time, they won't have the luxury of internal debate. They'll be too busy trying to survive."

Chapter 36

False Peace

The morning after the emergency meeting, the atmosphere at IISF headquarters felt deceptively calm. It was a fragile peace, one that Georgiy Garbuz knew could shatter at any moment. He sat in his office, staring at the reports from the previous day's meeting, his mind racing with the implications of everything that had transpired. The confrontation with Dr. Andrei Volkov and his faction had ended in a truce, but the underlying tensions remained. The cracks were still there—barely visible, but ready to widen with the slightest pressure.

Garbuz leaned back in his chair, rubbing his temples. He had managed to keep the IISF intact, but the unity he had fought for was tenuous at best. His thoughts drifted to the conversation with Elena Markov the night before. She had been right—there was only so much pressure the organization could take before it fractured completely.

A knock on the door pulled Garbuz from his thoughts. Elena stepped into the office, her expression serious, though there was a calmness to her demeanor that helped ground him.

"How are you holding up?" she asked, taking a seat across from him.

"I've had better days," Garbuz replied with a weary smile. "But we survived the meeting. That's something, I guess."

Elena nodded, though her eyes remained sharp, focused. "We did. But this isn't over. You saw the way Volkov was looking at you. He's not convinced, Georgiy. And neither are some of the others. They're standing by you for now, but if anything else goes wrong, they'll be the first to push for a change."

Garbuz sighed, running a hand through his hair. "I know. It's like we're balancing on a knife's edge. One wrong move and the whole thing comes crashing down."

Elena leaned forward, her voice soft but firm. "That's why we have to stay ahead of this. We can't afford to be complacent. Orlov is going to come after us again, and when he does, we need to be ready. We can't wait for him to make the first move."

Garbuz gave her a knowing look. "You think he'll strike soon?"

"I know he will," Elena said, her tone resolute. "We embarrassed him with the last launch. His sabotage failed, and we pulled off a success right in front of the world. He won't let that go unanswered."

Garbuz leaned back in his chair, staring up at the ceiling as he considered her words. He knew she was right. Orlov wasn't the type to sit back and watch. He was already plotting his next move, and if the IISF wasn't prepared, they could be caught completely off guard.

"Elena," Garbuz said after a long pause, "if Orlov attacks again, we need a plan. We can't just react. We need to anticipate. If we wait for him to strike, we'll always be playing catch-up."

Elena nodded. "I've been thinking the same thing. We need to go on the offensive. Take the fight to him instead of waiting for him to come to us."

Garbuz raised an eyebrow. "You have something in mind?"

"Not yet," Elena admitted. "But I've started working on a few ideas. It'll take time to put the pieces together, but I'm confident we can hit him where it hurts."

Garbuz's lips pressed into a thin line. He admired Elena's determination, but he wasn't sure if going on the offensive was the right move. Volkov had made it clear that a more aggressive strategy could escalate the conflict even further, and the last thing the IISF needed was to get caught in a war with Russia.

"We'll need to be careful," Garbuz said, his voice thoughtful. "If we push too hard, we risk provoking Orlov into something even worse. And we're not ready for an all-out conflict."

Elena's expression softened slightly. "I understand. But we can't afford to sit back either. If we wait, he'll pick us apart piece by piece. We need to find a way to strike without escalating. Something that cripples his ability to hurt us, but doesn't push him over the edge."

Garbuz was silent for a moment, weighing her words carefully. He had to admit, Elena had a point. Waiting for Orlov to strike first would only leave them vulnerable. But the risk of escalating the conflict was real, and if they pushed too far, they could end up in a situation far worse than they had ever imagined.

Finally, Garbuz nodded. "Start working on it. But we'll move cautiously. We can't afford to make mistakes."

Elena smiled faintly, relief flickering across her face. "I'll keep you updated."

As she stood to leave, Garbuz watched her go, his mind still racing. They had bought themselves a little time with the emergency meeting, but he knew it wouldn't last. The fragile peace they had managed to secure was just that—fragile. And all it would take was one more strike from Orlov to shatter it completely.

In another part of the IISF complex, Sable observed from a distance as the team regrouped after the emergency meeting. The mood in the building was one of cautious optimism—Volkov and his faction had agreed to stand with Garbuz for now, and the immediate threat of a schism had been averted. But Sable knew better than to believe that the peace would last. Orlov's strategy was working, and it was only a matter of time before the next phase of the plan unfolded.

As Sable moved through the halls, they kept a close eye on Volkov. The scientist's doubts were still present, even though he had agreed to Garbuz's terms during the meeting. Sable approached Volkov as he walked toward his lab, offering a quiet word of support.

"You handled yourself well yesterday," Sable said in a low voice. "Garbuz knows he can't ignore you now. But don't let your guard down. We're not out of the woods yet."

Volkov glanced at Sable, his expression thoughtful. "I know. Garbuz may have kept things together for now, but if Orlov strikes again, the pressure will be too much. I don't know how long we can keep this up."

Sable nodded, their voice carefully measured. "You're right. And that's why we need to start thinking about the future. Garbuz is doing what he can, but if the IISF is going to survive, we need to be prepared for all possibilities. Including leadership that's willing to make hard decisions."

Volkov didn't respond immediately, but Sable could see the wheels turning in his mind. The scientist had been on the edge of rebellion for weeks, and while he had stepped back for now, Sable knew that it wouldn't take much to push him forward again.

"Just keep that in mind," Sable said, offering a subtle smile. "We'll need people like you to lead when the time comes."

Volkov nodded slowly, his eyes distant as he continued walking. Sable watched him go, satisfaction flickering across their face. The seeds had been planted, and it was only a matter of time before they took root.

Chapter 37

The Next Strike

Far from the measured discussions at IISF headquarters, President Vasily Orlov was in the heart of Moscow, preparing for his next move. His fingers tapped lightly against the armrest of his chair as he listened to Viktor Karpov outline the details of their next assault on the IISF. The sabotage of the satellite launch had been a setback, but Orlov had always known that it was only the beginning. Now, it was time to step up the pressure.

Karpov stood by the large display screen in Orlov's private office, a map of key IISF facilities spread across the globe glowing in front of him. Each site was marked with precise details, highlighting weaknesses in their infrastructure—vulnerabilities that Orlov's agents could exploit.

"We're ready to move," Karpov said, his voice steady. "The teams are in place, and our cyber units have already begun infiltrating their systems. This time, we'll hit them where it hurts the most. Simultaneous strikes—no time to react."

Orlov's gaze was fixed on the map, his mind calculating the outcome of each move. He had spent years studying Garbuz, learning his tactics, his weaknesses. Garbuz was a survivor, but Orlov knew that everyone had a breaking point.

"And the timing?" Orlov asked, his voice low and controlled.

"We'll coordinate it down to the second," Karpov replied. "The first attack will target their communications network, followed by strikes on their research labs in Germany and

South America. We'll disrupt their logistics, delay their upcoming missions, and cripple their ability to respond. By the time they realize what's happening, it'll be too late."

Orlov nodded, a small, satisfied smile crossing his face. "Good. Garbuz has been too comfortable. He thinks that surviving one sabotage attempt means he can handle whatever we throw at him. Let's show him how wrong he is."

Karpov gave a brief nod and left the room to finalize the preparations, leaving Orlov alone with his thoughts. The tension between Russia and the IISF was no longer just a matter of political posturing—it had become a war of attrition, and Orlov intended to win. He knew that Garbuz was struggling to keep his organization together, and with each new attack, the IISF would become weaker, more fractured.

All he had to do was keep applying pressure, and eventually, the cracks would turn into a full collapse.

At IISF headquarters, the day had begun like any other. The team was still working through the aftermath of the emergency meeting, and although the mood was tense, there was a sense of cautious optimism that they had averted a larger crisis. But that optimism would not last.

It began with a small glitch. A routine status check on the IISF's global communications network revealed a slight delay in satellite uplinks. At first, it seemed like nothing more than a technical issue—an easily fixable error that happened from time to time.

But as the minutes passed, the problem escalated. One by one, the IISF's primary communication satellites began to go offline, cutting off key research facilities and international partners from the central hub at headquarters.

Elena Markov was in the command center when the first alerts began flashing across her console. She frowned, leaning closer to the screen as she tried to make sense of the data.

"Communications down in Germany," she said aloud, her voice drawing the attention of the nearby technicians. "And South America is reporting similar issues. Something's wrong."

She began issuing orders, directing her team to investigate the disruption, but even as they worked, the situation worsened. Within minutes, the IISF's entire satellite communications network had been compromised, leaving them isolated from their most important facilities around the world.

"Elena, we've got another problem," one of the technicians called out, panic rising in his voice. "The propulsion lab in Munich just went dark. We've lost all contact."

Elena's heart sank. "What do you mean, 'dark'? Have we been hacked?"

The technician shook his head, his face pale. "It's not just the network. The facility's offline. No power, no backup systems. We can't reach anyone there."

Elena's hands clenched into fists as she realized what was happening. This wasn't a technical malfunction—it was an attack.

She tapped her earpiece, connecting directly to Garbuz's office. "Georgiy, we've got a situation. Multiple facilities are going offline. This isn't random. Orlov's attacking us again."

Garbuz was on his feet the moment he heard Elena's voice. The calm of the morning shattered as the full scale of Orlov's assault became clear. The IISF was under siege, and they were losing control fast.

He stormed into the command center, his face set in a grim expression as he took in the chaos. Red alerts flashed across every screen, with technicians scrambling to regain control of the compromised systems. The global map displayed on the central screen showed critical IISF facilities going dark, one by one.

"How bad is it?" Garbuz demanded, his voice cutting through the noise.

Elena's expression was grim. "We're losing communication across the board. Orlov's cyber units must've hacked into our satellite network. We've already lost Munich and South America. If we don't act fast, we're going to lose everything."

Garbuz's mind raced as he processed the information. Orlov had struck with precision, hitting them where they were most vulnerable. Without communication, they were blind—unable to coordinate their missions, research, or even basic operations. And if the sabotage at the Munich lab was any indication, Orlov wasn't just targeting their technology. He was coming after their infrastructure as well.

"Get me a secure line to our ground teams," Garbuz ordered. "We need to lock down every facility we can. If Orlov's agents are inside, we have to stop them before they do more damage."

Elena nodded and immediately began issuing orders to the security teams stationed at IISF facilities around the world. But the damage was already spreading. Reports flooded in from other locations—explosions at the propulsion lab in Munich, a cyber breach in the logistics center in South America, and a power outage at the communications hub in Australia.

Garbuz watched the reports come in with a sinking feeling. This wasn't just an attack—it was an all-out assault, designed to overwhelm the IISF and leave them scrambling in the dark.

"We can't keep up with this," Elena said quietly, her voice filled with frustration. "He's hitting us on all fronts. We're trying to plug every hole, but the attacks are too coordinated."

Garbuz's mind raced. They needed to regain control, but Orlov had them on the defensive. Every second they spent reacting to the attacks put them further behind.

"We can't let him dictate the terms," Garbuz said, his voice filled with urgency. "We need to disrupt his operations—now. If we let him keep the initiative, we're finished."

Elena looked at him, her expression conflicted. "You're talking about going on the offensive? Right in the middle of this?"

Garbuz nodded, his decision made. "Yes. If we don't stop him, he'll pick us apart piece by piece. We need to hit him back—hard."

In the midst of the chaos, Garbuz called for an emergency strategy session with his senior team. The room was filled with tension as Elena, Dr. Volkov, and the other senior staff gathered to hear Garbuz's plan. The attacks were still ongoing, but Garbuz knew that they couldn't afford to wait. They needed to strike back before Orlov could land a killing blow.

"We're under attack from all sides," Garbuz said, addressing the group. "Orlov's strategy is clear—he's trying to overwhelm us, isolate us, and take us down facility by facility. If we keep reacting, we'll lose. We need to go on the offensive."

Volkov, who had been silent until now, finally spoke. "Going on the offensive right now is risky, Georgiy. We're already spread thin. What makes you think we can afford to launch an attack while we're still under siege?"

Garbuz met Volkov's gaze, his voice firm. "Because if we don't, we'll lose everything. Orlov won't stop until we're crippled. We need to hit him where it hurts, disrupt his operations, and force him to pull back. If we wait any longer, he'll win."

The room fell silent as Garbuz's words sank in. Volkov's expression was unreadable, but he didn't argue further.

Elena stepped forward, her face set with determination. "If we're going to do this, we need to be smart about it. We can't just throw everything we have at Orlov and hope for the best. We need to target his operations directly, cripple his ability to keep attacking us."

Garbuz nodded. "Agreed. We'll focus on taking out his communications network and disrupting his logistics. If we can cut off his ability to coordinate his attacks, we can buy ourselves the time we need to regain control."

The team quickly moved into action, coordinating their plan to strike back at Orlov's operations. It was a dangerous gamble, but Garbuz knew that it was their only chance to turn the tide.

Chapter 38
The IISF Strikes Back

The command center at IISF headquarters buzzed with controlled chaos as Georgiy Garbuz and his senior team finalized their preparations for the counteroffensive. The screens on the walls displayed real-time updates from around the world—satellites offline, research labs sabotaged, communications jammed. Orlov had crippled their operations, but Garbuz was determined to regain control. This was their only chance to strike back before Orlov overwhelmed them entirely.

Garbuz stood in front of the central console, scanning the data coming in from their compromised facilities. His mind was racing, calculating every possible outcome, weighing the risks against the rewards. He knew that the decision to go on the offensive was dangerous, especially with the IISF's infrastructure already under siege. But there was no other option. They had to stop Orlov before he destroyed everything they had built.

"We're ready," Elena Markov said, stepping up beside him. Her voice was calm, but the intensity in her eyes betrayed the gravity of the situation. "Our teams have identified the targets. Orlov's communications network is vulnerable, and if we hit his logistics hubs, we can cripple his ability to launch further attacks."

Garbuz nodded, turning to face the rest of his senior staff. Dr. Andrei Volkov stood near the back of the room, his arms crossed as he watched the preparations unfold. His expression was unreadable, but Garbuz could sense his unease.

"Are we certain about this?" Volkov asked, his voice laced with caution. "We're already stretched thin. If this fails, we'll be in an even worse position. Orlov's already crippled our communications. What if we can't recover?"

"We won't have to," Garbuz replied, his tone firm. "If we pull this off, Orlov won't be able to keep up his attacks. We'll cripple his supply lines, disrupt his network, and buy ourselves the time we need to rebuild. But if we wait, we'll be finished."

Volkov hesitated for a moment, then nodded slowly. "All right. But we need to be prepared for a quick retreat if things go south. We can't risk losing more than we already have."

"Agreed," Elena said. "Our cyber team is ready to deploy countermeasures if Orlov retaliates. And we've reinforced the remaining security at our facilities to buy us time."

Garbuz glanced at Elena, his confidence bolstered by her unwavering resolve. "Let's do this."

As the operation began, the command center shifted into high gear. Garbuz watched from the central console as his team launched a series of cyber counterattacks against Orlov's communications network. Captain Martinez, who had successfully led the mission to disarm the sabotage at the satellite launch, was now coordinating the ground teams.

The IISF's first target was a series of communications hubs located in Eastern Europe—critical nodes in Orlov's sprawling network. These hubs allowed Orlov's forces to coordinate their attacks across multiple regions, and if the IISF could take them offline, it would severely limit Orlov's ability to respond.

"We've breached their firewall," one of the cybertechs reported, his fingers flying across the keyboard. "Orlov's encryption is tough, but we're making progress."

Elena nodded, her eyes fixed on the screen. "Focus on disabling their command channels. If we can sever their connection to the ground teams, Orlov won't be able to coordinate his attacks."

As the cyber team worked, Garbuz turned his attention to the second phase of the operation: targeting Orlov's logistics hubs. The IISF had identified several key facilities in remote parts of Russia—warehouses, transport centers, and supply depots that fed Orlov's operations. A strike here would disrupt his entire supply chain.

"Captain Martinez, how's the ground team?" Garbuz asked, his voice steady but tense.

Martinez's voice crackled through the comms. "Our units are in position near the first logistics hub. We're ready to move on your command."

"Proceed with caution," Garbuz said. "Hit them hard, but don't expose yourselves. We can't afford any losses."

Martinez acknowledged the order, and Garbuz watched as the feed switched to a live view from the ground teams. The operatives moved swiftly and silently through the remote Russian countryside, closing in on Orlov's supply lines. Garbuz's heart pounded as the tension mounted. The success of this operation depended on precision, on timing, on everything going perfectly.

The first strike came swiftly. As the cyber team breached Orlov's communications network, a series of targeted disruptions rippled through his channels. Orlov's forces, now isolated from central command, scrambled to respond, their once-coordinated attacks thrown into chaos.

In Russia, Captain Martinez and his ground team launched their assault on the logistics hub. Explosions echoed through the facility as the IISF operatives neutralized the guards and sabotaged key supply routes. Flames lit up the night sky as the team planted explosives on the transport vehicles, cutting off Orlov's ability to move supplies.

"We've disabled their transport fleet," Martinez reported, his voice crackling through the comms. "The facility is compromised. Moving to the extraction point."

Garbuz exhaled a breath he hadn't realized he was holding. It was working. For the first time since Orlov's attacks had begun, the IISF was on the offensive, hitting back with precision and force.

But the success was short-lived.

Even as the IISF celebrated their victories, Orlov's retaliation came swift and brutal. In Moscow, Orlov had anticipated that Garbuz would strike back, and he was prepared. As soon as his communications network was compromised, Orlov ordered a direct counter-attack—one that targeted the heart of the IISF's operations.

"Georgiy," Elena called out from the console, her face tight with alarm. "We've got incoming signals—Orlov's launching a counteroffensive. He's targeting our headquarters."

The words sent a chill through Garbuz. Orlov was no longer just playing defense. He was going for the kill.

"Scramble all defenses," Garbuz ordered, his voice rising as the room erupted into action. "I want every available resource focused on stopping that attack. We can't let him breach our systems."

The command center lit up with activity as technicians and security personnel worked frantically to fortify their defenses. But Orlov's attack was relentless. His cyber teams launched wave after wave of assaults on the IISF's remaining infrastructure, targeting their power grids, backup systems, and critical data stores.

"We're losing ground," one of the cybertechs shouted. "They're penetrating our firewalls faster than we can patch them."

"Elena!" Garbuz called out, his voice filled with urgency.

"I'm on it," Elena replied, her fingers flying across the keyboard. "I'm rerouting power to the auxiliary systems, but we're not going to last much longer if this keeps up."

The room was filled with the hum of alarms and the flashing red of emergency lights. The situation was deteriorating fast, and Garbuz knew that they were on the edge of a full systems collapse.

As the command center descended into chaos, Garbuz made a decision. It was risky, but it was their only chance to survive Orlov's counterattack.

"Elena, I need you to prepare for a system shutdown," Garbuz said, his voice hard.

Elena looked at him in shock. "A shutdown? Georgiy, if we shut down now, we'll be completely vulnerable. We'll lose everything."

Garbuz shook his head. "We'll lose everything if we don't. Orlov's going to break through our firewalls, and if that happens, he'll have access to all our data. We can't let that happen. If we shut down the main systems and run on backups, we might be able to isolate the breach."

Elena hesitated, clearly torn, but she nodded. "All right. I'll initiate the sequence. But once we shut down, we're flying blind."

"Better blind than exposed," Garbuz replied. "Do it."

Chapter 39

The System Shutdown

The lights in the IISF command center flickered as Georgiy Garbuz made his fateful decision. The main systems had to be shut down to stop Orlov's cyberattacks from penetrating their core infrastructure. As the room buzzed with activity, there was a palpable sense of urgency and fear. Garbuz's heart pounded in his chest as he watched his team prepare for the shutdown. Every second counted, and he knew they were moments away from losing everything.

Elena Markov stood at the central console, her fingers flying over the controls as she initiated the sequence. The large screens in the command center flashed red, displaying warnings that their systems were about to go offline.

"System shutdown in T-minus sixty seconds," one of the technicians called out, his voice shaky.

"Everyone, prepare for backup protocols," Elena ordered, her voice commanding but tense. "We're going dark in one minute."

Around the room, the team scrambled to secure what they could. Data was rapidly being backed up to isolated servers, and the security team was reinforcing the physical defenses at key IISF facilities. But they all knew that once the main systems went offline, the entire organization would be vulnerable.

Garbuz glanced at the digital countdown on the screen—forty-five seconds. The tension was almost unbearable, but he kept his face calm. Now wasn't the time to let fear take hold. He needed to show his team that they could pull through this, even if he wasn't entirely sure himself.

"Elena," Garbuz said quietly, moving to stand beside her. "Are we sure the backups will hold?"

"They'll hold," Elena replied, though the uncertainty in her voice betrayed her. "We've isolated the critical data. Orlov's team won't be able to access it, but we'll be flying blind until we can get the main systems back online."

Garbuz nodded, gripping the edge of the console as the countdown reached twenty seconds. The lights flickered again, and an uneasy quiet fell over the room as everyone waited for the inevitable.

"We're almost there," Elena whispered, her eyes fixed on the screen.

The countdown hit zero, and suddenly, everything went dark. The overhead lights shut off, the hum of the machinery died, and the screens blinked out, leaving the room bathed in an eerie red glow from the emergency backup lights.

Garbuz stood still, listening to the quiet murmur of voices as his team adjusted to the sudden darkness. The command center, which had been buzzing with activity only moments before, now felt like a tomb.

"Elena?" Garbuz called out softly, straining to hear over the faint sound of emergency alarms.

"I'm here," she replied, her voice steady. "Backups are active. We've lost the main systems, but the core data is secure. We'll need at least an hour to bring everything back online—maybe more."

Garbuz closed his eyes for a moment, exhaling slowly. They had bought themselves some time, but they were far from safe.

"All right," Garbuz said, raising his voice so the entire room could hear him. "We've shut down to stop Orlov's attack, but this isn't over. We'll bring the systems back online as soon as we can, and when we do, we need to be ready for anything. Stay focused. Stay sharp."

There were murmurs of agreement from around the room, though the tension remained thick. Everyone knew they were vulnerable, and if Orlov chose to strike again during the shutdown, there would be little they could do to stop him.

Meanwhile, in Moscow, President Vasily Orlov paced in his private office, frustration radiating from him. He had been watching the attack unfold through encrypted channels, monitoring the progress of his cyber units as they broke through IISF firewalls. Everything had been going according to plan—until Garbuz had ordered the shutdown.

"They shut down their systems," Orlov muttered, glaring at the live feed on his screen. "Garbuz knew we were close."

Viktor Karpov, who had been standing nearby, nodded. "They're running on backup protocols now. It'll slow them down, but we've lost our window to breach their core systems."

Orlov clenched his fists, his jaw tightening in frustration. "They're vulnerable right now. Their systems are offline, their defenses down. We need to press harder."

Karpov hesitated for a moment. "Our cyber teams are regrouping, but without the main systems online, the IISF is running blind. We've cut off their communications, but they'll recover if we give them time. A direct strike on their facilities might be our best move."

Orlov's eyes narrowed. "I want ground teams ready to move. Hit their labs in Germany and South America again. Make sure they can't recover."

Karpov nodded and moved to relay the orders. Orlov turned back to his screen, watching the red dots that marked IISF facilities around the world. Garbuz had been clever, but Orlov knew that he couldn't keep the organization afloat much longer. The shutdown had bought Garbuz time, but it had also left him more vulnerable than ever.

Back at IISF headquarters, the minutes dragged by as Garbuz and his team waited for the systems to come back online. The silence was oppressive, broken only by the occasional beep from the backup generators and the whispered conversations among the staff.

Garbuz sat down at the central console, rubbing his temples as the weight of the situation pressed down on him. His mind raced with questions: Was Orlov preparing another attack? Would their backup systems hold? Could they regain control before Orlov broke through again?

Elena sat beside him, her eyes scanning the screens that flickered with only minimal data. "We're holding for now," she said quietly. "But we can't stay like this forever. Orlov knows we're vulnerable."

Garbuz nodded, his eyes dark. "We're sitting ducks until the systems come back online."

Elena's expression softened. "You made the right call, Georgiy. If we hadn't shut down, Orlov would've had access to everything."

"I know," Garbuz replied, though the doubt still lingered in his voice. "But the longer we stay in the dark, the more time he has to hit us. We can't afford to lose another facility."

As if on cue, a technician rushed over, his face pale. "We've just received reports—Orlov's ground teams are mobilizing. They're heading for our facilities in Munich and South America."

Elena's eyes widened. "We've reinforced security, but if they hit us with ground teams, we won't be able to hold them off for long."

Garbuz stood up, the urgency returning to his voice. "Get me Captain Martinez. We need to lock down those sites immediately. Have the remaining security teams prep for an assault. We can't lose those labs."

The technician nodded and rushed off, leaving Garbuz and Elena to face the grim reality: Orlov was preparing to strike again, and this time, it wouldn't be through cyberspace.

As the IISF security teams prepared for the incoming assault, Garbuz and Elena worked furiously to bring the systems back online. The backup generators were holding, but the main power grids were still offline, and their ability to coordinate a defense was limited.

"Martinez is ready," Elena said, relaying the message from the field. "He's stationed at the Munich facility with reinforcements. South America is more vulnerable, but we've sent additional teams there as well."

Garbuz clenched his fists, feeling the pressure mounting. They were racing against time. If they couldn't restore the systems before Orlov's ground teams arrived, they risked losing two of their most important research facilities—along with everything inside.

"Tell Martinez to hold the line," Garbuz ordered, his voice tense. "We're going to get the systems back up, and once we do, we'll hit Orlov where it hurts."

Elena nodded, though her eyes betrayed the gravity of the situation. "I'll do what I can. But if Orlov's teams breach the labs…"

Garbuz didn't need to hear the rest. He knew what was at stake. The IISF was hanging by a thread, and Orlov was preparing to cut it.

Chapter 40

The Decision

The storm was coming.

At IISF headquarters, the emergency lights cast a faint red glow across the command center as the staff worked in near silence, save for the occasional soft murmur of voices and the steady hum of the backup generators. Georgiy Garbuz stood in the center of the room, his eyes glued to the status monitors as they flickered with minimal data. The tension was suffocating. They had shut down to prevent Orlov's cyberattack, but now, the IISF was blind, vulnerable, and exposed.

"Elena, status on the power grid?" Garbuz asked, his voice calm but strained.

Elena Markov glanced up from her console, her fingers still moving over the controls. "We're making progress, but we're not there yet. It's going to take another twenty minutes to bring the main systems back online. Backup protocols are holding, but we don't have full access to external communications or security feeds."

Garbuz nodded, feeling the weight of the clock ticking down. Twenty minutes felt like an eternity.

"We don't have twenty minutes," he muttered, knowing full well that Orlov wouldn't wait that long to strike again.

Just then, the door to the command center slid open, and Captain Martinez stepped inside, his face set in grim determination. He had been in constant contact with the IISF's security teams on the ground, organizing the defenses as Orlov's forces closed in.

"Orlov's ground teams are on the move," Martinez reported, stepping up to the central console. "Our scouts have spotted enemy units near the outskirts of Munich, and we're picking up chatter that indicates a coordinated strike. They'll hit the Munich propulsion lab and the South American logistics center at the same time."

Garbuz's eyes darkened. Munich and South America—two of the IISF's most critical facilities. If Orlov took those sites, the damage to their operations would be catastrophic.

"How long do we have?" Garbuz asked.

"Not long," Martinez replied. "They'll be in range within the hour. We've fortified our defenses at both sites, but the teams are outnumbered. We're running short on manpower, and without full communications, we're relying on field radios and shortwave signals. If they hit us hard, we might not hold."

Garbuz cursed under his breath. They had anticipated cyberattacks, sabotage, and political pressure—but now they were facing a direct military-style assault. And with the systems down, they couldn't coordinate the defenses effectively.

"Elena, how much longer?" Garbuz asked again, his frustration starting to show.

"I'm working as fast as I can," Elena replied, her voice tight. "We'll get the systems back, but it's going to take time. There's no way to rush this."

"Then we hold," Garbuz said firmly, turning back to Martinez. "Tell our teams to dig in and hold the line. We can't afford to lose those facilities."

Martinez nodded, pulling up his comms to relay the orders to the field. Garbuz watched him for a moment, then turned to Elena.

"We can't let Orlov take Munich or South America. If we lose those sites, we lose the heart of our propulsion research and logistics operations. Is there any way we can speed this up?"

Elena met his eyes, her face serious. "Not without risking a complete crash. We're already running on minimal power. If we push too hard, we could fry the backup systems."

Garbuz took a deep breath, weighing his options. They were in a race against time, and the outcome would determine the future of the IISF. He knew that if they couldn't restore the systems in time, the defenses would be overwhelmed.

"We'll have to buy ourselves time," Garbuz said finally. "Martinez, keep the ground teams updated. I don't care what it takes—hold those facilities."

On the ground outside the Munich propulsion lab, the air was thick with anticipation. The IISF security teams, led by Captain Martinez, had fortified their positions, turning the lab into a defensive stronghold. Makeshift barricades had been erected, and the few armed personnel they had were stationed at key points around the perimeter.

Martinez checked his rifle, his jaw set with determination as he surveyed the landscape. The German countryside was quiet, the only sound being the occasional rustle of leaves in the wind. But he knew that silence wouldn't last. Orlov's forces were out there, closing in, and it wouldn't be long before the battle began.

"Captain, we've got movement on the eastern ridge," one of the scouts reported through the comms. "Looks like at least two squads, heavily armed."

Martinez raised his binoculars, scanning the ridge in the distance. Sure enough, dark shapes moved through the trees, advancing toward their position. He could feel the tension rising among his men as they realized the enemy was close.

"Stay sharp," Martinez ordered, his voice calm. "They'll be coming in fast. Hold your positions and don't let them breach the perimeter."

The first shot rang out moments later, the sharp crack of gunfire echoing through the valley. Orlov's forces, dressed in tactical gear and moving with precision, launched their assault, pushing toward the propulsion lab with alarming speed.

The IISF defenders returned fire, but they were outnumbered and outgunned. Orlov's ground teams advanced in waves, using smoke and flash grenades to disorient the defenders. Martinez shouted orders, directing his team to fall back to secondary positions as the enemy closed in.

"Hold the line!" Martinez yelled, his voice rising over the sounds of battle. "Don't let them through!"

But it was a brutal fight. Orlov's forces were relentless, and despite the IISF's best efforts, they were slowly being pushed back. Martinez knew they couldn't hold forever, but he also knew they had no choice. If they lost Munich, it would be a devastating blow.

Meanwhile, in South America, the situation was equally dire. The logistics center—a sprawling complex deep in the jungle—was under siege. The IISF security team stationed there was smaller and less equipped than the team in Munich, and they were struggling to hold the line against a coordinated assault from Orlov's forces.

The jungle provided some cover, but the enemy's superior numbers and firepower gave them the advantage. IISF operatives huddled behind crates and cargo containers, returning fire as Orlov's troops moved in from multiple directions.

Lt. Rodriguez, the leader of the South American team, was fighting to keep morale up. "We can't let them take the depot," he said through gritted teeth, firing at an enemy soldier. "If they get control of our supply chain, it's over."

But the odds were against them. Orlov's forces had already breached the outer defenses, and now they were closing in on the main logistics center.

Back at IISF headquarters, Garbuz could feel the weight of every second that passed. Reports from Munich and South America were coming in sporadically, filled with the sounds of gunfire and explosions. His teams were holding, but just barely.

"Elena, we're running out of time," Garbuz said, his voice low. "We need those systems back online—now."

Elena didn't look up from her console. "I know, Georgiy. I'm almost there."

Garbuz's jaw clenched as he listened to the latest update from Martinez. Orlov's forces were pushing harder than expected, and both sites were on the verge of being overrun.

"We can't hold much longer," Martinez's voice came through the comms, crackling with static. "They're throwing everything they've got at us."

"Just a little longer, Martinez," Garbuz said, gripping the console. "We're almost there."

As if on cue, the command center's lights flickered back to life. The hum of the main systems returning online filled the room, and the screens flashed as the IISF's infrastructure began to recover.

"We're back," Elena said, her voice filled with relief. "Main systems are online. We have full access."

Garbuz's heart pounded as he turned to the screens. "Get our defenses up. Reestablish contact with Munich and South America."

The command center sprang into action, the technicians working frantically to bring their systems back online. But Garbuz knew that even with the systems restored, they were still in the fight of their lives.

Chapter 41

Turning the Tide

The air in the command center was heavy with tension. Georgiy Garbuz stood over the main console, his face illuminated by the flickering screens displaying the damage reports from the Munich propulsion lab and the South American logistics center. The IISF had barely survived Orlov's coordinated assault, and now they faced a future that seemed more uncertain than ever.

"The propulsion lab is crippled," Elena Markov said quietly, standing at Garbuz's side. Her eyes were fixed on the screen, where the extent of the destruction was laid out in stark numbers. "Half the research equipment is gone, and what's left is either damaged o r offline. We're looking at months—maybe longer—before we can fully recover."

Garbuz exhaled slowly, his gaze hard. He knew the loss of the propulsion lab would have a devastating impact on their upcoming mission—the IISF's first manned journey into deep space. The mission had been in development for years, a beacon of hope that was supposed to unify the organization and demonstrate to the world that the IISF was still the leader in space exploration. Now, that hope felt fragile.

"And South America?" Garbuz asked, though he already knew the answer.

Elena shook her head. "Not much better. The logistics center is operational, but we've lost a lot of personnel. Orlov hit us hard. Our supply network is crippled, and we're running on emergency reserves."

The weight of the situation pressed down on Garbuz's shoulders. They were supposed to be preparing for the most ambitious mission in human history, but instead, they were struggling just to keep the organization from collapsing. He ran a hand over his face, trying to push back the rising tide of frustration.

Before he could speak, the door to the command center slid open, and Dr. Andrei Volkov stormed in, his face flushed with anger. The scientist barely spared a glance at Elena before focusing his gaze on Garbuz.

"This is a disaster, Georgiy," Volkov spat, his voice tight with fury. "The propulsion lab is in ruins. Our deep space mission is dead in the water unless we make drastic changes now."

Garbuz bristled at the accusation but kept his voice measured. "I'm aware of the situation, Andrei. We're doing everything we can to recover."

"Everything we can?" Volkov's eyes flashed. "You've been too reactive, always one step behind Orlov. We should have anticipated these attacks. Now, thanks to your hesitation, we're on the brink of failure."

The tension in the room thickened as Volkov's words hung in the air. Elena stepped forward, ready to defend Garbuz, but Garbuz raised a hand, stopping her. He understood Volkov's frustration—he felt it himself—but they couldn't afford to let this turn into an internal fight.

"We're still moving forward with the mission," Garbuz said firmly. "We'll repair the damage to the propulsion lab, and the deep space launch will proceed as planned. This is our chance to show the world that we can rise above Orlov's sabotage."

Volkov let out a bitter laugh. "Proceed as planned? Have you even looked at the damage reports? Half our propulsion technology is gone. We're supposed to be days away from launching humanity's first mission into deep space, and you want to pretend that everything is fine? We're not ready. We're not even close."

"We'll adapt," Garbuz shot back, his voice sharpening. "We've come too far to back down now."

Volkov shook his head, his frustration boiling over. "Adapt? We don't have time to adapt. Orlov is preparing to launch a competing mission with the BRICS alliance, and we're sitting here patching up the wreckage of our own facilities. If we don't take action—decisive action—we'll lose everything."

The room fell into a tense silence. Garbuz stared at Volkov, the weight of his words settling over him. He knew that Volkov was right, at least in part. The damage to their facilities was severe, and the deep space mission was on the verge of collapsing under the strain. But abandoning it wasn't an option. If they canceled the mission now, Orlov would win. The BRICS alliance would dominate, and the IISF's role as a leader in space exploration would be over.

"Elena," Garbuz said quietly, turning to her. "What's the status of the spacecraft? Are we still on track for launch?"

Elena nodded, though her expression was grim. "The spacecraft is intact, and the crew is ready, but we've had to make adjustments due to the propulsion setback. It's going to be a tight schedule, and any further delays could jeopardize the mission. We've also been monitoring security—there's been chatter about a possible sabotage attempt on the launch itself."

"Sabotage?" Volkov's eyes widened. "Do you have proof?"

Elena shook her head. "Nothing concrete, just signals and chatter from Orlov's network. But we can't ignore the possibility. If Orlov sabotages the spacecraft, it could be catastrophic."

Garbuz's mind raced as he absorbed the information. The risks were multiplying. Not only was the deep space mission threatened by technical failures, but now there was the looming threat of sabotage. Orlov wasn't just trying to cripple their operations—he was trying to destroy the entire mission before it could even begin.

"We'll increase security," Garbuz said, his tone decisive. "Double-check every system on the spacecraft, run thorough background checks on all personnel, and keep an eye on any unusual activity near the launch site. This mission cannot fail."

Volkov crossed his arms, his expression still skeptical. "And what about the BRICS mission? If they launch before us, we're done. We can't beat them if we're limping across the finish line."

"We'll launch first," Garbuz said firmly. "We'll show the world that the IISF is still leading the charge."

Volkov stared at him for a long moment, then nodded grudgingly. "Fine. But if we don't see significant progress in the next few days, I'm going to start questioning whether you're the right person to lead this organization."

Garbuz didn't respond. He didn't need to. The challenge had been laid out clearly, and he knew that Volkov wasn't the only one who was losing faith. The internal divisions within the IISF were growing deeper, and if they didn't succeed soon, those divisions could tear the organization apart.

Unbeknownst to Garbuz and Volkov, Sable, Orlov's sleeper agent within the IISF, was quietly observing the escalating tensions. Sable had been subtly manipulating Volkov for weeks, pushing him toward greater frustration with Garbuz's leadership. Now, as the deep space mission faced potential sabotage, Sable saw an opportunity to accelerate their plans.

In the shadows, Sable sent a coded message to Orlov, detailing the internal strife and the vulnerabilities in the IISF's operations. Orlov's plan was working. The cracks within the organization were widening, and it was only a matter of time before they crumbled.

Sable smiled to themselves as they watched Volkov walk away from Garbuz, tension radiating from every step. It wouldn't be long now. The deep space mission might just be the final blow to Garbuz's leadership—and to the IISF's future.

Chapter 42

The BRICS Rivalry

Garbuz sat at his desk in the dimly lit office, staring at the wall of screens in front of him. Reports from across the world flooded in—updates on the deep space mission, the status of the crippled facilities, and encrypted communications from their international partners. Each report felt like a ticking clock, counting down the time they had left to prove themselves. He couldn't afford another mistake.

A sharp tone cut through the silence, signaling an incoming secure call. Garbuz glanced at the console—it was Senator Warner from the United States. He exhaled deeply before answering.

"Georgiy," Warner's voice crackled through the comms. "We need to talk. I just got off the phone with members of the Senate committee. They're not happy with how things are going at the IISF. The attacks, the setbacks with your facilities... it's all looking very bad from where we stand."

Garbuz sat back, rubbing his temples. He knew this call was coming but had hoped for more time. "We're aware of the issues, Senator. We're making repairs as we speak, and our systems will be back up soon. The mission is still on track."

Warner's voice grew colder. "On track? Georgiy, this isn't just about the mission. It's about confidence—international confidence in the IISF. The United States has invested billions in this organization, and people are starting to ask if it's worth it. With the BRICS alliance moving forward with their own deep space mission, we're in danger of losing our position. If that happens, Congress won't hesitate to pull the plug."

Garbuz's jaw clenched at the mention of the BRICS mission. It was no secret that Orlov had orchestrated their rise to challenge the IISF's dominance, and now they were positioning themselves to lead the global race into deep space. If the BRICS mission launched first, the IISF's credibility—and its funding—would be in jeopardy.

"We're preparing our countermeasures against Orlov," Garbuz said, forcing confidence into his voice. "We'll strike back, and the mission will launch as planned. The IISF won't let BRICS take the lead."

Warner sighed. "I hope you're right. But let me be clear: you're on thin ice, Georgiy. The committee is already drafting proposals to reallocate resources if the IISF doesn't deliver. We don't have time for more delays."

The call ended abruptly, leaving Garbuz staring at the black screen. Thin ice. He could feel it beneath his feet—the tension, the growing doubts, the weight of expectations. And now, with the BRICS mission looming, they had even less time than he thought.

The comms beeped again, pulling him out of his thoughts. This time, it was President Zhang of China.

Garbuz straightened up in his chair and answered. Zhang's calm but firm voice filled the room.

"Mr. Garbuz, I'm contacting you with grave concerns from Beijing," Zhang said without preamble. "The recent attacks on your facilities have raised serious questions about the IISF's ability to maintain operational security. We are also aware of your current difficulties in launching the deep space mission. China, as you know, has been a key financial backer of the IISF. But given recent developments, there is growing sentiment within our government that perhaps our interests would be better served elsewhere."

Garbuz tensed, sensing where this conversation was going. "We're addressing the situation, President Zhang. The damage to our facilities is being repaired, and the deep space mission is still moving forward. We've implemented additional security measures to prevent further sabotage."

Zhang's tone remained neutral, almost clinical. "I'm glad to hear that. However, we are also aware of the BRICS alliance's plans. Their mission is proceeding smoothly, and there are talks of launching within the next few months. The question, Mr. Garbuz, is whether the IISF can stay ahead of them. If not, China may need to reconsider its role in the IISF."

It was a threat, thinly veiled but unmistakable. Garbuz's mind raced. Losing China's support would be disastrous. They had been one of the IISF's biggest financial contributors, and their technological collaboration had been crucial to the success of the mission.

"We will launch first," Garbuz said, his voice steady but strained. "I give you my word. The IISF will lead humanity's first manned mission into deep space."

There was a pause on the other end, then Zhang's voice returned, softer but no less serious. "I sincerely hope that you can keep that promise, Mr. Garbuz. For the sake of our continued partnership."

The line went dead, and Garbuz leaned back in his chair, letting out a long breath. The BRICS alliance was moving faster than anticipated, and the pressure was mounting. He needed to act quickly, or the IISF would lose more than just credibility—it would lose its place in history.

As the day wore on, the reality of the BRICS mission weighed heavily on Garbuz's mind. The BRICS alliance, with Orlov pulling the strings, was positioning itself to seize the lead in space exploration. Their mission had been shrouded in secrecy, but what little intelligence they had gathered suggested that BRICS was on the verge of launching a crewed mission to deep space—perhaps even sooner than the IISF.

Garbuz called an emergency meeting with Elena, Volkov, and several key members of the senior staff. They gathered in the command center, their faces tight with concern.

"Let's get right to it," Garbuz began, addressing the group. "We've got a serious problem. The BRICS alliance is preparing to launch their own deep space mission, and if they launch before us, we're finished. We'll lose our funding, our partnerships, and our leadership position. We can't let that happen."

Elena nodded, her face drawn with stress. "I've been monitoring the chatter. BRICS is moving fast, and Orlov is backing them every step of the way. If they launch before us, it will be a global statement that we've lost control."

Volkov crossed his arms, his expression dark. "And meanwhile, we're scrambling just to keep our own mission on track. Munich is a mess, and the sabotage threat is still very real. We can't afford to rush into this launch without making sure everything is secure."

Garbuz exhaled, feeling the weight of the decisions before him. Every choice seemed to lead to another risk. "We don't have the luxury of time. If we delay, BRICS will launch first. And I'm not willing to hand them that victory."

"But what about the sabotage?" Elena asked. "We still don't know who Orlov has inside the IISF. If there's even a chance the spacecraft has been compromised, we're putting the entire mission—and the crew—at risk."

Garbuz was silent for a moment, the words hanging in the air. The threat of sabotage had been looming for weeks, and despite their best efforts, they hadn't been able to uncover who, if anyone, was plotting against them. They had doubled security, checked and rechecked the spacecraft's systems, but the uncertainty remained.

"We're going to move forward," Garbuz said finally, his voice resolute. "We'll launch first, no matter what. But we're going to take every precaution. Volkov, I need you to oversee the final security sweep of the spacecraft. Nothing gets overlooked."

Volkov's expression softened slightly, though the tension in his voice remained. "I'll handle it. But if we find anything out of place, we'll have to delay. We can't risk lives just to stay ahead of BRICS."

Garbuz nodded. "Understood. We'll do this right. But we *will* do it."

Unbeknownst to Garbuz, Sable, Orlov's sleeper agent, had already begun setting the next phase of their plan into motion. After the emergency meeting, Sable sent a secure message to Orlov, informing him of the IISF's decision to move forward with the launch despite the sabotage threat.

Orlov's response was immediate: accelerate the sabotage. If the IISF's mission failed—if their spacecraft suffered even a minor malfunction during launch—it would be the final blow to Garbuz's leadership. The world would turn to the BRICS alliance, and the IISF would crumble.

Sable knew that the timing had to be perfect. If they could trigger the sabotage just as the IISF was about to launch, it would devastate Garbuz's credibility and pave the way for the BRICS mission to take center stage.

The pieces were falling into place, and Sable was ready to strike when the time came.

Chapter 43
Volkov's Growing Frustration

The corridors of IISF headquarters buzzed with a low hum of activity as the organization prepared for its most critical operation yet. Despite the recent damage and setbacks, the deep space mission was back on schedule. But beneath the surface, the growing tension within the organization simmered, threatening to boil over.

In a conference room adjacent to the command center, Elena Markov, Dr. Andrei Volkov, and several senior officers gathered for a briefing on the final security sweep of the spacecraft. Garbuz had tasked Volkov with ensuring that every inch of the spacecraft was secured before launch, a responsibility that weighed heavily on the already-stressed scientist.

Volkov stood at the front of the room, projecting a series of technical schematics on the wall as he outlined the findings of the initial inspections.

"We've checked and double-checked the propulsion systems, life support, and the communication arrays," Volkov began, his voice steady but tired. "So far, everything seems to be in order. But there's one area we're concerned about—the software governing the navigation system. We've detected some anomalies."

Elena's brow furrowed as she leaned forward. "Anomalies? Could they be part of the sabotage attempt we've been fearing?"

Volkov exhaled, his hands gripping the edge of the table. "It's possible. We've isolated the issue, but it's subtle—too subtle for anyone without inside knowledge to manipulate. My team is working on it, but the fact that we found it this late in the process raises red flags."

The room fell silent as everyone absorbed the weight of Volkov's words. Elena could see the stress etched on his face, the toll the last few weeks had taken on him. He had been under immense pressure—not just to ensure the success of the deep space mission, but to also navigate the growing tensions within the IISF.

"Do you think this is Orlov's doing?" Elena asked, her voice low.

Volkov's eyes met hers, and for a moment, he looked uncertain. "I don't know. But whoever planted this knows the spacecraft inside and out. If we hadn't found it now, the mission would have been doomed."

Elena felt a chill run down her spine. They were so close to the launch, and yet danger still lurked within their own ranks. "We'll need to run a full investigation," she said. "If this is sabotage, it means Orlov has a mole—someone deep inside the IISF."

Volkov nodded grimly. "That's what I'm afraid of."

Meanwhile, back in Garbuz's office, the situation was no less tense. Garbuz sat at his desk, staring at a report from the Munich facility that detailed the extensive damage to their propulsion research. The costs of the attack were staggering, and they still hadn't recovered fully.

The door slid open, and Garbuz looked up to see Sable enter, carrying a set of data pads. As Orlov's sleeper agent, Sable had played their role perfectly, posing as a loyal member of the IISF while quietly sowing discord and confusion.

"Reports from the Munich lab," Sable said, handing the data pads to Garbuz. "We're still behind schedule on propulsion, but they're pushing forward as fast as they can."

Garbuz took the data pads without a word, his mind elsewhere. He couldn't shake the feeling that they were running out of time. The BRICS alliance was moving quickly, and the pressure from international governments was intensifying. The deep space mission was supposed to be a moment of triumph, a symbol of hope for the future. But now it felt like a gamble—one that could easily end in disaster.

Sable watched Garbuz closely, sensing his anxiety. "The team is ready for the launch," Sable said softly. "We're prepared. This mission can still be the turning point."

Garbuz looked up, meeting Sable's eyes. "I want to believe that. But with everything going on—the attacks, the sabotage threat—it feels like we're balancing on the edge of a knife."

Sable smiled faintly, masking the satisfaction they felt. Garbuz was right to be afraid. The final sabotage plan was already in motion, and if all went well, the IISF would fall apart from within.

"We just need to stay focused," Sable said, their voice soothing. "Once the mission launches, everything will change. We'll show the world that the IISF is still the leader in space exploration."

Garbuz nodded, but he still felt the unease gnawing at him. He trusted his team, but the threat of sabotage lingered like a shadow over everything they did.

In the spacecraft hangar, Volkov was overseeing the final checks on the spacecraft. His team worked methodically, combing over every detail to ensure that the anomalies in the navigation software had been corrected. Volkov couldn't shake the feeling that they were missing something—something important.

As the engineers worked, Volkov's mind wandered back to his earlier conversation with Elena. If there truly was a saboteur within the IISF, they would have to act fast to prevent any further damage. But who could it be? And how deep did Orlov's influence run?

One of the engineers approached Volkov, handing him a tablet with the final diagnostics. "Everything checks out now, sir," the engineer said. "We've isolated the navigation anomalies and patched the system. It should be ready for launch."

Volkov nodded but didn't feel the sense of relief he had been hoping for. "Run the test simulations one more time," he ordered. "I want to be absolutely sure there are no more surprises."

As the engineer moved away, Volkov's thoughts turned dark. The upcoming launch was meant to be a moment of victory, but if anything went wrong, it would be catastrophic. And if someone within their own ranks was working against them, there was no telling what could happen.

That night, Sable made their move. In the quiet hours, long after most of the staff had left the headquarters, Sable accessed the internal systems one last time. They had waited for the right moment, and now, with the mission just days away, it was time to act.

Sable navigated the secured network with ease, implanting a final command in the space-craft's navigation software. It was a subtle change, almost invisible, but it would trigger at the worst possible moment—during the launch sequence. By the time anyone realized what had happened, it would be too late.

With the command successfully executed, Sable stepped back from the console, satisfied. The trap was set. Garbuz and his team would never see it coming.

The next morning, Garbuz gathered the senior staff for one final briefing before the launch. Volkov, Elena, and Sable stood at the table, reviewing the final preparations. Everyone looked exhausted, worn down by weeks of relentless pressure and the constant threat of sabotage.

"We're ready," Elena said, though her voice lacked the usual confidence. "The spacecraft has been cleared, and the crew is on standby. We've run every check possible."

Volkov nodded but remained tense. "I've double-checked the navigation system myself. It should be secure now. But we can't ignore the possibility that Orlov will make a move during the launch."

Garbuz's gaze hardened. "We're not letting Orlov stop us. This mission goes forward. I want security doubled at the launch site. No one gets near that spacecraft unless they've been cleared by Elena or me personally."

Sable remained silent, watching the exchange. Everything was in place. The mission would launch, but it would not end the way Garbuz expected.

Chapter 44

Countdown to Launch

The hours leading up to the launch were some of the most tense the IISF had ever experienced. The towering spacecraft sat on the launchpad, gleaming under the harsh lights as the final pre-launch checks were completed. For months, the deep space mission had been seen as the pinnacle of humanity's ambition, but now it felt more like a last, desperate gamble.

In the command center, Georgiy Garbuz stood at the main console, his eyes locked on the live feed of the spacecraft. The crew had boarded and were running through their final procedures. The control room was filled with the hum of voices and the steady tapping of keyboards as the IISF team worked under immense pressure.

Next to him, Elena Markov monitored the communication lines with the launch team. She glanced at Garbuz, her expression filled with concern, though she kept her voice steady. "All systems are operational. Final checks are coming through, but we're still green across the board."

Garbuz nodded, though his jaw was tight with tension. They had done everything they could to ensure the mission's success, but he couldn't shake the nagging doubt in his mind. They still hadn't identified the saboteur, and there was always the possibility that something had slipped through.

"We can't afford any mistakes," Garbuz said quietly. "This launch has to go perfectly. If anything happens out there…"

Elena didn't need him to finish the thought. The pressure was overwhelming, and the consequences of failure were unthinkable. Not only was this mission critical for the IISF, but the entire world was watching. If the mission failed—if even a single thing went wrong—Orlov and the BRICS alliance would claim victory, and the IISF would be finished.

"Stay focused," Elena said, placing a hand on Garbuz's arm. "We've done everything we can. We just need to trust the team."

Garbuz exhaled slowly, nodding. He had to trust his people. This mission was bigger than any one individual. The crew was already in position, and the launch sequence would begin soon. There was no turning back now.

Down on the ground, at the launch site, the crew inside the spacecraft were strapped into their seats, performing their final system checks. Commander Daniel Matthews, the mission's lead astronaut, ran through his checklist with precision. Next to him, Dr. Emily Hoss, the lead scientist for the mission, monitored the spacecraft's systems with calm professionalism.

"Navigation online. Guidance systems confirmed," Commander Matthews said, his voice clear over the comms. "All readings are nominal."

"Copy that, Commander," came the voice from mission control. "You are go for final countdown."

Dr. Hoss glanced at Matthews. "Looks like we're all set," she said, her voice steady despite the tension in the air. "After everything we've been through, we're finally about to make history."

Matthews gave her a small smile. "One step closer to the stars."

Back in the command center, Dr. Andrei Volkov stood near one of the secondary consoles, his face lined with stress. He had overseen the final security checks personally, but the tension in his gut hadn't eased. Something still felt off. He knew the sabotage threat was real, and despite all their precautions, there was always the possibility that they had missed something.

As the minutes ticked down, Volkov moved to the console to review the data streams one more time. His fingers flew over the controls as he checked the spacecraft's navigation systems. Everything looked normal, but then, a small anomaly appeared on his screen—a flicker in the data stream.

Volkov's heart skipped a beat. It was the same kind of anomaly he had noticed earlier, the one they had thought was fixed. His mind raced. Could the saboteur have planted something deeper into the system?

"Elena!" Volkov called out, his voice sharp. "I've found something. There's an anomaly in the navigation data. I think it's sabotage."

Elena rushed over to his console, her eyes scanning the screen. "What are you talking about? We fixed this."

Volkov shook his head, his face pale. "It's still there. It's subtle, but I can see it. This isn't an error—someone planted this. If we don't act fast, it could trigger during launch."

Elena's blood ran cold. The launch was moments away. If Volkov was right, they were about to send the spacecraft into deep space with a sabotaged navigation system.

"We need to stop the launch," Volkov said urgently, his voice filled with dread. "If that anomaly activates mid-flight, the crew won't be able to correct their course. It could send them off-target—or worse."

Garbuz overheard the conversation and hurried over. "What's going on?"

"Elena and I found something in the navigation system," Volkov explained quickly. "I think it's sabotage. We need to stop the launch now."

Garbuz's mind raced. If they aborted the launch now, it would be a global humiliation for the IISF. But if Volkov was right, sending the crew into space with a compromised navigation system could be catastrophic.

The room fell into a tense silence as Garbuz weighed the decision. The countdown clock showed less than five minutes to launch. His heart pounded in his chest as he glanced at the live feed of the spacecraft. The crew was ready. The world was watching.

"Elena, how certain are you?" Garbuz asked, his voice tight.

Elena hesitated, then shook her head. "I trust Volkov's instincts, but we haven't confirmed anything. We're running out of time."

Volkov's eyes were wide with urgency. "Georgiy, if we don't stop the launch, we could lose the crew. It's not worth the risk."

The decision hung heavily in the air. Garbuz knew that an aborted launch would be a public relations disaster, handing Orlov and the BRICS alliance a victory. But he also knew that launching the mission without confirming the sabotage could lead to something far worse—losing the crew and the mission itself.

"Cut the feed," Garbuz said suddenly, his voice firm.

Elena and Volkov looked at him in shock. "What?" Elena asked, confused.

"Cut the live feed to the public," Garbuz ordered, his eyes hard. "We're going to run one last check before we make the final call. If we abort the launch, we'll do it quietly. No need for the world to see us panic."

Elena nodded, quickly relaying the order to the communications team. The live feed to the media was cut, leaving the IISF with a few precious minutes to investigate further.

Volkov continued running diagnostics, scanning the navigation system for any sign of foul play. His hands trembled as the countdown continued. "There's something here," he muttered to himself. "I can feel it."

But the clock was ticking down. Garbuz knew that every second counted, and they couldn't delay much longer.

"Commander Matthews, stand by," Garbuz said into the comms, his voice steady. "We're running one final check."

As the minutes ticked away, a flicker of movement caught Elena's eye from across the room. Sable stood by one of the consoles, seemingly observing the proceedings. But something in their posture seemed off—too relaxed, too calm.

Elena's eyes narrowed. In the chaos of the last few weeks, they hadn't had time to properly investigate the potential sabotage, but Sable had been in the periphery of every major event. Could they have been the one to plant the sabotage?

Suddenly, Sable turned and made their way toward a side exit. Elena's instincts kicked in. She quickly motioned to one of the security officers and whispered, "Follow them."

The officer nodded, moving quietly toward the exit as Sable disappeared into the corridor. Elena's heart raced. Could they have finally found the saboteur?

Chapter 45

A Race Against Time

The seconds ticked by, each one dragging the IISF closer to an irreversible decision. In the command center, Georgiy Garbuz stood motionless, eyes locked on the countdown clock as it edged closer to launch. The weight of the moment bore down on him—the launch was mere minutes away, but the threat of sabotage loomed over everything.

"Elena, any word?" Garbuz asked, his voice tight with urgency.

Elena Markov stood beside him, her eyes darting between the data streams and the communication lines. Dr. Andrei Volkov was still running the final checks on the navigation system, but time was running out. Every second felt like an eternity.

"Volkov is still investigating," Elena replied, her brow furrowed with tension. "He hasn't confirmed anything yet, but he's sure there's something there. We need more time."

Garbuz's fists clenched at his sides. More time. It was the one thing they didn't have. The world was waiting for this launch—a symbol of hope and progress, and the IISF's chance to prove they still led the race to deep space. But sending the crew out with a sabotaged navigation system could end in catastrophe.

Behind them, the countdown clock continued its relentless march toward zero.

Meanwhile, in the dimly lit corridors of IISF headquarters, Sable moved swiftly, slipping through side passages away from the command center. They knew the clock was ticking—not just for the launch, but for them. It wouldn't be long before someone noticed their absence, and by then, they needed to be far away.

The security officer Elena had dispatched followed quietly, keeping their distance but never letting Sable out of sight. The air was tense, and the officer could feel the adrenaline coursing through them. If Elena's suspicions were correct, Sable wasn't just an observer—they were the saboteur.

Sable turned a corner, disappearing into a service hallway that led toward the lower levels of the facility. The officer quickened their pace, moving quietly, their hand resting on the holster at their hip.

As Sable reached the end of the corridor, they paused, glancing over their shoulder. For a brief moment, their eyes met the officer's, and the realization hit them—they'd been made.

Without warning, Sable broke into a sprint, darting toward the far exit. The officer swore under their breath and gave chase, their footsteps echoing down the narrow hallway.

"Command, this is security," the officer called into their comms as they ran. "I'm in pursuit of Sable. Suspected saboteur, heading toward the lower levels. Need backup!"

Back in the command center, the atmosphere was thick with tension. Volkov was typing furiously, his eyes scanning lines of code as he combed through the spacecraft's navigation system. The anomaly was still there, lurking beneath the surface, but identifying its exact cause was proving difficult.

"We're running out of time," Elena muttered, her voice tight with frustration. She glanced at the countdown clock—less than two minutes to launch. "Volkov, we need an answer. Now."

"I'm working on it," Volkov replied through gritted teeth, his fingers flying over the keys. "There's definitely something here, but it's buried deep in the system. Whoever did this knew exactly how to hide it."

Garbuz's eyes flicked to the live feed of the spacecraft. Inside, the crew was strapped in, unaware of the turmoil unfolding on the ground. Commander Daniel Matthews and Dr. Emily Hoss were running their final system checks, calm and professional as ever. But Garbuz knew that any hesitation now could mean disaster.

"Elena," Garbuz said, his voice firm. "Prepare the abort sequence. If we don't have a clear answer in the next sixty seconds, we're pulling the plug."

Elena's heart raced. "Understood," she said, though the weight of the decision hung heavy in the air.

At the console, Volkov's face suddenly lit up with recognition. "I've found it!" he exclaimed, his voice filled with both relief and dread. "It's a hidden command buried in the navigation software—it's set to trigger a course correction mid-flight. If we hadn't caught it, the spacecraft would have been thrown off course, sending the crew into deep space without a way to recover."

Elena's eyes widened. "Can you remove it?"

Volkov's fingers flew over the keys. "I'm already on it. But it's not a simple fix. I need time to fully disable it."

Garbuz's heart pounded as the countdown clock hit one minute. They were out of time. He had to make the call now.

"Elena, prepare to abort—"

Before he could finish the sentence, the command center doors burst open. The security officer rushed in, breathing heavily. "We've got Sable," they said between gasps. "They're the saboteur. They were trying to leave the building."

Garbuz's eyes narrowed, his mind racing. Sable. The quiet, unassuming agent who had been right under their noses all this time. Orlov's influence had run deeper than he'd imagined.

"Sable's been taken into custody?" Elena asked, her voice sharp.

The officer nodded. "Yes, but there's no telling how much damage they've done already."

Garbuz's pulse quickened. Sable was in custody, but the sabotage had already been set in motion. The crew was at risk. With less than a minute left, they needed to act.

"Elena, Volkov, what's our status?" Garbuz asked, his voice commanding but tense.

Volkov looked up from his console. "I've disabled the command, but the system still needs a full reboot to ensure it's clean. I can do it remotely, but we need a few more minutes."

Garbuz swore under his breath. They didn't have a few more minutes. The clock was down to thirty seconds.

"Elena, abort the launch," Garbuz ordered, his decision made. "We can't take the risk."

Elena's fingers hovered over the abort controls, but before she could act, the comms crackled to life.

"Commander Matthews to ground control," came the voice of the mission commander. "We're seeing some unusual readings up here. Navigation system just flagged an error. Can you confirm?"

Garbuz hesitated, his mind racing. Volkov had disabled the sabotage, but the navigation system was still unstable. If they launched now, they could fix it in-flight—or they could face disaster.

"We're confirming now, Commander," Garbuz replied, his voice steady despite the chaos.

Volkov's eyes were locked on the screen. "The system's clear," he said finally, his voice barely above a whisper. "We're green."

Garbuz's heart raced as the countdown hit ten seconds.

"Launch is a go," he said firmly, locking eyes with Elena.

The command center erupted into activity as the final seconds of the countdown ticked away. On the screens, the spacecraft's engines roared to life, the ground shaking as the massive vehicle prepared to leave the Earth behind.

"Five… four… three… two… one… liftoff!"

The spacecraft soared into the sky, a brilliant trail of fire and smoke streaming from its engines. The command center watched in silence as the vessel climbed higher, breaking through the atmosphere and into the vastness of space.

Garbuz stood frozen, his eyes glued to the screen. He could barely breathe as the spacecraft disappeared from view, the roar of the engines fading into nothingness.

"We have liftoff," Elena said softly, her voice trembling with relief. "The mission is underway."

For a moment, there was only silence in the command center. Then the room erupted into applause, the tension of the last few hours releasing in a wave of exhilaration.

But Garbuz didn't celebrate. His mind was still reeling from the discovery of Sable's sabotage. They had stopped it in time, but the threat had been far too close for comfort. Orlov's reach had nearly derailed their greatest mission.

As the crew settled into orbit, Garbuz knew one thing for certain: this mission was only the beginning. The dangers of space were still ahead, and Orlov wasn't done yet.

Chapter 46
The Journey Begins

The vast, endless expanse of space stretched out before the IISF spacecraft, its silver hull reflecting the distant light of stars as it drifted deeper into the unknown. Inside, the crew of humanity's first manned mission into deep space was adjusting to the reality of their journey. The initial exhilaration of liftoff had faded, replaced by the quiet hum of the spacecraft's systems and the weight of their monumental task.

Commander Daniel Matthews floated in the cockpit, his hands deftly navigating the controls as he ran through the post-launch systems check. He glanced at the large display screen, which showed the spacecraft's current trajectory—a perfect arc through the solar system, destined for the far reaches of deep space.

"All systems green," Matthews said, his voice calm as he relayed the report to Mission Control. "Propulsion stable. Guidance online. Life support systems at full capacity."

In the seat beside him, Dr. Emily Hoss, the mission's lead scientist, was monitoring the spacecraft's environmental systems. Her fingers hovered over her tablet, reviewing the air quality, water filtration, and power consumption. Everything appeared nominal, but she felt a lingering unease. The sabotage threat hadn't left her mind, and despite the repairs made before launch, she knew they couldn't relax just yet.

"Roger that, Commander," came the reply from Mission Control. Elena Markov's voice was calm, but Matthews could sense the tension behind her words. "You're on course. Proceed with the next phase of the mission plan."

Matthews turned to Hoss. "How are we looking?"

She nodded, though her eyes remained fixed on the screen. "Everything's stable for now. But I'm keeping a close eye on the life support systems. I don't like what we've been seeing in the data."

Matthews frowned. "The anomalies Volkov found?"

Hoss glanced at him, her expression serious. "Yeah. We patched the system before launch, but I've noticed a few minor irregularities in the oxygen levels. It's nothing critical yet, but it's enough to make me uneasy."

Matthews leaned back, staring at the display. They were only hours into the mission, and already there were signs that things weren't as smooth as they seemed. "Keep monitoring it. I don't want any surprises."

In the narrow confines of the living quarters, Lt. Jason Park, the mission's engineer, floated near the communication console. He was reviewing the signals coming from Earth—routine check-ins with IISF Mission Control, telemetry data, and status updates from their support teams. But something strange caught his eye.

A faint signal was embedded in the background noise of their communication channels—too weak to be normal, too erratic to be natural. Park frowned and adjusted the controls, isolating the signal to get a better reading.

"Commander," Park called over the comms. "I'm picking up something strange in our communications array. It's not strong, but there's a signal buried in the noise."

Matthews floated over to the console, his brow furrowed as he examined the data. The signal was faint, barely a blip on the system, but it was there. "Any idea what it is?"

Park shook his head. "Could be interference, but it's too regular for that. I'm running diagnostics now, but this might be related to the sabotage Volkov warned us about."

Matthews' jaw tightened. The word *sabotage* hadn't been spoken aloud since launch, but it had never left any of their minds. They had made it into space, but the danger wasn't over.

"Keep monitoring it," Matthews said, his voice low. "If it starts to affect our comms, we'll have to take a closer look. And don't mention this to the others yet. No need to raise alarms until we know what we're dealing with."

Park nodded, but the unease in his eyes mirrored what Matthews was feeling. The deep space mission was off to a historic start, but something wasn't right.

Back in the cockpit, Hoss continued monitoring the life support systems. The irregularities in the oxygen levels persisted, but no alarms had gone off yet. Still, something gnawed at her.

Hoss brought up the environmental control logs, tracing the data backward. Everything had been normal during pre-flight checks, but after launch, the irregularities had started—small fluctuations in the air mixture, nothing dangerous but enough to raise questions.

"Commander, I've got something," Hoss said, her voice more tense than she intended. "The oxygen levels are fluctuating, and I think it's linked to the sabotage."

Matthews' face darkened. "How bad is it?"

"It's not critical yet, but if this trend continues, we could start seeing degradation in the life support systems over time. We might have a few days before it becomes a problem, but it's hard to say for sure."

Matthews nodded, considering their options. "Let's keep it under observation for now. I don't want to jump to conclusions, but we can't ignore this either."

Hoss agreed, but the anxiety in her chest wouldn't go away. "If it gets worse, we'll have to take more drastic measures."

Matthews was about to respond when the comms crackled to life.

"Commander Matthews, this is Mission Control," came Elena's voice. "We've detected an anomaly in the data stream coming from your navigation system. Is everything alright on your end?"

Matthews exchanged a glance with Hoss. "We've been seeing some minor irregularities in life support, but nothing we can't handle. Navigation looks stable on our end. Is there something specific we should be looking for?"

There was a brief pause before Elena's voice returned. "We're seeing a slight shift in your trajectory. It's subtle, but it could be related to the sabotage we detected pre-launch. We're running a full diagnostic on our end, but you might want to prepare for manual corrections if it persists."

Matthews' pulse quickened. A shift in trajectory? That was no small error—it could change everything about the mission.

"Understood, Mission Control," Matthews replied, his voice steely. "We'll prepare for manual control if needed."

As the comms went silent, Matthews turned to Hoss, who was already pulling up the navigation data. The numbers were small, but the deviation was real. It wasn't enough to raise alarms yet, but it was growing.

"This isn't good," Hoss muttered, her eyes scanning the data. "If this continues, we'll be way off course before we even reach the mission's halfway point."

Matthews took a deep breath, his mind racing. "Let's prep for a correction. We can't afford to lose our trajectory now."

In the command center back on Earth, Garbuz paced anxiously as Elena monitored the data coming from the spacecraft. The news of the trajectory shift had hit hard—if the spacecraft veered too far off course, the entire mission would be jeopardized. And that wasn't even considering the life support irregularities or the suspicious signal Park had detected.

"Any word from the crew?" Garbuz asked, his voice low but tense.

"They're aware of the trajectory issue," Elena replied, her fingers moving quickly over the console. "Matthews is preparing to make a manual correction if the deviation continues."

Garbuz nodded, his mind working overtime. The mission had barely begun, and already they were facing multiple issues. The sabotage they had thought was neutralized clearly had deeper consequences than they anticipated. If things continued to spiral, they would have to make a difficult decision—press forward, risking the crew's safety, or turn back and admit defeat.

"We need to stay ahead of this," Garbuz said, his voice hard. "Get Volkov back on the diagnostics. I want to know if this is something we missed or if it's part of Orlov's sabotage plan."

Elena glanced at Garbuz, her eyes betraying her concern. "And if it is?"

Garbuz didn't answer right away. His gaze was fixed on the live feed of the spacecraft drifting through the black void of space, so far from Earth that it almost seemed surreal.

"If it is," Garbuz said finally, his voice grim, "we deal with it. We didn't come this far just to turn back."

Chapter 47

Into the Unnkown

The spacecraft floated silently through the endless void, a lone beacon of human ambition as it ventured farther from Earth than any mission before. But inside, the crew of the IISF was growing increasingly uneasy. The anomalies in the systems had started small, but now they were becoming harder to ignore.

In the cockpit, Commander Daniel Matthews watched as the slight trajectory shift that had been detected earlier continued to worsen. Despite multiple checks, the navigation system was still reporting erratic data, making it difficult to maintain their course.

"Mission Control, this is Commander Matthews," he said, his voice steady but tense. "We're seeing a persistent deviation in the navigation data. I'm preparing to initiate manual control to correct the trajectory."

The response from Earth came quickly. Elena Markov's voice was calm, though Matthews could hear the underlying concern. "Roger that, Commander. We're seeing the same data here. Proceed with manual correction. We'll monitor from our end."

Matthews exhaled slowly, knowing what was at stake. Their mission depended on hitting precise coordinates, and if the trajectory continued to drift, they would miss their window to reach the deeper regions of space. He glanced at Dr. Emily Hoss, who was monitoring the ship's other systems. She had been keeping a close eye on the life support, where the irregularities were becoming harder to dismiss.

"Emily, anything new on life support?" Matthews asked, his fingers hovering over the manual control inputs.

Hoss shook her head, her expression grim. "The oxygen levels are still fluctuating, but it's within safe limits for now. I don't think we're in immediate danger, but it's not stable. We'll have to keep monitoring it."

Matthews nodded. "Alright, let's focus on the course correction for now. If we lose our trajectory, none of this will matter."

The crew gathered in the cockpit, each member focused on their respective roles as Matthews prepared to take manual control of the navigation system. Lt. Jason Park, the mission's engineer, was already troubleshooting the signal interference he had detected earlier, but he hadn't found the source yet.

"We're ready, Commander," Park said, his hands moving quickly over the controls. "The system is set for manual input. You should have full control now."

Matthews' grip tightened on the control stick as he took a deep breath. The weight of responsibility hung heavily on his shoulders. The trajectory deviation was small, but if left unchecked, it would spiral out of control, sending them hopelessly off course.

"Let's do this," he muttered, his fingers moving steadily to initiate the manual course correction.

The spacecraft responded to his touch, a slight shift in its orientation as the thrusters fired to adjust their path. For a moment, the display screen showed a slight improvement, the deviation beginning to correct itself. But then, without warning, the navigation system blinked red—an error message flashed across the screen, and the ship's course shifted again, even more erratically than before.

"What the—?" Matthews gripped the control stick tighter, trying to wrestle the system back under control. "The system's fighting me!"

Park rushed to his console, furiously typing commands. "I'm seeing the same thing. The navigation software is overriding the manual input. I'm trying to isolate the problem, but this isn't normal."

Hoss' eyes widened as she stared at the fluctuating data on her screen. "This has to be part of the sabotage. There's no other explanation."

Matthews gritted his teeth. "Can we cut the system entirely and operate manually without the software?"

Park hesitated. "We can, but it's risky. Without the software, we'll be relying entirely on manual inputs, which could leave us vulnerable to any other hidden issues in the system. If there's more sabotage we haven't caught, things could get a lot worse."

"We don't have much choice," Matthews said, his voice firm. "If we don't fix this trajectory now, we're not going to make it to our target."

As the crew fought to regain control of the spacecraft, back on Earth, the tension inside IISF Mission Control was palpable. Garbuz stood behind Elena, watching the live data stream from the spacecraft with mounting anxiety. The deviation in the trajectory had worsened, and now the navigation system was showing signs of catastrophic failure.

"Elena, what's happening?" Garbuz asked, his voice low but urgent. "Why is the system fighting the manual input?"

Elena's fingers moved quickly over the console as she tried to diagnose the problem. "It's not just a simple glitch. The sabotage we detected earlier may have been deeper than we thought. I think there's another hidden command in the system that's preventing the crew from taking full control."

Garbuz cursed under his breath. Sable's sabotage had clearly been more sophisticated than they had realized. If they couldn't regain control of the spacecraft's trajectory, the entire mission would be in jeopardy.

"Can we override it from here?" Garbuz asked, desperation creeping into his voice.

Elena shook her head. "Not remotely. The crew will have to disable the system manually. But doing that while maintaining their course is going to be a challenge."

The room was silent for a moment as Garbuz considered the options. They were out of time. Either the crew regained control, or the mission would fail.

"Elena, get me Matthews," Garbuz said, stepping closer to the console.

Moments later, Matthews' voice crackled through the comms. "This is Matthews. We're trying to regain control of the navigation, but it's not responding. I'm ready to cut the system entirely and go manual."

Garbuz exhaled slowly, knowing the risk but seeing no other option. "Do it, Commander. Cut the system and take manual control. We're with you."

Inside the spacecraft, Matthews braced himself. "Alright, team," he said, his voice steady. "We're cutting the navigation system. This is going to get bumpy."

With a nod from Hoss and Park, Matthews initiated the manual override, effectively cutting the ship's navigation software from the control loop. The ship lurched slightly as the autopilot disengaged, leaving the crew entirely dependent on manual controls.

For a brief moment, everything went silent. The hum of the ship's systems continued, but the navigation display went blank. Matthews held his breath, hoping the maneuver had worked.

"Is it stable?" Hoss asked, her hands gripping the console tightly.

Matthews checked the controls. The ship's thrusters had stopped firing erratically, and the trajectory had begun to stabilize. "It looks like it," he said, relief flooding his voice. "We've regained manual control."

Park, still monitoring the system diagnostics, looked more skeptical. "We're stable for now, but I'm worried about what else we haven't seen yet. If there's another layer of sabotage, it could hit us when we least expect it."

Matthews nodded grimly. "We'll deal with that when it comes. For now, we need to stay on course."

As the crew began to settle back into their routine, the lingering sense of unease remained. They had survived the initial sabotage, but the knowledge that something else could be lurking in the ship's systems weighed heavily on all of them.

"Mission Control, this is Commander Matthews," he said into the comms. "We've regained control of the navigation, but we're keeping a close watch on the other systems. We don't know what else might be compromised."

Elena's voice came back almost immediately. "Understood, Commander. We're monitoring everything from here. Stay vigilant."

Matthews floated back from the console, allowing himself a moment to relax. The first crisis had been averted, but deep down, he knew the journey ahead was only going to get more challenging.

Back in IISF headquarters, Garbuz leaned against the console, the weight of the situation pressing down on him. They had avoided disaster for now, but the mission was far from secure. The crew was on their own in the vast emptiness of space, with a sabotaged spacecraft and unknown threats still looming.

"Elena," Garbuz said quietly, his eyes still fixed on the live feed. "We need to stay ahead of this. Whatever else Sable planted in that ship, we need to find it before it finds them."

Elena nodded, though she looked just as tense. "We'll keep digging. But we're in uncharted territory, both literally and figuratively. If there's more sabotage, we're racing against the clock to find it."

As the mission pressed deeper into space, Garbuz knew one thing for certain: they were all walking a razor's edge. And the deeper the mission went, the higher the stakes became.

Chapter 48

The Unseen Threat

As the spacecraft stabilized, the crew exhaled, but the relief was short-lived. The manual control had restored order for the moment, but every member of the team felt the shadow of further sabotage looming over them. The reality of deep space—silent, cold, and hostile—only magnified their isolation, and the knowledge that they were navigating in a compromised vessel weighed heavily.

Commander Daniel Matthews floated in the cockpit, his eyes fixed on the starry expanse outside the window. He felt the pressure of the mission more keenly than ever. Deep space wasn't forgiving, and now they knew that Orlov's influence had followed them even into the black unknown.

"Navigation's holding," Lt. Jason Park said from the engineering station. His voice was calm, but Matthews could hear the fatigue creeping in. "But we need to watch the systems like hawks. If there's another hidden command, we might not have time to react."

Matthews gave a slow nod. "Keep monitoring. I don't want any more surprises."

Nearby, Dr. Emily Hoss finished running diagnostics on the environmental systems. She had been keeping a close eye on the oxygen levels ever since the irregularities first appeared, and while the readings were stable for now, she couldn't shake the feeling that something was off.

"Oxygen levels are fluctuating again," Hoss reported, her tone cautious. "Not enough to set off alarms, but it's the same pattern as before. The life support system is holding, but it's... erratic."

Matthews moved over to her console, his eyes scanning the data. "Could this be another part of the sabotage?"

Hoss shrugged, her face tight with concern. "It's hard to say. If it is, it's been designed to be subtle, just enough to slowly destabilize the system over time. We won't notice until it's too late."

Matthews cursed softly under his breath. "We can't afford to lose life support. We need to dig deeper into this. I want you to run a full analysis. If there's any sign of tampering, we need to fix it now."

Hoss nodded and got to work, though she knew it wouldn't be easy. The sabotage had been designed to evade detection, and every minute they spent in space increased the chances that something else could go wrong.

As Hoss began her analysis, Park turned his attention back to the communications console. The strange signal he had detected earlier still lingered in the background, faint but persistent. It was almost as if something—or someone—was watching them.

"Commander, that signal I mentioned before—it's still there," Park said, his voice uneasy. "It's not affecting our communications directly, but it's embedded in the noise. It's regular, like a pulse."

Matthews' brow furrowed as he joined Park at the console. "Can you isolate it? I want to know if this is something external, or if it's coming from inside the ship."

Park nodded, his hands moving quickly over the controls as he worked to pinpoint the source. The signal was weak, barely registering on the instruments, but it was definitely there. After a few minutes, Park leaned back in his seat, his face grim.

"It's coming from inside the ship."

Matthews felt a chill crawl down his spine. "Inside?"

"Yeah," Park confirmed. "It's originating from one of the auxiliary systems—could be communications or telemetry. I think this might be another layer of the sabotage. Whoever planted it wanted to make sure they could monitor us."

Matthews clenched his fists, the pieces falling into place. Sable's sabotage hadn't just been about disrupting their systems. It had been a way for Orlov to keep an eye on them, to track their progress and, if needed, intervene.

"Can we shut it down?" Matthews asked, his voice tight.

Park hesitated. "I can isolate it, but I'm worried about what happens if we cut the signal. If it's connected to something else in the system, shutting it down could trigger another malfunction—or worse."

Matthews' mind raced. They were already walking a fine line with the navigation system and life support. If cutting the signal triggered another failure, it could be catastrophic. But leaving it active meant Orlov could continue to monitor their every move.

"We can't let them watch us," Matthews said, his voice low but firm. "Do what you need to do to isolate the signal. Just be careful—we don't need another system going down."

Park nodded, though the tension in the air was palpable. He began working to isolate the signal, but the uncertainty of what it might trigger weighed heavily on him.

As the hours passed, the crew remained on high alert. The strain of the mission—and the growing awareness of the sabotage—began to take its toll. Inside the cramped quarters of the spacecraft, every small sound, every flicker of the systems, set their nerves on edge.

In the common area, Dr. Hoss floated near the window, her arms crossed as she stared out into the blackness. Lt. Jason Park joined her, his expression weary after hours of working to isolate the mysterious signal.

"You think we'll make it?" Park asked quietly, his voice breaking the silence.

Hoss turned to him, her face thoughtful. "I think... we'll have to. There's no turning back now."

Park gave a tired smile, though it didn't reach his eyes. "I'm just worried about what we haven't found yet. There could be more sabotage buried in the system, just waiting to activate. And out here... we're on our own."

Hoss nodded. "I know. But we're trained for this. We'll find a way."

But even as she said the words, she couldn't shake the doubt creeping into her mind. The sabotage had already caused so many problems—if there was more lurking in the system, how long could they hold out before something went wrong?

As the crew continued to investigate the ship's systems, back on Earth, the IISF command center was buzzing with activity. Garbuz stood with Elena Markov, watching the live data stream coming from the spacecraft. The navigation issue had been resolved for the moment, but the mysterious signal detected by Park was causing concern.

"Elena, what's the status on the signal?" Garbuz asked, his voice tight with tension.

Elena shook her head, her eyes scanning the data. "It's coming from inside the ship, but we can't pinpoint exactly where. Park is working to isolate it, but there's a risk that cutting it could trigger something else. It's a delicate situation."

Garbuz rubbed his temples, the stress of the mission weighing heavily on him. Every decision felt like a gamble. The sabotage had already pushed the crew to the edge, and now they had to deal with the possibility that Orlov was still watching them from afar.

"We can't let Orlov control this mission," Garbuz said, his voice resolute. "Tell Matthews to isolate the signal, but they need to be ready for anything. If this is a trap, we need to be prepared."

Elena nodded, relaying the orders to the crew. As the minutes passed, Garbuz felt the weight of his decision pressing down on him. If the signal was part of a larger plan to sabotage the mission, cutting it could be the only way to save the crew. But if it triggered something worse, it could spell disaster.

Back on the spacecraft, Park floated over to the communications console, his fingers moving quickly as he prepared to isolate the signal. He could feel the eyes of the crew on him, each of them tense as they waited to see what would happen next.

"Alright," Park said, his voice steady despite the tension in his chest. "I'm going to isolate the signal now. If anything goes wrong, we'll have to act fast."

Matthews nodded from his seat at the navigation console. "Do it."

Park's hands moved over the controls, and with a final press of a button, he cut the signal.

For a moment, there was silence. The hum of the spacecraft's systems continued as normal, and nothing seemed to change. The crew exchanged cautious glances, wondering if they had finally neutralized the threat.

But then, without warning, the ship lurched violently. Alarms blared, red lights flashing across the control panels as the life support system began to fail.

"What the hell—?" Hoss cried out, her eyes wide as she looked at the environmental controls. "We're losing oxygen!"

Park frantically tried to reverse the isolation, but the system was locked. "It's a failsafe! Cutting the signal triggered it!"

Matthews gripped the controls, his heart pounding. "We need to get that system back online—now!"

Chapter 49
Life Support Crisis

The shrill alarm echoed through the cramped corridors of the spacecraft as the red lights flashed in warning. The life support system was failing, and the crew of the IISF's first deep space mission was staring down the unthinkable—a loss of oxygen.

Commander Daniel Matthews acted instinctively, immediately strapping himself into his seat as he relayed commands. "Everyone, secure yourselves! Hoss, what's the status on life support?"

Dr. Emily Hoss, her fingers moving rapidly over the environmental control panel, tried to keep her voice steady despite the panic rising in her chest. "We're losing oxygen at an accelerated rate—air filtration is down! CO2 levels are rising. We've got minutes before it starts impacting the crew."

Matthews swore under his breath, the weight of the situation pressing down on him. "Park, can we reverse what we just did?"

Lt. Jason Park, the mission's engineer, was already trying, his hands flying over the console as he attempted to restore the system. "I'm locked out," he said, his voice tight with frustration. "The isolation triggered some kind of failsafe. The life support system is responding like we're under attack—like it's shutting down to contain damage."

Hoss glanced at the readouts, her face grim. "If we don't get air circulation back online, the carbon dioxide will reach dangerous levels in less than ten minutes."

"Ten minutes?" Matthews echoed, his eyes wide. They had less than ten minutes to fix this, or they would start losing consciousness.

Matthews hit the comms button to Mission Control. "Mission Control, this is Commander Matthews. We've got a critical failure in life support—oxygen is dropping fast. We're trying to reverse it, but the system's locked us out. We need help, fast!"

Back in the IISF command center, the atmosphere shifted from tense to chaotic. The sound of the alarms from the spacecraft blared over the speakers, sending a ripple of fear through the room. Elena Markov's eyes widened as she watched the live feed from the crew—Park was furiously working on the consoles, and Hoss was desperately monitoring the oxygen levels.

Garbuz leaned over Elena's console. "What just happened? How did cutting the signal trigger this?"

Elena's fingers flew over the keyboard as she reviewed the data. "It looks like the failsafe was embedded deep in the life support system. Sable must have rigged it to activate if the signal was cut. This was a contingency—designed to make sure the crew couldn't survive if they disabled the monitoring systems."

Garbuz's expression darkened. Sable's sabotage had been far more intricate than they'd imagined. "Can we override it from here?"

Elena shook her head, her face pale. "We don't have direct control over life support—it's localized on the ship. The crew has to fix this themselves."

Garbuz clenched his fists. "Tell Matthews to use the emergency oxygen supply if they can't fix it in time. We need to buy them some time to get the system back online."

Elena relayed the message, her voice calm but urgent. "Commander Matthews, initiate emergency oxygen protocols. You need to buy yourselves time to get the system back online."

Inside the spacecraft, Matthews didn't hesitate. "Hoss, engage emergency oxygen supplies. We need to slow the drop while we figure this out."

Hoss quickly initiated the emergency procedure, and moments later, there was a faint hiss as the ship's backup oxygen tanks began pumping air into the cabin. It wasn't a permanent solution, but it would slow the depletion long enough for them to find a fix.

"We've bought ourselves a few more minutes," Hoss said, her voice tight with tension. "But the emergency oxygen won't last long. We need to fix the primary system."

Park's eyes were glued to the screen in front of him, desperately trying to unlock the life support controls. "I'm in the failsafe code now, but it's encrypted. Whoever set this up knew what they were doing. This is more than just a simple lockdown."

"Can you bypass it?" Matthews asked, his voice low but urgent.

Park's jaw clenched. "I'm trying, but it's going to take time. I don't know if I can crack it before we run out of air."

The cabin felt claustrophobic, the hiss of the emergency oxygen reminding them that time was running out. Hoss continued monitoring the air quality, but the CO2 levels were still rising.

Matthews looked around at his crew—Hoss, Park, and the other members of the team were all working furiously, but he could see the fear in their eyes. He knew that if they didn't fix this soon, it would be the end of the mission—and their lives.

"Do what you can, Park," Matthews said. "We're not going down without a fight."

Back on Earth, Garbuz was pacing, his mind racing. Elena was working with her team to analyze the sabotage, trying to find any weakness that could help the crew regain control of their life support systems.

"We need to get ahead of this," Garbuz muttered. "Sable's sabotage was meant to kill them if they disabled the monitoring. There has to be a way to disable the failsafe without triggering another lockdown."

Elena's fingers paused on the console as she studied the encryption. "There is one thing. It's risky, but… we could try to force a full system reboot. It would reset the failsafe and potentially bring the life support system back online."

Garbuz's eyes narrowed. "What's the risk?"

"If the reboot fails, the entire system could stay offline permanently," Elena replied, her voice grave. "It's a last-ditch effort. But with the failsafe engaged, the crew's manual overrides won't work. This might be their only chance."

Garbuz didn't hesitate. "Tell them."

Elena relayed the message to the spacecraft, her voice calm but filled with urgency. "Commander Matthews, we've got a plan, but it's risky. You can attempt a full system reboot—it should reset the failsafe and bring life support back online. But if the reboot fails, the entire system could stay down."

Matthews looked at Hoss and Park, both of whom wore expressions of grim determination. They all knew the risks, but time was running out, and they didn't have any other options.

"We're doing it," Matthews said, his voice hard. "Park, prepare for a full reboot."

Park moved swiftly, entering the commands to initiate a full system reboot. The ship's lights dimmed, and the hum of the environmental systems slowed as the ship prepared to shut down.

"Here we go," Park said, his voice tense. "Initiating reboot in three… two… one."

The spacecraft went completely silent.

The crew floated in the dark, the only sound the faint hiss of the emergency oxygen as they waited. Every second felt like an eternity, the weight of the decision hanging over them. If the reboot failed, the system would remain offline, and the emergency oxygen would run out soon.

Matthews glanced at Hoss, who was watching the life support monitors with a grim expression. The CO2 levels continued to rise, though more slowly, and they were running out of time.

"Come on," Park muttered under his breath as he waited for the system to come back online. "Come on…"

The hum of the environmental system returning to life was like a lifeline.

Lights flickered back on, and the control panels illuminated as the life support system rebooted. Hoss immediately checked the oxygen levels.

"It's back online," she said, her voice filled with relief. "Life support is operational. CO2 levels are stabilizing."

A collective sigh of relief filled the cabin as the crew realized they had narrowly avoided disaster. Park floated back from the console, his face pale but relieved. "We're back in business."

Matthews exhaled, a weight lifting from his chest. "Good work, everyone. Let's make sure we stay ahead of this from now on."

With the immediate crisis averted, the crew allowed themselves a brief moment to recover. Hoss checked the environmental systems again, ensuring everything was stable. The ship was back under their control, but the knowledge that they had nearly lost it hung heavily over them.

Matthews floated over to the cockpit window, staring out into the vast expanse of space. They were still on course, their journey far from over, but they had survived a major threat. Orlov's sabotage had nearly killed them, but they had fought back.

But the victory felt hollow. Matthews knew there could be more sabotage waiting for them, buried deeper in the ship's systems. They had weathered this storm, but the mission was still fraught with danger.

"We're still in this," Matthews said quietly to himself, his gaze fixed on the distant stars. "We're still in the fight."

Chapter 50

Uneasy Calm

The spacecraft hummed softly once again, its systems stabilized after the harrowing life support crisis. The crew floated in the narrow confines of the ship, the relief of survival tempered by the knowledge that the danger wasn't over. The damage from Orlov's sabotage still hung over them like a storm cloud, and every flicker of the control panels, every minor glitch in the systems, set their nerves on edge.

Commander Daniel Matthews rubbed his temples, feeling the strain of the last few hours. They had narrowly avoided disaster, but his mind was already spinning with what might come next. The sabotage had been sophisticated—too sophisticated to think that Sable had acted alone. There was still the possibility of other, hidden dangers lurking in the systems.

"We're stable," Dr. Emily Hoss reported, her voice calm but tinged with exhaustion. She floated beside the environmental controls, running final checks to ensure the life support system was truly back online. "CO2 levels are under control, and oxygen production is steady again."

Matthews nodded, though his mind was already elsewhere. "Good. But we need to keep a close eye on everything. There could be more triggers hidden in the system."

Hoss gave a grim nod in agreement. "I'll run constant diagnostics, but you're right—we can't assume this is over."

Across the cockpit, Lt. Jason Park was finishing up his own checks on the ship's communication and navigation systems. After cutting the strange signal that had triggered the failsafe, he had restored their comms and made sure their navigation was stable again. But like the rest of the crew, he knew there was no guarantee they wouldn't face another crisis.

"We're getting a strong signal from Mission Control," Park said, his eyes scanning the data. "No sign of interference, but I'm going to monitor it closely. After everything we've seen, I don't trust anything right now."

Matthews floated over to join Park at the communication console. "We need to get an update from Earth. Mission Control will want to know the status of the ship, and we need to know if they've uncovered any more intel about Orlov's plans."

Park nodded and opened the comms link. "Mission Control, this is Commander Matthews. Life support crisis has been resolved, but we're still on high alert for any further sabotage. How's it looking on your end?"

At IISF Mission Control, the tension hadn't eased. The life support failure had sent ripples of fear through the command center, and even though the crew had survived, the sense of impending disaster still lingered.

Elena Markov leaned over her console, her fingers still dancing over the controls as she monitored the spacecraft's data. Every sensor reading and system report was scrutinized for signs of further tampering. The crew's survival had been a narrow escape, but they weren't out of danger yet.

Garbuz stood beside her, arms crossed, his expression grim. "We've got to assume Orlov's sabotage goes deeper than what we've seen so far. There could be more hidden traps waiting to trigger."

Elena nodded, though her focus remained on the data. "We're running full diagnostics on every system, but it's difficult to pinpoint what we're looking for. The sabotage has been subtle so far, designed to trigger only under specific conditions. Sable was clever—this was planned well in advance."

Garbuz's jaw tightened at the mention of Sable. The revelation of a sleeper agent within their ranks had shaken him deeply. Even now, with Sable in custody, the consequences of their betrayal were still being felt.

"Have we learned anything from Sable?" Garbuz asked, his voice low but sharp.

Elena paused before answering. "Not yet. Sable's refusing to talk. Whatever Orlov promised, it's enough to keep them silent."

Garbuz swore under his breath. "We need answers. If there's another layer of sabotage on that ship, we're sending those astronauts into a death trap."

As he spoke, the comms crackled to life, and Matthews' voice came through. "Mission Control, this is Commander Matthews. Life support crisis has been resolved, but we're still on high alert for any further sabotage. How's it looking on your end?"

Elena quickly responded. "Commander, we're still digging through the data on our end. No new signs of sabotage yet, but we're running deeper checks on the remaining systems. We'll let you know if we find anything. In the meantime, proceed with extreme caution."

Matthews' reply was steady. "Understood. We're staying vigilant up here. Keep us updated."

The comms went silent again, and Elena turned to Garbuz. "They're back online for now, but the crew's on edge. They know this isn't over."

Garbuz nodded, his mind racing. "It's not just them. Orlov's next move could be even worse. We need to be ready."

Back on the spacecraft, the crew gathered in the common area for a much-needed breather. Despite the quiet hum of the systems, there was an unspoken tension in the air. Every member of the team knew they had just survived a brush with death, and the uncertainty of what lay ahead weighed heavily on them.

Dr. Emily Hoss floated near the window, her eyes fixed on the distant stars. She had been trained for the dangers of space, but the thought of sabotage—from their own ranks, no less—was a new kind of threat.

"You think we'll be able to find the rest of it?" she asked, glancing at Lt. Jason Park.

Park shrugged, his face lined with fatigue. "We've caught two layers of sabotage so far. There's no telling how many more are buried in the system. We just have to keep looking."

Commander Matthews floated nearby, watching his crew with concern. He could see the exhaustion in their faces, the fear in their eyes. They had trained for every conceivable challenge space could throw at them, but no one had prepared them for the enemy within.

"We'll handle it," Matthews said, his voice firm. "Whatever Orlov's thrown at us, we'll find it. We've come too far to turn back now."

Park nodded, though the doubt in his eyes remained. "I just hope we have enough time."

As the crew worked to secure the spacecraft, far from Earth, Dmitry Orlov sat in a private room in the BRICS alliance command center, a slight smile playing on his lips. The news of the life support crisis had reached him hours ago, and while the IISF crew had survived, Orlov wasn't concerned.

"They may have fixed the first layer of sabotage," Orlov said, speaking to one of his top advisors. "But Sable's work was thorough. The deeper layers are still waiting to be uncovered."

His advisor nodded, a grim look on their face. "And the BRICS mission? We're still on schedule?"

Orlov's eyes gleamed. "Of course. The BRICS mission will launch soon, and once it does, the IISF will be left scrambling. They're already fighting for survival. We'll claim the lead in space exploration while they're busy dealing with their own internal collapse."

The advisor hesitated for a moment before speaking. "What if they succeed? What if the IISF crew makes it through?"

Orlov's smile faded, his expression hardening. "Then we'll make sure they don't."

As the spacecraft drifted deeper into the void, Park's eyes flickered to a small blinking icon on his console. He frowned and floated closer, quickly scanning the data.

"Commander," Park called, his voice tight with urgency. "I think I've found something."

Matthews was at his side in an instant. "What is it?"

Park pointed to the data stream on his console. "This—there's a section of the system that's been locked down. I can't access it, but it looks like it's tied to the ship's propulsion systems. If this is another layer of sabotage, it could trigger a failure in our engines."

Matthews' eyes narrowed as he stared at the data. "You're saying we could lose propulsion?"

"If the system is compromised, yeah," Park said grimly. "And out here, without propulsion, we're dead in the water."

Hoss floated over, her face pale. "Can we fix it?"

Park hesitated. "I don't know yet. I can try to bypass the lockout, but if I trigger something else…"

The crew exchanged glances, the gravity of the situation sinking in. They had survived the sabotage of the life support system, but now their very ability to move through space was in jeopardy.

Matthews made the decision. "Do it, Park. We can't risk losing propulsion. Whatever happens, we deal with it."

Park nodded, his hands already moving over the controls. "I'll get us through this."

Chapter 51

Propulsion in Peril

The quiet hum of the spacecraft's systems was once again drowned out by the sense of impending doom. The crew floated silently, the weight of their newest discovery pressing down on them. With the life support system stabilized, they now faced another potential disaster—this time, with their propulsion systems. If they lost their engines in deep space, they wouldn't just be stranded; they'd be doomed.

Commander Daniel Matthews hovered near the console, watching Lt. Jason Park as he carefully worked on bypassing the lockdown that had sealed off part of the propulsion system. Every move felt like a gamble, and Matthews knew they couldn't afford another crisis like the one they'd just survived.

"You've got this, Park," Matthews said quietly, trying to instill confidence in his engineer. "We can't let this take us down."

Park nodded, his focus laser-sharp. "I'll do what I can, but if this is another layer of sabotage, we need to be prepared for anything. It could be set to trigger a catastrophic failure if I mess with it."

"We don't have a choice," Dr. Emily Hoss chimed in, her voice strained. "If we lose propulsion, we won't be able to adjust our course or maintain stability. We'd drift into the void."

The crew knew what that meant—without propulsion, they would have no way of returning to Earth. It was an outcome they couldn't afford to face.

Park's hands moved swiftly over the controls, inputting a series of commands. "Alright," he said, his voice tense. "I'm starting the bypass now. If there's any hidden command tied to the propulsion system, we'll know in the next few seconds."

Matthews and Hoss exchanged a glance, the silence in the cockpit suffocating as they waited.

Back on Earth, at IISF Mission Control, Elena Markov was monitoring the data stream from the spacecraft closely. The propulsion system anomaly had thrown the entire command center into high alert, and the stakes couldn't be higher.

"They're trying to bypass the lockout now," Elena reported to Georgiy Garbuz, who stood nearby, his eyes fixed on the live feed. "But if this is sabotage—"

"I know," Garbuz said quietly. "One wrong move and they could lose everything."

Elena's hands tightened on the console as she watched the propulsion diagnostics roll across the screen. The ship's thrusters were stable for now, but the hidden lockout was preventing the crew from fully accessing the system. It was as if a trap had been set, waiting to spring at the worst possible moment.

"We need a backup plan," Garbuz said, his voice laced with tension. "If they lose propulsion, how long before the mission becomes unsalvageable?"

Elena glanced at the screen, her face grim. "If they lose propulsion completely, they'll have days before they run out of fuel for essential functions. After that... they'd be adrift. And if Orlov's sabotage is worse than we think, they could lose control much sooner."

Garbuz clenched his fists. Sable's sabotage had been far more extensive than they had ever anticipated, and the crew was paying the price. He felt a deep sense of responsibility for sending them into this situation. The future of the IISF—and the entire mission—was hanging by a thread.

Inside the spacecraft, the tension was unbearable. Jason Park's hands moved steadily, even though his heart was racing. The lockdown on the propulsion system was tougher than he expected, but he was making progress.

"I'm almost there," Park said, his voice taut with concentration. "I've bypassed most of the security measures, but there's one final lock. It's encrypted—more sophisticated than what we've seen so far."

Matthews floated closer, watching over Park's shoulder. "Can you break it?"

"I can try," Park replied. "But if it's booby-trapped, the moment I crack it, we could lose propulsion—or worse."

"We don't have another option," Matthews said firmly. "We need propulsion to stay on course."

Park took a deep breath, his fingers hovering over the final commands. "Here goes nothing."

He entered the code.

For a moment, nothing happened. The system hummed quietly, the encrypted lock holding steady. Then, suddenly, the console flickered, and a warning flashed across the screen—PROPULSION SYSTEM OVERRIDE ACTIVATED.

"Damn it!" Park shouted, his eyes wide with alarm. "It's triggering the failsafe!"

The ship lurched violently, the sudden jolt knocking the crew off their feet as the propulsion system sputtered to life. Alarms blared across the cabin, red lights flashing as the ship veered slightly off course.

"We're losing control of the engines!" Park yelled, his hands flying over the controls. "It's locked us out again—this time completely!"

Matthews grabbed onto a nearby handle, stabilizing himself as the ship bucked under the strain. "Park, shut it down! We need to stop this before the engines blow!"

"I can't!" Park shouted back. "The system's not responding!"

As the spacecraft lurched and strained, Hoss frantically checked the navigation and propulsion systems. The engines were firing erratically, threatening to destabilize the ship's course. If they couldn't regain control, they would either burn through their fuel or send the ship spiraling off into deep space.

"We're losing fuel at an alarming rate," Hoss reported, her voice strained. "If we don't stop this, we'll run out of propellant in minutes."

Matthews slammed his fist against the console, frustration boiling over. "Park, there has to be another way. Can we bypass the entire propulsion system?"

Park's hands were shaking as he continued working. "I'm trying to isolate the manual override—if we can shut down the engines completely, we might be able to reboot them, but there's no guarantee we'll get them back online."

"Do it," Matthews ordered. "We don't have any other choice."

Park nodded, taking a deep breath before entering the manual shutdown commands. The engines whined loudly, the strain on the ship becoming unbearable, before everything went silent.

The crew floated in the eerie stillness as the hum of the propulsion system disappeared. The alarms stopped, and the red lights faded as the ship stabilized, its engines now offline.

For a long moment, no one spoke.

"Engines are down," Park said finally, his voice barely a whisper. "We've got manual control, but we're dead in the water for now."

Hoss checked the fuel levels and navigation data, her face pale. "We've lost a lot of fuel. If we don't get the engines back online soon, we won't have enough to reach our destination."

Matthews floated back from the console, his mind racing. They had managed to stop the sabotage—for now—but the ship was crippled. Without propulsion, they were stranded, and the chances of fixing the system were slim.

As the minutes passed, the crew's sense of relief was replaced by a growing dread. They had averted immediate disaster, but the realization that they were now drifting in space—without propulsion—was settling in. The mission, which had been filled with so much hope and promise, was beginning to feel like a death sentence.

"We need to come up with a plan," Matthews said, gathering the crew around him. "We've got enough fuel left to make one more push—if we can get the engines back online."

Hoss crossed her arms, her face grim. "But if we don't fix the system before then, we'll use the last of our propellant and still be stranded."

Park looked exhausted. "I'm going to keep working on the propulsion systems, but the lockdown was designed to cripple us. Whoever set this up knew what they were doing."

Matthews clenched his fists, his frustration simmering beneath the surface. "We're not giving up. We're going to fix this. We didn't come this far to let Orlov's sabotage win."

Hoss nodded, though her eyes betrayed the growing doubt she felt. "We'll do everything we can, Commander."

Far from the struggling IISF spacecraft, Dmitry Orlov watched as the next stage of his plan unfolded. His operatives had confirmed that the sabotage had worked—the IISF's first manned mission into deep space was now crippled, and their chances of survival were rapidly dwindling.

"Their propulsion system is offline," Orlov's advisor reported. "They're stranded."

Orlov smiled, his eyes gleaming with satisfaction. "Good. The longer they remain stranded, the more vulnerable they become. And while they fight to survive, the BRICS alliance will launch their own mission, seizing the lead in space exploration."

His advisor nodded. "What if the IISF manages to fix their systems?"

Orlov's smile faded slightly, his expression hardening. "Then we'll ensure they don't make it home."

244

Chapter 52

Confronting the Breakdown

The dim, sterile lights in the spacecraft's cockpit cast a harsh glow over the crew as they gathered to assess the damage. The weight of their isolation had never felt more real, with the silence of space pressing in on them and the uncertainty of their future hanging heavily in the air.

Commander Daniel Matthews floated near the control console, his face grim as he examined the propulsion system's diagnostics. The engine shutdown had kept them from burning through the last of their fuel, but the damage was severe. If they didn't repair the system, they would drift aimlessly through space.

"Give it to me straight, Park," Matthews said, turning to Lt. Jason Park, the mission's engineer. "What are our options?"

Park's face was drawn with exhaustion, his eyes darting over the diagnostics. "The lockdown triggered a failsafe that burned out part of the circuitry," he explained, tapping the screen. "Most of it is fried beyond repair, and we're low on replacement parts. We could try rerouting power, but it's a delicate job. One wrong move, and we could short out the whole system."

"And if we don't repair it?" asked Dr. Emily Hoss, her voice steady but laced with worry.

Park glanced at her, his expression bleak. "Then we're stuck. Without propulsion, we're not going anywhere. We'd be at the mercy of our trajectory, which means we could drift into deep space with no way to adjust our course."

The gravity of his words settled over them, and the crew exchanged uneasy glances. They were closer to the edge of survival than ever, and the mission's importance was starting to feel like a distant concern. Now, it was about staying alive.

"Alright," Matthews said, his voice taking on a note of resolve. "What's the best plan for rerouting the power?"

Park pulled up the ship's schematics on the console. "We can pull parts from non-essential systems. It's risky, but it'll give us a shot at restoring limited propulsion. If we're careful, we might have enough to regain control of our course."

"Then let's get started," Matthews said, nodding. "I'll work with you on the rerouting. Hoss, I need you to run simulations and make sure we're not overlooking anything. Every step has to be precise."

Hoss agreed, though her face was tight with concern. "If we're taking from non-essentials, it'll leave us exposed. Life support and comms will be running on thin power reserves."

Matthews looked at her, his gaze steady. "We'll manage. Let's move."

As they began their repairs, the crew's tension became palpable. Working in silence, Park and Matthews dismantled parts from the non-essential systems, carefully extracting the components they needed. Each movement felt precarious, as if the slightest miscalculation could lead to catastrophe.

Hoss monitored the simulations from a nearby console, her brow furrowed as she ran calculation after calculation. But as the hours wore on, the strain began to take its toll.

"We're looking at hours of work, minimum," Park muttered, a note of frustration slipping into his voice. "And that's assuming we can keep the systems balanced."

Hoss glanced up, her tone sharper than she intended. "Complaining about it isn't going to help, Park. We're all exhausted."

Park shot her a look. "I'm just saying we need to be realistic. Orlov's sabotage was designed to trap us. These aren't just simple malfunctions—he's boxed us in with every contingency."

Hoss's jaw tightened. "I get it, Jason. But we don't have the luxury of dwelling on that now. We've beaten the odds before. Let's focus on solutions, not the scale of the problem."

Matthews interjected, his voice calm but firm. "Enough. We're all feeling it, but let's keep it together. We've got a job to do."

The silence resumed, tense but determined, as they returned to their work. It was clear that while they shared the same goal, the stress and fear were beginning to fray their unity.

After hours of painstaking work, Park and Matthews managed to reroute enough power to restore partial functionality to the propulsion system. They gathered around the control console, looking at the data feed that showed their progress.

"Alright," Park said, adjusting the display. "We've rerouted enough power to attempt a low-thrust ignition. It's not much, but it should be enough to get us back on course."

Hoss ran a final diagnostic. "It's going to be close. The propulsion system is fragile, and we don't know how long it'll hold up under strain."

Matthews nodded, acknowledging the risk. "Then we make every move count. Let's prepare for a course correction. This is our one shot to stabilize our trajectory."

He turned to face the crew, his voice taking on a note of encouragement. "We've all been pushed to the limit, but we're still here. We've already overcome so much, and we'll overcome this too."

The crew responded with a renewed sense of determination, the gravity of their mission reignited by Matthews' words. Though the outcome was uncertain, they knew they had to give everything to survive.

Chapter 53

Support from Earth

At IISF Mission Control, the air was thick with tension. Data streams from the spacecraft flickered across dozens of screens as the ground crew watched the live telemetry feed, their expressions tight with worry. News of the propulsion failure and the subsequent makeshift repairs had left the entire command center on edge.

Elena Markov glanced at the wall-mounted monitor, where Commander Daniel Matthews' status report was displayed alongside critical system readouts. She turned to Georgiy Garbuz, who stood nearby, his gaze locked on the screen.

"Propulsion repairs are underway," she said quietly, "but we're still not sure how long the patch will hold. They're balancing on a knife's edge."

Garbuz's face was drawn with worry. He had always understood the risks of space travel, but Orlov's sabotage had pushed those risks to new extremes. The crew was enduring trials no astronaut should face.

"We need to give them more than good luck," Garbuz replied. "If this patch fails, we could lose them. We need to rally support for a contingency."

Elena nodded. "I agree. But the international community is already losing faith in the IISF's ability to lead a secure mission. We're facing heavy criticism from allies, particularly the BRICS-aligned countries, who are pushing their own agenda."

Garbuz's eyes narrowed, his mind already spinning with options. "Then we take the diplomatic approach—lean on allies who still believe in this mission and get them on-board with a rescue plan. We can't sit idle while our people are stranded."

Garbuz and Elena initiated a secure call with Senator Warner, President Zhang, and representatives from key international partners. The virtual meeting quickly became heated as the situation on the spacecraft was reviewed.

"Georgiy, this mission has been one problem after another," Senator Warner said, his expression skeptical. "First the sabotage, then the propulsion failure. We're already funneling significant resources into this, and frankly, the IISF hasn't proven capable of keeping this mission on track."

President Zhang leaned forward, her gaze icy. "The BRICS alliance has made it clear that we're ready to lead. If the IISF can't assure the safety of this crew, we're prepared to step in and support alternative missions."

Garbuz's jaw clenched, but he kept his tone even. "Senator, President Zhang, we're fully aware of the gravity of the situation. This isn't just about the IISF or BRICS; this is humanity's first deep space mission. We have a responsibility to ensure the crew returns safely, and that means exploring all options, including a rescue mission if necessary."

Senator Warner's expression softened slightly, though he remained guarded. "A rescue mission would take months. It's a monumental commitment. Can you guarantee it would make a difference?"

Garbuz looked directly into the camera. "What I can guarantee is that the crew will keep fighting as long as they have hope. And if we support them, we give them every chance to complete the mission and return safely. Abandoning them is not an option."

The silence that followed was tense, each leader processing Garbuz's words. Finally, Warner gave a nod.

"We'll provide initial support," he said, his voice cautious but committed. "But the IISF needs to prove that it can keep the crew stable. If there are further setbacks, we'll have to re-evaluate our position."

President Zhang remained silent, her expression unreadable, but she didn't object. Garbuz knew it wasn't a victory, but it was a step in the right direction.

Back on the spacecraft, Matthews was in the cockpit, preparing for the next phase of the propulsion repairs, when the comms crackled to life.

"Commander Matthews, this is Elena. We have some updates for you," she said, her voice steady, though he could hear the strain beneath it. "The international community has agreed to support a contingency plan. A rescue mission is under preliminary discussion, though the timeline would be lengthy."

Matthews exchanged a glance with Dr. Emily Hoss and Lt. Jason Park, who had paused their work to listen.

"Good to hear, Elena," Matthews replied, his tone a mixture of relief and caution. "But we both know it could take months to reach us."

"We're aware," Elena replied, her voice softening. "But it's a lifeline. We're doing everything we can on our end to support you, and you've got the full backing of IISF Mission Control. You're not alone in this."

Matthews felt a renewed sense of determination settle over him. The reassurance from Earth was a reminder that their struggle wasn't in vain and that others were fighting for them.

"Thanks, Elena. We'll keep working on the propulsion. We're not giving up," Matthews said, his voice resolute.

After the call ended, Matthews turned to his crew, who looked visibly relieved by the news. The prospect of a rescue mission, however distant, was a glimmer of hope.

The crew gathered in the common area, a tight space barely large enough for the team but offering a brief moment of reprieve. For the first time since the sabotage began, they allowed themselves to hope.

Park adjusted a strap on his gear, his expression thoughtful. "A rescue mission... even if it takes months, it's a lifeline. Knowing we're not out here completely alone—it changes things."

Hoss nodded, her expression softening. "It gives us something to hold onto. If Earth is willing to back us, then we owe it to them and ourselves to keep pushing forward."

Matthews looked around at his team, his gaze intense. "They believe in us, but that's only because we've proven we're worth believing in. We're going to keep working on the propulsion, and we're going to make it through this."

The crew nodded in agreement, a renewed determination in their eyes. For the first time since the propulsion crisis began, they felt they had a fighting chance. They were more than just a stranded crew—they were pioneers, representing the best of humanity's resilience and courage.

Chapter 54
Against the Void

The silence inside the spacecraft was broken only by the steady hum of life support and the faint clicking sounds of Lt. Jason Park working to stabilize the propulsion system. The crew had spent hours meticulously rerouting power and cannibalizing non-essential components to restore partial functionality, and now they were approaching the moment of truth.

Commander Daniel Matthews floated near the main console, watching Park's every movement, his gaze intense but focused. This was their last shot. They had one attempt to restore propulsion—one attempt to keep the mission alive.

"Alright, I've bypassed the damaged circuits and rerouted power from the non-essential systems," Park said, his voice barely above a whisper as he finished connecting the final wires. "We should be able to initiate a low-thrust ignition, just enough to adjust our trajectory."

Dr. Emily Hoss moved closer, her eyes darting between the console and Park's face. "How much fuel will we have left after this?"

Park took a breath, his face lined with tension. "Not much. This ignition will burn through a good portion of our reserves. We'll have enough for one more major maneuver after this—if we're lucky."

Matthews nodded, a steely resolve in his eyes. "Then we make it count. Are we ready?"

Park glanced at Hoss, who gave a tense nod. "As ready as we'll ever be."

Matthews took his place at the main console, positioning his hands over the controls. He glanced at his crew, each of them bracing for the outcome. "Initiating low-thrust ignition in three... two... one..."

The spacecraft shuddered slightly as the propulsion system roared to life, sending a low, rumbling vibration through the cabin. Matthews held his breath as he watched the readings on the console. The thrust was minimal, just enough to adjust their trajectory, but the strain on the system was evident.

"Thrust is holding," Park reported, his eyes fixed on the data feed. "We're burning through fuel faster than expected, but it's stabilizing."

Matthews nodded, adjusting the controls to keep their trajectory steady. The engines hummed, pushing the ship gently forward. It was working—barely, but it was working.

But just as hope began to build, the console flashed a warning. ENGINE TEMPERA-TURE CRITICAL. The propulsion system's temperature was spiking, a clear sign that the patched circuits were struggling under the load.

"We're overheating," Hoss said urgently. "If we push it any harder, we risk a total burnout."

Matthews gritted his teeth. They were so close, but the risk of a complete failure loomed large. "Park, can we cool it down?"

"I'm trying to reroute the cooling system, but it's already maxed out," Park replied, his fingers flying over the controls. "This is about as much as we're going to get."

The crew exchanged anxious glances. They had achieved a minor course correction, but it wasn't enough to put them back on track completely. If they shut down now, they'd need their last fuel reserves to attempt a second maneuver—a gamble that could leave them entirely stranded if it failed.

"Commander," Hoss said softly, her gaze steady. "We might not get another chance."

Matthews took a deep breath, his mind racing. Pushing the system further risked burning out the engines completely, but if they stopped now, they might never have enough fuel to realign their course. Either option was a gamble—but with lives on the line, Matthews knew he had to choose.

"Let's throttle down, but don't shut it off entirely," Matthews decided. "If we can keep it running just enough to maintain the adjustment, we might buy ourselves the time we need."

Park adjusted the engine's thrust, lowering it just enough to keep the temperature from spiking further. The rumble of the engines softened, but the gentle push was enough to keep them on course. The crew remained silent, each of them holding their breath as the system strained under the low-thrust burn.

Minutes passed, the tension thick as the crew watched the readings, hoping the system would hold. Hoss checked the fuel reserves, her eyes darting between the fuel gauge and the engine temperatures.

"We're just about there," she murmured, her voice a mix of relief and anxiety. "Trajectory correction is within safe parameters."

The console blinked green as their course finally stabilized. The propulsion system had held, and the spacecraft was now on a viable path. Matthews let out a breath he hadn't realized he'd been holding.

"We did it," he said, the relief in his voice evident. "Hoss, Park—solid work. That was as close as it gets."

Park slumped back, wiping a hand across his forehead. "That patch won't hold forever, but it'll buy us time."

The crew exchanged looks, exhaustion mingling with relief. For the first time in days, they allowed themselves a moment to feel the victory, however small it was.

As the crew savored their accomplishment, the comms crackled to life. Elena Markov's voice came through, a tone of restrained excitement in her words.

"Commander Matthews, this is Mission Control. We've been monitoring your course adjustment—excellent work," she said, her voice filled with pride. "Your trajectory is stabilized, and you're on track. The support teams here are already analyzing your next steps."

Matthews smiled, his spirits lifted by the support from Earth. "Thank you, Elena. We couldn't have done it without the backup plan. The crew here gave it everything they had."

Elena's voice softened. "We know, Commander. And everyone here is behind you. We're running diagnostics on your propulsion output and fuel reserves now. We'll be in touch with recommendations."

Matthews nodded, glancing at his crew. "Copy that. We're holding steady for now."

As the comms went silent, the crew felt a renewed sense of purpose. They weren't out of danger, but they had a path forward. And for the first time since the crisis began, they felt a spark of hope.

With their course stabilized, Matthews gathered the crew in the common area, where they could talk through their options. Though they had made significant progress, their journey was far from over.

Hoss floated nearby, her arms crossed as she surveyed the crew. "We've bought ourselves time, but we have to be smart about what comes next. Our fuel reserves are dangerously low, and the propulsion system is still unstable. If we face another malfunction, we might not have the resources to fix it."

Park nodded in agreement. "It's true. We're on borrowed time with this patch. We have to conserve every bit of power we can."

Matthews listened carefully, his face thoughtful. He knew the risks, but he also knew they couldn't afford to sit idle.

"We'll focus on fuel conservation and limited power usage," he decided. "No unnecessary systems will be used until we know exactly what our resources look like. And we stay on alert for any signs of additional sabotage. If Orlov has more surprises in here, we're not letting them catch us off guard."

The crew nodded, a renewed determination in their eyes. They had survived the sabotage so far, and with Mission Control backing them, they felt ready to push forward, no matter the obstacles.

Chapter 55

A Rival Mission

Far from the stranded IISF crew, Dmitry Orlov stood in his office at the BRICS command center, overlooking a bustling control room preparing for the launch of BRICS's own deep space mission. Confidence radiated from him; the IISF's mounting troubles played perfectly into his hands, positioning BRICS to make history as the first alliance to reach deep space and return successfully.

As Orlov reviewed the launch preparations, one of his advisors approached, a cautious expression on her face. "Sir, there's been a development. Our team has detected a security breach in the BRICS system diagnostics."

Orlov's brow furrowed as he turned to face her. "A security breach? Explain."

"It's subtle but significant. There are unusual command sequences buried in our system logs, similar to the sabotage patterns we saw in the IISF's data," she said, hesitating. "We believe it could be connected to the same network that planted Sable within IISF."

Orlov's face darkened. He had prided himself on staying one step ahead, controlling every aspect of his plan. But now, the realization struck: his own mission might be compromised. "Are you saying that Sable's network could have infiltrated BRICS?"

"It's possible, sir," the advisor replied, her voice tense. "The sequences are encrypted, and the commands are designed to be undetectable under normal conditions. Whoever did this went to great lengths to avoid detection. If it's anything like the IISF sabotage, there could be layers we haven't uncovered."

Orlov clenched his fists, his jaw tightening. The power struggle between IISF and BRICS had driven him to orchestrate complex operations, but now he was faced with the possibility that those he'd entrusted with his vision might be turning against him.

"Contain this immediately," Orlov ordered, his voice laced with anger. "I want every diagnostic report combed through, and I want anyone with access to sensitive data investigated. If there's a traitor in our ranks, we'll root them out."

The advisor nodded, hurrying off to carry out his orders. Left alone, Orlov's confidence wavered, his mind racing through the implications. A sabotage within BRICS would destroy his chances of seizing the space exploration lead, and if the IISF discovered his vulnerability, it could shift the balance of power.

Despite the breach, Orlov pushed forward with his plan, determined to outmaneuver any remaining threats. In the days leading up to the BRICS launch, he gathered his top advisors to finalize the preparations, intent on taking control of the deep space race once and for all.

As they reviewed the launch protocols, one advisor raised a critical point. "Sir, if there's still an active sabotage network within BRICS, launching this mission could expose us to significant risk. Our teams are monitoring the system closely, but if there's any hidden sabotage, it could be catastrophic."

Orlov's gaze hardened. "We don't have time for second-guessing. Every moment we delay is an opportunity for IISF to recover. This mission goes forward as planned."

The advisors exchanged tense glances, but no one dared argue. Orlov's word was final, and despite their reservations, they prepared to launch. Orlov knew that delaying would weaken their position, but the growing suspicion within his ranks hinted at fractures he hadn't anticipated. He realized that control—both over BRICS and his own allies—was slipping, and the stakes were rising.

Back on the IISF spacecraft, Commander Daniel Matthews and his crew had settled into a cautious routine of monitoring their fragile systems, holding steady on the adjusted trajectory. They were managing to conserve power and fuel, but the strain of constant vigilance was beginning to wear on them.

In the midst of their watch, the comms unexpectedly crackled to life. Elena Markov's voice came through, but there was something different in her tone—an urgency they hadn't heard before.

"Commander Matthews, we've received intelligence that could change the course of this mission," Elena said, her voice low but steady. "IISF's security team has detected vulnerabilities in the BRICS systems, similar to the patterns used in the sabotage against your crew. It's likely that Orlov's mission is also compromised."

Matthews exchanged a look with Dr. Emily Hoss and Lt. Jason Park, their expressions reflecting the same shock he felt. If Orlov's team was dealing with sabotage, the race for deep space supremacy was no longer just between two alliances—it was a battle within each organization.

"Do we have any details on the sabotage in BRICS?" Matthews asked, his mind racing with possibilities.

"Not yet, but our intelligence team is analyzing the data," Elena replied. "If we can find a way to use this information, it could change the game. Orlov's mission might be just as vulnerable as yours, if not more so. This could give us the edge we need to complete your mission without interference."

Matthews absorbed this, a cautious optimism growing in him. For the first time, it felt like they had a card to play against Orlov. If BRICS faced the same risks, it would weaken Orlov's grip on the mission, leveling the playing field for IISF.

"Understood, Elena. Keep us updated. We'll continue conserving resources and maintain our current trajectory," Matthews said, his voice steady. "If Orlov's mission is compromised, it might buy us the time we need."

After the comms cut off, Hoss let out a slow breath. "If this intelligence is correct, Orlov's plan is backfiring."

Park nodded, a small smile appearing on his face. "Serves him right. Maybe now we have a fighting chance."

Matthews smiled, a glimmer of hope rekindling within him. They had endured the worst that Orlov had thrown at them, and now, it seemed, his own arrogance might be his undoing.

The crew's optimism was short-lived. As they continued their repairs and system checks, a warning light suddenly flashed on the console—a low-pressure alert in one of the life support conduits.

Hoss quickly ran diagnostics, her face going pale as the data streamed in. "We're losing oxygen," she reported, her voice tense. "It's slow, but if we don't fix this, we'll be at critically low levels within a few days."

Matthews cursed softly, feeling the renewed strain weigh heavily on him. They had barely stabilized their propulsion, and now their life support was once again in jeopardy. "Can we isolate the leak?"

"I'm trying," Hoss replied, her fingers moving quickly over the console. "But the damage is in a hard-to-reach section. We'll need to shut down part of the system to access it, which means we'll lose more oxygen in the process."

Park glanced at Matthews, the gravity of the situation sinking in. "This could be part of Orlov's sabotage. A slow leak would be hard to detect, designed to weaken us over time."

Matthews nodded, his mind already working through their options. They had overcome the odds before, but with every system under strain, their margin for error was razor-thin. "Let's prioritize the repair. If we can stop the leak, we'll buy ourselves the time we need."

As the crew prepared to tackle the leak, the significance of the moment wasn't lost on them. The threats they faced were relentless, but they had made it this far together, and they weren't about to give up.

Matthews gathered the crew, his expression resolute. "We've faced sabotage, system failures, and now an oxygen leak, but we're still here. We're still fighting. Orlov may have planned every step of this, but he didn't account for our resilience."

Hoss nodded, her face determined. "We're all in, Commander."

Park gave a thumbs-up, a small smile on his face. "Let's fix this."

With renewed purpose, the crew set to work, each of them focused on their respective tasks. Despite the odds, they knew that as long as they worked together, they could face whatever challenges lay ahead. They were more than just astronauts on a mission—they were a team, bound by purpose and grit.

As they worked to stabilize the life support system, they knew the coming days would test them even further. But for now, they pressed forward, determined to overcome every obstacle between them and their mission.

Chapter 56

A Leap of Faith

Inside the cramped and dimly lit confines of the spacecraft, tension was reaching its breaking point. The newly detected oxygen leak had thrown the crew into high alert yet again. With every breath, they were aware of the precious resource slipping away, the clock ticking down on their chance to survive.

Commander Daniel Matthews floated near the control console, watching Dr. Emily Hoss and Lt. Jason Park as they worked to locate and seal the leak. The hours of constant vigilance were taking their toll; exhaustion was evident on every face.

"We've isolated the area," Hoss reported, her voice a mixture of relief and urgency. "The leak is coming from a weakened connection in the life support's central conduit. It's in a hard-to-reach spot, and we'll have to shut down part of the oxygen system to reach it safely."

Matthews nodded, knowing they didn't have another option. "Do it. Let's minimize our oxygen use as much as possible. Park, get the tools ready and prep the system for partial shutdown."

Park was already moving, floating toward the equipment storage unit where he retrieved the tools they'd need for the delicate repair. The room felt colder as they prepared to cut off part of the life support, but the team's determination remained strong.

As Park secured his tools, Hoss glanced at him. "We'll have to be fast. The moment we initiate the shutdown, oxygen levels are going to drop, and we'll be cutting it close."

"Understood," Park replied, his jaw clenched. "We've come this far—let's not let a slow leak take us down."

With Hoss at the control console, the countdown to the partial shutdown began. Matthews floated beside her, his gaze steady but intense. This wasn't just another repair—it was a fight for survival.

"Shutting down life support in three... two... one," Hoss announced, her hands poised over the controls. With a swift motion, she deactivated the life support system in the affected area, and the hum of the air filtration fell silent.

Immediately, the air felt thinner, the silence amplifying their awareness of every breath. The crew was fully aware that they were now operating on limited oxygen reserves, with only minutes to spare.

"Park, you're up," Matthews said, giving him an encouraging nod.

Park floated to the access panel, carefully unscrewing it to reveal the inner workings of the life support system. Sweat formed on his brow as he focused on the task, his hands moving with precision despite the mounting pressure.

"I see the damage," Park reported, his voice tense but focused. "The conduit is cracked. I'll need to seal it manually."

"Be careful," Hoss urged, watching him closely. "A misstep could damage the other systems."

Park nodded, barely breathing as he maneuvered a thin adhesive patch over the crack. He pressed down, activating the seal, his hands steady as he waited for the patch to harden.

"Almost there..." he whispered, his voice barely audible.

The seconds felt like hours, but finally, Park looked up, relief in his eyes. "The patch is holding. Conduit is sealed."

As soon as Park confirmed the seal, Hoss moved to restore the life support system. Her fingers flew over the controls, reactivating the filtration and oxygen supply.

With a soft hum, the system came back online. The cool, oxygen-rich air flowed back into the cabin, and the crew let out a collective sigh of relief as the atmosphere began to stabilize.

"Oxygen levels are returning to normal," Hoss reported, her voice filled with relief. "We've got full containment again. The leak is sealed."

Matthews placed a hand on Park's shoulder, a rare smile breaking through his otherwise serious expression. "You did good work, Park. You all did."

The crew shared a moment of quiet satisfaction, each of them taking in the weight of what they had just accomplished. Against all odds, they had managed to stave off another threat to their survival.

As the crew caught their breath, the comms crackled to life. Elena Markov's voice filled the cabin, her tone warm with pride and admiration.

"Commander Matthews, we just received your status update on the life support repair. The entire IISF team is behind you—we know you're fighting for every breath, and you're proving why you were chosen for this mission."

Matthews glanced at his crew, their faces brightening at the words of support from Earth. "Thank you, Elena. It's a team effort. We're not giving up, no matter what Orlov throws at us."

Elena's voice softened. "And we're with you every step of the way. We're coordinating all possible resources to keep you safe and have some additional intel that might give you an advantage. The sabotage in BRICS seems to be unraveling faster than we anticipated. It could weaken Orlov's position sooner than expected."

A spark of hope flickered in Matthews' eyes. If Orlov's own mission was destabilizing, it could buy them precious time to complete their own objectives and return to Earth.

"Keep us updated, Elena," Matthews replied. "We're holding our course. And thanks… we'll need all the support we can get."

With the life support system stabilized and a fresh wave of encouragement from Earth, the crew gathered in the common area for a rare moment of calm. The string of crises had left them exhausted, but the knowledge that they had endured every challenge renewed their determination.

Hoss leaned against the wall, her eyes closed as she took a deep, steadying breath. "I didn't think a simple breath of air would ever feel like a victory," she murmured with a tired smile.

Park gave a quiet chuckle, nodding. "Funny how survival brings things into perspective. We're out here holding on by a thread, but we're still here."

Matthews looked at his team, his expression solemn but proud. "We've pushed through some of the toughest situations imaginable. I know it hasn't been easy, but if we keep working together, we'll make it back. We'll show Orlov that no amount of sabotage can break this mission."

They all nodded in agreement, their spirits rekindled by the small but meaningful victory. The moments of calm were few and far between, but they embraced it, each crew member drawing strength from one another.

After a long silence, Hoss spoke up, her voice barely above a whisper. "Whatever happens… I'm grateful to be here with you all."

The rest of the crew echoed her sentiment, a quiet understanding passing between them. They were more than just a team—they were a family forged in the fire of adversity.

Meanwhile, in Moscow, Orlov sat in silence, watching the monitor as the IISF's trajectory realigned perfectly, overcoming his final sabotage attempt. His plans to disrupt the mission had failed. In the quiet, his frustration turned into a cold, unyielding resolve.

"They have made their choice," he said finally. "Contact the generals overseeing the operations in Ukraine. Increase the offensive. Make it known that the West's actions have provoked this response—and that we are ready to do whatever it takes to assert our position."

As the orders were relayed, the aggression intensified on the ground. Each failure in space was mirrored by new devastation closer to home, the stakes raised higher as Orlov sought to reassert dominance, if not in space, then in the territories nearest to him.

Chapter 57

Hope on the Horizon

With life support stabilized and oxygen levels back to normal, the crew felt a newfound sense of calm and cautious optimism. However, their journey was far from over, and every system in the spacecraft was still running on borrowed time. Fuel reserves were low, and the propulsion system—held together with improvised repairs—remained their last fragile lifeline.

Commander Daniel Matthews gathered the crew in the cockpit for a briefing on their next step. The success of the oxygen repair had given them precious time, but their ultimate objective was still ahead of them, and it would require one final course correction.

"Alright, team," Matthews began, his gaze steady as he looked at each of his crew members in turn. "We've managed to stabilize life support and restore partial propulsion, but we're nearing the edge of our fuel reserves. Our next move will be a controlled burn to adjust our course and get back on track to complete the mission."

Lt. Jason Park nodded, his face serious as he reviewed the propulsion system's latest diagnostics. "The propulsion patch is holding, but it's delicate. Any course correction will push the system to its limit. We're looking at our last significant burn."

Dr. Emily Hoss raised a hand, her expression cautious. "Once we initiate this course correction, what's our contingency plan if something goes wrong?"

Matthews considered her question carefully. "This course correction will set our trajectory for the remaining leg of the mission. If we experience a failure during the burn, we may not have enough fuel to attempt a second correction, which means... this is it. It's all or nothing."

The weight of his words settled over the crew. They had come too far to turn back now, but the risks were undeniable. If they could complete this final course correction, they would stand a chance at completing the mission—and if luck was on their side, returning home.

The crew began preparing for the course correction, checking every system, every bolt, and every connection. The propulsion system had already undergone tremendous stress, and this final burn would test the limits of their repairs.

Park floated beside the propulsion controls, carefully rechecking his calculations. "I'll keep the burn at minimum thrust and monitor the system temperature. We'll shut it down at the first sign of trouble."

Hoss moved to the control console, her fingers deftly navigating through diagnostics as she adjusted the life support system to conserve oxygen during the burn. "The air filtration and cooling systems are prepped. I'll manage the power distribution, so we're running as lean as possible."

Matthews watched them both, his mind racing through every possible outcome. They had survived sabotage, system failures, and the brink of suffocation. But this final maneuver would either see them to safety or seal their fate.

"Alright," Matthews said, his voice low but steady. "We've been through a lot, and I trust each of you to keep us moving forward. We'll initiate the burn on my mark."

The crew took their positions, the cockpit filled with a tense silence as they waited for Matthews' signal.

With the crew ready and every system as prepared as possible, Matthews took a steadying breath and began the countdown. "Commencing burn in three... two... one... engage."

Park activated the thrusters, and a soft hum vibrated through the ship as the propulsion system came to life. The low, steady thrust sent a gentle pressure through the cabin, nudging the spacecraft along its adjusted trajectory. The data on the console showed that the ship was holding its course.

"We're on track," Park reported, his eyes glued to the diagnostics. "Temperature is climbing, but it's within manageable levels. Fuel consumption is steady."

Matthews watched the console, his heart pounding as he monitored the delicate balance of the burn. The propulsion system was fragile, and every passing second felt like a minor victory.

Then, just as the system began to stabilize, a warning light blinked on the console—a low-fuel alert.

"We're down to critical fuel levels," Hoss reported, her voice calm but urgent. "At this rate, we'll need to end the burn in less than thirty seconds."

Matthews clenched his jaw, weighing their options. They were just short of reaching the full course correction, but pushing any further could burn through the last of their reserves.

"Park, prepare to shut it down on my mark," Matthews ordered, his voice steady. "We'll cut the burn as close as possible without running dry."

The seconds ticked by, each one ratcheting up the tension in the cabin as the fuel levels dipped lower. Finally, when they had reached the threshold, Matthews gave the command.

"Cut the burn—now!"

Park deactivated the thrusters, and the propulsion system powered down. The cabin was silent once again, save for the soft hum of life support and the occasional beep of the diagnostic consoles.

Matthews scanned the trajectory readouts, exhaling a breath of relief as the system displayed their updated course.

"We're back on track," he said, his voice breaking the tension. "We did it."

The crew exchanged glances, a wave of relief washing over them. Despite every obstacle, they had managed to complete the final course correction. For the first time since the mission had nearly fallen apart, they allowed themselves a moment to feel hopeful.

"We're running on fumes, but we're moving in the right direction," Park said with a weary smile.

Hoss nodded, a tired but genuine smile on her face. "We're not out of the woods, but that was one of the biggest hurdles. If the systems hold, we might just pull this off."

Matthews took a deep breath, feeling the weight of the past weeks finally lifting, if only slightly. "I'm proud of all of you. This mission was designed to test the limits, but I don't think anyone could have anticipated just how far we'd be pushed."

He glanced around at his crew, each of them embodying the resilience that had kept them alive. They had faced down every challenge together, and now, for the first time, the end of the mission felt within reach.

The comms crackled to life once more, and Elena Markov's voice came through. There was a note of restrained excitement in her tone that immediately caught Matthews' attention.

"Commander Matthews, we've been tracking your telemetry from here, and we can confirm that your trajectory is now on course to reach the mission's destination. Well done, crew. This was an incredible maneuver."

Matthews smiled, feeling a sense of validation. "Thank you, Elena. We're hanging in there."

"There's more," Elena added, a hint of suspense in her voice. "We've received intelligence that Orlov's mission may be delayed. His team has encountered unexpected difficulties, which could give you the lead."

The crew exchanged glances, their exhaustion momentarily replaced by renewed energy. If Orlov's mission was faltering, they had a real chance to complete their mission objectives first.

Hoss's eyes sparkled with cautious optimism. "If Orlov is losing ground, we might actually make it. We've worked through every obstacle he's thrown at us."

"Keep us updated on his status, Elena," Matthews said. "We're going to stay the course, but any edge we have is one we'll use."

"Understood, Commander," Elena replied. "Everyone here is rooting for you. You're proving that IISF is capable of anything, even in the face of sabotage."

As the comms cut out, Matthews turned back to his crew. "Let's keep our focus. We have a lot of work left, but this is our mission, and we're going to see it through."

With the course set and the mission objectives within sight, the crew returned to their stations, each of them more determined than ever. The road ahead was still fraught with risk, and the systems remained fragile. But they had overcome every challenge so far, and they were prepared to face whatever came next.

As they set to work on preparations for their mission destination, the reality of their achievements began to sink in. They were no longer just astronauts on a mission; they were survivors, representing humanity's endurance and spirit in the face of adversity.

Matthews floated near the observation window, watching the stars drift by, a sense of purpose filling him. No matter the odds, they would see this mission through—both for the IISF and for each other.

Chapter 58

The Edge of the Unknown

The IISF spacecraft drifted into the uncharted region of deep space, a vast darkness stretching endlessly before them. Every member of the crew knew that this was the final leg of their journey—the destination that had driven them through sabotage, failures, and countless repairs. They were about to make history, and the weight of that knowledge hung heavily in the cabin.

Commander Daniel Matthews stood at the control console, watching the data feed as they approached the mission's destination. The navigational systems displayed the coordinates, marking their entry into a zone no human spacecraft had ever reached.

"Almost there," Matthews said, his voice low, as though speaking any louder would disturb the fragile silence of space. He glanced at Dr. Emily Hoss and Lt. Jason Park, each of whom was deeply focused on their tasks.

Hoss, monitoring the readings from their sensors, looked up with a nod. "We're entering the designated coordinates. Radiation levels and particle densities are spiking, but they're within expected ranges."

Park floated beside the propulsion system, checking the readings to ensure the final adjustments held. "Engines are holding steady. We'll reach our target point in less than five minutes."

Matthews nodded, his face a mixture of relief and awe. "We're about to achieve what no one else has. Let's make sure we do it right."

As the crew made their final approach, each member moved into action, preparing for the scientific and technological objectives they had been assigned.

Hoss activated the sensor array, her fingers moving quickly over the controls as she calibrated the equipment. "Beginning data capture on the surrounding particles and radiation levels. I'll collect samples as well, though we may have to run further analysis on Earth."

The data flowed across her console, displaying information about radiation types, gravitational anomalies, and particle compositions. Each readout was groundbreaking, a testament to the crew's dedication and perseverance.

Meanwhile, Park checked on the beacon deployment system. The IISF's mission included placing a relay beacon at this location, marking it as a point of interest for future exploration.

"Beacon is ready for deployment," Park said, glancing over at Matthews. "Once it's active, it'll send a signal back to Earth, marking our location."

Matthews gave a nod of approval. "Deploy it."

Park activated the controls, and with a slight jolt, the beacon released, floating gently away from the ship. Moments later, the console lit up with a soft green light as the beacon began emitting a signal.

"We're live," Park reported, a faint smile breaking through the exhaustion on his face. "The beacon's signal is locked. Earth will know exactly where we are."

Matthews allowed himself a rare moment of pride. This was a milestone, not just for their mission but for humanity. They had overcome near-impossible odds, and now their efforts would serve as a marker for future explorers.

With the beacon deployed and the data collection underway, Matthews initiated a communication with IISF Mission Control. Despite the challenges they had faced, he wanted to share this moment with the people who had supported them from millions of miles away.

"Mission Control, this is Commander Matthews," he said, his voice carrying a note of pride. "We have reached the mission's destination. Beacon is deployed, data collection is underway, and the crew is safe. The IISF's objectives are in progress."

Elena Markov's voice came through the comms, the excitement in her tone evident. "Commander Matthews, this is incredible news. You've made history today, and the whole world is watching. The IISF team couldn't be prouder."

Matthews exchanged glances with his crew, feeling a rush of emotion. They had survived so much together, and now, despite everything, they were fulfilling the mission's purpose.

"Thank you, Elena," he replied. "And thank the whole team for standing by us. We couldn't have done this alone."

Elena's voice softened, her pride clear. "We'll pass it along, Commander. The crew here will be thrilled to hear from you. Your accomplishments are a testament to what we can achieve when we work together."

As the crew settled into the rhythm of data collection, Hoss's console beeped softly, alerting her to an unexpected reading. Frowning, she adjusted the controls to focus on the anomaly—a faint but structured signal, coming from somewhere nearby.

"Commander, I'm picking up a signal," Hoss said, her tone cautious. "It's faint but definitely structured. This isn't random interference."

Matthews moved to her console, his face tense as he reviewed the readings. The signal was almost hidden within the surrounding noise, but there was a distinct pattern to it—a sequence that seemed to repeat in rhythmic intervals.

"Could it be coming from the beacon?" Matthews asked, although he knew it was unlikely.

Hoss shook her head. "No, the beacon's signal is distinct. This... this looks like it's coming from an external source. Something we didn't account for."

Park floated over, looking at the data with equal concern. "It could be an old signal, maybe something left behind by a previous probe or satellite?"

Hoss shook her head. "The frequency is unusual. I've never seen anything quite like it."

Matthews considered their options. They were on limited time, but this signal could be significant. "Record it for now, and we'll analyze it later. Our primary objective is to complete the mission, but let's not overlook this. It could be important."

Hoss nodded, her face reflecting the same curiosity he felt. "Understood, Commander. I'll log the data and keep monitoring for any changes."

As the crew continued their work, the mysterious signal lingered in the back of their minds—a reminder that the vast expanse of space held secrets far beyond what they had planned for.

Chapter 59

Mission Cleared

The IISF crew worked steadily, their movements precise and efficient as they executed the final stages of the mission. The quiet hum of the spacecraft's systems filled the silence, occasionally interrupted by diagnostic alerts and data pings as the crew collected and processed information from this unexplored region of space.

Commander Daniel Matthews floated near the observation window, looking out at the vast darkness surrounding them. Despite every challenge, they had reached this point, and the sense of pride was undeniable. But he knew they couldn't get comfortable; this mission was as much about survival as it was about discovery.

"Status check," Matthews called, his voice breaking the silence as he addressed his team.

Dr. Emily Hoss adjusted her sensors, studying the streams of data from the particle and radiation analyzers. "Readings are steady. We're detecting trace elements and radiation levels that are unlike anything we've recorded before. This data is going to be invaluable for future exploration."

Lt. Jason Park reviewed the diagnostics on the propulsion system, ensuring it would hold for their journey back. "The propulsion patch is stable, but we're on reserve capacity. Any strain from here on out could push us past our fuel limit."

Matthews nodded, knowing the delicate balance they were trying to maintain. "Let's finish strong. Every piece of data we send back could shape humanity's understanding of space."

With the primary objectives complete, Hoss initiated the transmission of their collected data back to IISF Mission Control. The packages included sensor readings, radiation profiles, and other data points that would be analyzed by scientists on Earth for years to come.

"Transmission started. IISF should have the full data package in under thirty minutes," Hoss reported, her fingers steady on the controls.

Moments later, Elena Markov's voice came through the comms, steady but carrying a hint of excitement. "Commander Matthews, we're receiving the data now. This information is a breakthrough—what you're sending is going to change the landscape of space exploration. The IISF team couldn't be prouder."

Matthews exchanged a glance with Hoss and Park, each of them sharing a look of quiet satisfaction. They had accomplished the mission under the most challenging conditions imaginable, and now their findings would contribute to humanity's journey into the cosmos.

"Thank you, Elena," Matthews replied. "It's been a team effort all the way, and we're glad to have made it here."

Elena's voice softened. "Your resilience has inspired everyone here. You're proof that we can go farther than anyone imagined."

After completing the data transmission, Matthews prepared a final message to Earth. This was his chance to capture the magnitude of their achievement and to leave a legacy for future missions.

"This is Commander Daniel Matthews of the IISF," he began, his tone calm but filled with pride. "We have reached our destination and completed our objectives. The data we've collected will deepen humanity's understanding of space and stands as a testament to the strength of collaboration and determination."

He looked over at Hoss and Park, who nodded in support. "This mission has tested us in every possible way, but we've persevered. Let this moment serve as a reminder to everyone back on Earth that exploration requires courage and resilience."

He paused, the weight of the journey settling over him. "We're coming home."

A quiet settled over the cockpit as the transmission was sent. Each crew member took a moment to reflect on the journey that had brought them here—through sabotage, repairs, and near disaster—to the edge of the unknown.

Meanwhile, on Earth, Dmitry Orlov sat in his office, watching as the IISF's success unfolded. The data transmitted by the IISF was already being celebrated, each discovery confirming that they had not only survived but succeeded in their mission. His jaw tightened as he considered the implications of their triumph.

Orlov's assistant entered, her expression cautious. "Sir, the IISF has completed their mission. International support for their program is rising, and some allies are already calling for expanded funding."

Orlov's eyes narrowed. The IISF's success was a direct threat to BRICS's plans, undermining his attempts to dominate the deep space race. He was already formulating a new plan to counter the IISF's momentum.

"This isn't over," Orlov muttered, his gaze darkening. "They've gained a small victory, but I'll make sure they don't get far."

Orlov dismissed his assistant and began making calls to his contacts within BRICS. He knew that if he wanted to regain control, he would have to escalate the competition in space—perhaps by employing methods even more drastic than before.

Back on the spacecraft, Matthews and the crew began the final preparations for departure. The fuel reserves were low, and the patched propulsion system was holding, but barely. They would have only one chance to initiate the return journey.

"Park, run a final check on the propulsion system," Matthews ordered. "Hoss, double-check that all data logs are secure and that the beacon transmission is stable."

"Data logs and beacon are secure," Hoss confirmed, her fingers tapping over the console as she performed her final checks.

Park's face was cautious as he completed the diagnostics on the propulsion system. "We're running on reserves. This will be a single burn, and if anything goes wrong, we won't have the fuel for a second attempt."

Matthews nodded, the weight of the moment settling over him. "Understood. We'll make it count."

The crew moved into position, each of them aware that this was their final opportunity. If anything failed now, their survival would be left to chance.

With all systems checked and rechecked, Matthews took his place at the controls, his expression resolute. "Initiating return sequence. Final burn in three... two... one."

Park activated the propulsion system, and the spacecraft gave a soft lurch as it began its journey home. The hum of the engines reverberated through the cabin, a gentle yet powerful reminder that they were on the edge of survival, every bit of power accounted for.

"We're holding steady," Park reported, his eyes fixed on the console as he monitored the fuel and engine status. "Fuel is low, but we're on course."

Hoss nodded as she monitored the systems. "Everything's looking stable. If we hold this trajectory, we'll be in range for pickup as planned."

The tension in the cabin lessened, replaced by a quiet determination. They had accomplished their mission and set their sights on home, but each of them knew that the journey was far from over.

Chapter 60
The Future of Space Exploration

As the IISF crew set their course for home, the atmosphere at IISF Mission Control was one of celebration and relief. Their success had already become a global sensation, with news outlets broadcasting the crew's accomplishments. But even as the world cheered, tensions simmered beneath the surface.

In the conference room at IISF Headquarters, Elena Markov and Georgiy Garbuz prepared for a high-stakes video call with international leaders, including Senator Warner from the United States and President Zhang of China. The IISF's achievements were undeniable, but BRICS leaders were increasingly vocal about the need to regulate future IISF missions.

As the screen flickered to life, Senator Warner's face appeared, joined by President Zhang and other representatives. Each leader's expression was tense, the applause for the IISF crew's success underscored by a cautious reserve.

"Congratulations on a successful mission, Georgiy," Senator Warner began, his tone formal but supportive. "The achievements of your crew are remarkable. They've set a new standard for exploration."

Garbuz nodded, his expression calm but wary. "Thank you, Senator. This mission was a triumph not only for the IISF but for everyone supporting the future of space exploration."

But before he could continue, President Zhang spoke up, her gaze sharp. "While we commend the IISF's success, it's clear that unilateral missions pose risks. We believe the BRICS alliance should be more involved in future planning to ensure that resources are managed responsibly and that no one nation dominates space exploration."

Warner's eyes narrowed slightly as he responded, "President Zhang, the IISF mission was an international collaboration. Our goal has always been to advance space exploration for all of humanity."

President Zhang's expression remained impassive. "Even so, the BRICS alliance has invested heavily in its own deep space programs. We cannot ignore the competitive nature of these missions, nor can we afford to let one organization lead without oversight."

Garbuz, sensing the rising tension, stepped in. "Let's focus on the bigger picture here. The IISF's mission has paved the way for future exploration—an endeavor that should unite us, not divide us."

The silence that followed was heavy. While Garbuz's words resonated with the leaders on screen, the undercurrent of rivalry was palpable. The space race had evolved beyond exploration; it was now a matter of power and influence.

As the call concluded, Garbuz turned to Elena, a look of determination on his face. "They're not going to let this go, Elena. Orlov and his allies will do everything they can to outpace us now."

Elena nodded, her expression somber. "And with Orlov's mission delayed, he'll be pushing BRICS leaders to go even further. This success is only the beginning of what will become a heated battle for control."

Garbuz let out a slow breath, the weight of the moment settling over him. "We'll need to be ready. The IISF has proven that it can succeed even in the face of sabotage, but the future of space exploration will require even greater resilience—and unity."

The two shared a brief, unspoken understanding. They were preparing for a race that would not only test their organization but could reshape the balance of global power. For now, their focus was on bringing the crew home safely. But they knew that once the crew was back, the IISF would need to expand its vision to defend its place in this new era of space rivalry.

Meanwhile, aboard the IISF spacecraft, the crew's journey continued, the familiar rhythm of routine taking hold as they settled into the long voyage back to Earth. The fragile propulsion system held, though each member knew that any error could push them past the limit of their resources.

Commander Daniel Matthews floated near the observation window, gazing out at the stars, each one a silent witness to their survival and determination. The journey home was a final test of endurance, both for their patched-up systems and their own mental resilience.

Dr. Emily Hoss and Lt. Jason Park joined him at the window, each lost in their own thoughts.

"It's strange," Hoss murmured. "After everything we've been through, it feels almost peaceful out here. But knowing what awaits us back home... it's like this is the calm before the storm."

Matthews nodded, sensing the unspoken worries they shared. They had survived sabotage and mechanical failures, but the political storm they were returning to felt just as dangerous.

"We've shown what we're capable of," Matthews said, his voice steady. "And no matter what politics try to take away from this, they can't erase what we've done out here. This mission was about proving we could endure anything."

Park looked over at him, a flicker of pride in his eyes. "Whatever happens next, Commander, I'm glad I was a part of this."

Matthews met his gaze, his voice soft. "We all should be."

Back on Earth, Dmitry Orlov was already strategizing his counterattack. In a private meeting with his closest advisors, Orlov outlined his vision for BRICS's next steps, a plan that would ensure they remained a dominant force in space exploration.

"Despite the IISF's success, we have an opportunity here," Orlov began, his tone confident but cold. "The IISF may have survived this mission, but the BRICS alliance has the resources to surpass them."

One of his advisors nodded. "With increased funding and more aggressive tactics, we can establish dominance before the IISF has a chance to recover."

Orlov's gaze turned steely. "This is no longer just about exploration. The race for space control is an extension of our power on Earth. We can't afford to fall behind, and we won't."

He outlined a proposal for an accelerated BRICS mission timeline, suggesting the development of new technologies that would outmatch the IISF's capabilities. But he knew that time was of the essence—every delay could widen the gap between BRICS and the IISF, making his own position more precarious.

On the IISF spacecraft, as the crew settled into the journey, a new transmission came through from Mission Control. Elena Markov's voice was steady, but a hint of gravity underscored her words.

"Commander Matthews, congratulations again on your achievements. I wanted to update you on the response back home. While the world is celebrating your accomplishments, the BRICS alliance is pushing for a more assertive role in space exploration."

Matthews exchanged a look with Hoss and Park, each of them understanding what the news meant. Their mission had inspired unity among some, but for others, it had ignited a rivalry that was just beginning.

Elena continued, her tone softening. "You've made history, and you've inspired millions. We can't predict what the future holds, but know that everyone here is behind you. You've set a standard no one can ignore."

Matthews took a breath, responding with quiet resolve. "Thank you, Elena. We understand what's at stake, and we're ready to face whatever comes next."

The transmission ended, and the crew sat in silence, the weight of their journey home taking on new significance. They were returning not just as explorers but as symbols of what was possible in the face of impossible odds. And they knew that their survival, in a way, had already fueled the next steps in a growing race.

With the message from Earth lingering in their minds, the crew resumed their routines, each step a testament to their resilience. The long, quiet journey was a reminder of both their accomplishments and the challenges yet to come.

Matthews looked out at the stars, his mind replaying the mission's trials, each one a reminder that they had achieved something extraordinary. But he knew their success would be tested as soon as they set foot back on Earth. For now, he allowed himself a brief moment to reflect, to feel the full weight of what they had accomplished.

"We're not just coming home," he murmured quietly to himself. "We're coming back stronger."

The journey was not over, but the crew knew they had made history, and the future of space exploration would be forever changed because of it.

CHAPTER 61

A New Era of Hope

As the IISF spacecraft continued its journey home, the international impact of the mission grew. Leaders worldwide were issuing statements, and news media buzzed with stories of the crew's survival and success, sparking debates, celebrations, and an undercurrent of tension that hinted at the competitive path ahead. The mission had become a symbol of resilience, and each announcement from IISF headquarters only fueled further fascination—and concern—about what humanity's future in space might h old.

In the IISF command center, **Georgiy Garbuz** and **Elena Markov** held a briefing for representatives from partner nations and media, addressing questions about the mission, the crew's well-being, and plans for future IISF endeavors.

"Commander Matthews and his crew have overcome unprecedented challenges," Garbuz began, his voice steady but filled with pride. "This mission stands as a beacon of what we can achieve through collaboration, courage, and unwavering commitment to exploration. We look forward to seeing the crew return safely and to analyzing the incredible data they've sent back to us."

Elena took over, addressing questions about the political ramifications. "While there are discussions to be had about cooperation and the direction of future missions, the IISF remains committed to exploration that benefits all of humanity."

A reporter raised a hand, asking, "With the BRICS alliance openly challenging IISF's lead in space, is there concern that this mission has sparked a new race—one that could increase tensions on Earth?"

Garbuz paused, his expression thoughtful. "There will always be competition. But this isn't a race to conquer—it's a mission to understand, to learn. The real challenge is ensuring that space remains a domain for growth, not division."

As the briefing continued, Elena noted the underlying worries on the faces of the attendees. The question was no longer if humanity would explore deeper into space, but who would control that exploration and how.

Back aboard the IISF spacecraft, **Commander Daniel Matthews** and his crew were adapting to the long journey home. In the cockpit, the subtle glow of their screens illuminated their faces as they monitored systems, reviewed data, and ran checks on the fragile propulsion system that had, so far, held up.

Dr. Emily Hoss floated near the observation window, gazing out at the dark, star-studded expanse. "Feels strange knowing we're going back," she said softly. "After everything, Earth almost feels like another world."

Matthews joined her, his own expression thoughtful. "There were moments I didn't know if we'd ever see it again. But now, the challenges waiting for us there feel as daunting as any we faced out here."

Lt. Jason Park, who was checking their remaining fuel reserves, turned to them. "Do you think they'll recognize what we accomplished? Or will it just become another point of contention?"

Matthews shook his head, a faint smile crossing his face. "Whatever political maneuvering goes on back home, what we did here can't be undone. And no matter how many obstacles Orlov or anyone else puts in our path, we proved that we could handle whatever space—and they—threw at us."

Hoss nodded, a look of pride in her eyes. "I guess that's all we can do—show them what's possible and hope the right people take notice."

The crew fell into a quiet routine, each member absorbing the weight of their journey. They had seen firsthand the vast unknowns of space, and that knowledge was a gift no one could take from them.

Back on Earth, **Dmitry Orlov** sat in a tense meeting with his BRICS advisors, each one offering their insights on the recent success of the IISF mission. The usual confidence in Orlov's gaze was replaced by simmering frustration. The IISF's victory had caught him off guard, and despite his own team's preparations, they were still steps behind.

One advisor leaned forward, her voice steady but firm. "Orlov, perhaps it's time we reconsider our strategy. Instead of investing heavily in building a separate Russian space agency, we could support the IISF directly. They've proven capable, and if we align with them, we might secure influence without direct competition."

Another advisor nodded in agreement. "Our resources are spread thin as it is. Supporting the IISF would allow us to tap into their research and infrastructure while shaping the course of their missions from within. Many other BRICS nations feel the same—they're interested in cooperation, not rivalry."

Orlov's jaw tightened, his fingers drumming the table. "You're suggesting we abandon Russia's independent role in deep space?"

The advisor nodded. "The IISF's success is undeniable. Their technology, resilience, and adaptability have proven effective. By consolidating our resources and joining the IISF, we can help drive their future missions. We would wield influence without bearing the full cost."

Orlov remained silent, considering their words. He knew that an alliance with the IISF would mean ceding some control but also gaining a seat at the table with a proven leader in space exploration. Yet the idea of letting go of Russia's independent ambitions left him cold.

But as his advisors continued pressing their point, he sensed the shifting tides. A reluctant decision began to form in his mind—a potential alliance that could extend Russia's reach without compromising BRICS's influence in space.

"Very well," Orlov finally said, his tone measured. "We'll explore options to support the IISF while ensuring our stake in their operations. If we're joining them, we do so with intent—to steer their path, not merely follow it."

The advisors exchanged approving glances, sensing that this shift could be the key to ensuring BRICS remained a powerful force in space exploration.

As the spacecraft entered the last leg of their journey, Matthews gathered his crew for a final recording—a message to be broadcast to Earth. This message, he knew, would encapsulate the essence of their mission.

"Today, we are closer than ever to returning home," he began, his voice calm but charged with emotion. "We left Earth to explore, to learn, and to survive against the odds. We've faced challenges beyond imagination, yet we've proven that together, we can endure."

He looked at Hoss and Park, who gave encouraging nods. "This mission wasn't just about one crew or one organization. It was about what humanity can achieve when we reach beyond ourselves. We're returning to Earth stronger, with knowledge that will pave the way for the future. May it be a future filled with unity and purpose."

He ended the recording, sending it to IISF headquarters with a sense of closure. The journey had shaped them, tested them, and ultimately, it had shown them that the real strength lay in resilience.

Chapter 62

A New Vision for Humanity

As the final transmission from the IISF crew reached Earth, messages of support poured in from every corner of the globe. Commander Daniel Matthews's words were broadcast live, inspiring a sense of unity and wonder. The message emphasized survival and exploration, and his closing words—"We're coming home"—stirred emotions worldwide. The crew's achievements had given people a vision of humanity's potential to reach beyond.

With the world's attention fixed on the Capitol steps in Washington, D.C., Georgiy Garbuz, head of the IISF, prepared to deliver a pivotal address. As he approached the podium, representatives from dozens of nations watched with anticipation, and countless citizens followed the broadcast from their homes. This was more than a celebration of exploration; it was a call to rethink the future of humanity.

Standing at the podium, Garbuz looked out at the gathered crowd and began to speak.

"Today, we find ourselves in a rare and historic moment," he began, his voice steady and filled with pride. "Thanks to the courage and resilience of the IISF crew, humanity has taken a profound step into deep space. Their journey was not only one of survival but also a testament to what we can accomplish when we come together."

He paused, letting the weight of his words settle over the crowd.

"We are on the edge of a new era. The discoveries made on this mission are just the beginning. The vastness of space holds immense potential—resources that could advance our science, revolutionize our industries, and create prosperity on Earth like never before. Imagine a future where the abundance of space provides free healthcare, free education, and an end to scarcity for every person on this planet."

The crowd listened in silence, his words sparking hope and imagination.

"But beyond resources," Garbuz continued, "space exploration is a path to unity and peace. We are reminded that, in the face of the unknown, our divisions fade. When we reach beyond Earth, we realize that we are all part of something greater than borders, nations, or politics. To build a future in space, we must foster a spirit of cooperation—a world where exploration is driven not by rivalry but by a common desire to build a better life for everyone."

Garbuz's voice grew stronger as he painted a picture of a world uplifted by the wealth of space, with the potential for a renewed focus on education, health, and prosperity for all.

"Imagine," he said, "a world where the resources from space bring healthcare to every corner of the Earth, where every child has access to the best education, and where poverty and hunger are relics of the past. This mission has shown us that space is not a luxury—it is a necessity, a frontier that promises solutions for the challenges we face."

He looked out over the crowd, his gaze steady. "And let this mission be a reminder that we have the power to choose. We can use space to build a better future for all or risk turning it into another stage for conflict. Let us remember what our crew out there is showing us—that space exploration requires unity, purpose, and vision."

The crowd was silent, captivated by the possibilities Garbuz presented. In his words, they saw a future where humanity worked together, free from the constraints that had divided them for so long.

"Today, we celebrate the courage of the IISF crew," he continued, "and as we await their return, let us commit ourselves to a vision of space exploration that prioritizes the welfare of all. Let their journey inspire us to lift one another up—to create a world worthy of the possibilities they are uncovering for us."

As he finished, applause broke out, echoing across the Capitol steps. The cheers represented hope, unity, and a vision of what humanity could achieve together. The IISF's mission had become more than an expedition; it had become a call to action, a promise of a brighter future fueled by peace, exploration, and shared purpose.

Garbuz stepped back from the podium, his expression resolute. The IISF had opened a door to the stars, and the world now stood at a crossroads. With the crew's message echoing in their minds and Garbuz's vision lighting the way, the world was ready to move forward with a new understanding of what humanity could accomplish when united.

Above, in the vast unknown, the crew continued their journey home, unaware of the movement their mission had ignited. Their return would mark not only their triumph but the beginning of a future shaped by unity, purpose, and an unshakable belief in humanity's potential.

AFTERWORD

Dear Readers,

Thank you for joining me on this journey through *Rise of the IISF*. This story explores the boundaries of human potential, international cooperation, and the challenges we face as we reach for the stars. Through the tale of the IISF crew's incredible mission and their battle against sabotage and adversity, we've witnessed how determination, unity, and courage can overcome even the most daunting obstacles in humanity's quest to explore the cosmos.

At the core of this book is a belief in education, opportunity, and the boundless potential of the human spirit. Our mission guides our efforts to build a future where everyone has access to learning and growth. As part of this vision, we are working towards initiatives that support underprivileged children in gaining access to education, with the dream of one day establishing space academies that open the door to the stars for all.

Every time you purchase this book, you're not just experiencing the story—you're helping to make these dreams a reality. Your support is driving us closer to a world where children everywhere can explore their full potential, and where progress and innovation benefit all.

Thank you for being a part of this journey. Together, we are building a future full of hope, discovery, and opportunity for generations to come.

Proudly sponsored by GarbuzSpace.com

Za Detey – For Kids!

Za Lyubov – For Love!

Live, Make, & Enjoy!